Tangled Beginning

TANGLED SERIES

SOPHIE ANDREWS

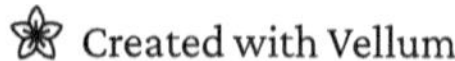 Created with Vellum

Content Note

Content Note: Tangled Beginning is the story of a golden retriever hero and the girl he'd follow to the ends of the earth with plenty of open door romance. Please be aware one of the main characters was cheated on and a secondary character is diagnosed with Huntington's disease. There are also multiple discussions about adoption.

I had no idea what Huntington's Disease was until a good friend was diagnosed. It is devastating, to say the least, but much like the characters in this story, we are taking it one day at a time. For more information on the disease or to make a donation, please go to the Huntington's Disease Society of America.

For the ones who need an escape...

CHAPTER ONE

Laney

We were down half a bottle of Malbec when I grabbed my phone for a birthday selfie with Gem to send to Bronte and Sam. "Let's show them what they're missing." Gem promptly stuck out her tongue, and I laughed, snapping a few pictures. "Beautiful."

Gem, Bronte, Sam and I had known one another since college. Though we were separated by state lines and differing job schedules, our friendship was bonded together by years of long talks, hours of crying and laughing, the usual breakups and make-ups, and endless sunsets and sunrises. But we hadn't all been in the same place together since Bronte had gotten married last summer. Fortunately, Gem's yoga retreat and conference was in San Francisco and coincided with my birthday so we could celebrate together.

"This is what twenty-eight looks like. Blurry and tipsy on wine before eight o'clock," Gem said, pointing to one particularly bad picture over my shoulder.

"I love it. I think it captures our spirit. Should we FaceTime them?"

She rolled her hand in a circle, gesturing *of course*.

A few minutes later, Bronte's and Sam's faces appeared on

my phone screen, and I ducked down so Gem could be in the frame too.

"Happy birthday, Laney doll!" Bronte crowed. She lived with her husband in Pennsylvania and couldn't take off work as a middle school teacher to make the cross-country trip.

"What are you up to?" Sam asked, her smile as bright as her purple-and-pink hair. She was in Austin, Texas, with her boyfriend while she finished up her PhD, and even though we'd all—the whole group, including husbands and boyfriends—celebrated New Year's Eve over Zoom a few weeks ago, it wasn't enough. I could never get enough of my girls.

I had lots of friends, tons of acquaintances, but I allowed very few people to really know me. And these three women were at the top of that list.

"We're having dinner at this fancy vegan restaurant," Gem said.

"I've been showing her around," I added.

Gem leaned into the phone with a mischievous grin. "And telling me about Ethan."

"Ethan?" Sam pursed her lips in thought. "As in, the heartbreaker?"

Gem nodded. "The high school heartbreaker."

"It was a hundred years ago," I said as if my best friends hadn't been there during those early college days when I'd tried to forget him by any means necessary, including, but not limited to, guys who were not good for me.

"He was the boy you..." Bronte lowered her voice as if the people in the restaurant would be able to hear her over the clatter of dinner service. "Lost your virginity to."

I rolled my eyes, wishing I'd never even brought it up to loud-mouthed Gem.

"She had a dream about him," the traitor told Sam and Bronte, leaning in close to the phone again.

I pushed my hair behind my shoulders. "It wasn't that big of a deal."

"Enough of a deal to tell me about it." Gem cocked an eyebrow at me. "And you know I think dreams mean something. Remember all those dreams I had while I was pregnant with Willow?"

On the phone screen, Sam waved her fingers. "Okay, let's hear it."

I gulped back the rest of my deliciously robust red wine. I wouldn't call myself a wine snob, but since I'd lived so close to wine country the last five years, I'd become picky. "Okay, so, in the dream, Bobby and I were fighting, and I ran out of the house all upset. And suddenly, Ethan was there, and we were eighteen again."

Bronte propped her chin on both of her fists like a child at story time. "Then what happened?"

"Nothing really. He hugged me, kissed me on the head, told me it was going to be okay. Then we ate hot dogs. I don't know where the hot dogs came from."

Gem shoved me over so she took up the whole frame. "I told her that her subconscious might be thinking about other options besides Bobby if it's going all the way back to high school."

"Are you thinking of other options?" Sam asked.

"Well…" I elbowed Gem out of the way. "I mean…it hasn't been easy lately, you know? Bobby's making more plans for New York City, and he's going to LA next week about a possible reality show idea for a new restaurant."

"Oh shit," Gem breathed out next to me.

Bronte frowned. "Yeah, that's a lot to deal with. I'm sorry."

I was used to it. We'd been together for three years. Bobby ruled a restaurant empire, a superstar chef with occasional guest-hosting gigs on the Food Network. He was handsome, charming, and Australian. What more could a girl want?

That was the question I'd been asking myself more and more lately.

When my friends frowned, I wrinkled my nose. "No, don't do that. It's fine. I'm fine." To prove it, I held up the bottle of wine, cheersing the screen before pouring more into my glass. When I moved to pour more into Gem's, she raised her palm over her glass. "You don't want anymore?"

"No. I'm good."

"Are you sure?" I shook the bottle a little. "We have at least two glasses left."

When Gem only offered me a closed-lips smile, I knew something was off and set the bottle back down. "You all right?"

Gem dragged her fork through her vegan basil and zucchini gnocchi. "Eh."

"Eh?"

"What's wrong?" Bronte asked, unable to see how pale Gem appeared when she pushed back the short bangs of her pixie cut.

"Gem's not feeling well," I said.

"Drink too much?" Sam guessed.

"Is it the food?" I asked. The more I considered it, the more obvious the clues seemed that my friend hadn't been feeling well. Since we'd met up this afternoon, Gem had pretty much let me jabber on when she usually would've been more energetic.

Gem held her water glass in her hand, her big, dark eyes scrutinizing it as if she wasn't sure if she should drink it or pour it over her head. After a moment, she pressed it to her forehead. "It's hot in here, huh?"

I shook my head. It wasn't hot at all. Mid-January in San

Francisco was mild, and the restaurant was cool enough for me to layer up.

"I...um..." Gem lifted her head, first meeting my gaze and then focusing on the phone screen. "I haven't felt right for the last few days, and now that I'm thinking about it..."

Seconds passed before Bronte, Sam, and I all spoke at the same time.

"Oh my god."

"Shut your face."

"You're pregnant."

"I don't know," Gem said, licking her lips a few times, and now she *really* looked sick. "I was tired, but I thought it was from travel and then from the retreat." She pressed her water glass to her forehead again.

"When was your last period?" Sam asked.

Gem spoke toward the table. "End of November."

"Is Jason getting his wish?" I asked, earning a laugh from everyone, including Gem. Her husband had said he wanted enough kids to field his own basketball team.

Bronte's eyes practically bugged out of her head in excitement. "Do you have a test? You have to take one right now. I'm dying."

"You're dying," Gem repeated with a smile that quickly faded, and she dunked two fingers into the water and dragged them across her opposite wrist. "I'm dying."

"Yeah, okay, okay." I grabbed my purse and flagged down the server. "We're going right now. I'll call a ride, and we'll stop by to grab a test."

"Let us know immediately," Bronte said.

Sam hiked her shoulders up to her ears. "Should I say good luck?"

"Save it for when I have to push out another one of Jason's big-headed babies."

Then I ended the call with a quick goodbye and hustled Gem out of the restaurant and into the waiting Lyft. With a pit stop for a Clearblue test, we were back at the two-bedroom condo Bobby and I shared in Russian Hill.

When I shoved the front door open, pointing to the half bath right off the entryway, Bobby popped his head up from the couch.

"Hey, babe."

"Hey," I said in a rush, throwing down my coat to toss Gem the test.

"How was dinner?"

"Great."

"Everything ok—"

I shut the bathroom door on Bobby's question and took the small cardboard box from Gem's fingers when she struggled to open it.

Gem bent over the sink. "I feel pukey."

"Because you're nervous, or because you puke a lot when you're pregnant?"

She leaned her elbows on the marbled counter, her head in her hands. "Probably both."

"Here." I held out one of the sticks, and Gem took it before unbuttoning her jeans.

Outside, Bobby knocked on the door. "Oi, everything okay in there?"

I opened the door a smidge, enough to meet my boyfriend's hazel eyes. "We'll be out in a few minutes."

He lowered his voice to a whisper. "Okay, love. Just checking." Then he winked and walked back to the living room, and I pivoted back around as Gem peed on the stick. She held the wrapper up for the garbage, and I took it, lifting the lid of the small trash bin in the corner.

"What the..." I tilted my head and leaned closer to the garbage.

"What?" Gem asked behind me.

Blinking, I lifted the used condom wrapper, my mind skidding to a stop. "I don't..."

Gem flushed the toilet. "What's that?"

But I couldn't answer. At the moment, finding words was like trying to solve a geometry proof.

In my periphery, I was aware Gem washed her hands and set a timer on her cell phone, but the reality of finding a Trojan wrapper in the bathroom garbage clouded my ability to even put a whole thought together. There were only broken fragments in my mind.

Bobby didn't use condoms.

I was on the pill.

My best friend was about to find out if she was pregnant.

Someone in this condo didn't want to get *someone else* pregnant.

That someone wasn't me.

And the someone else certainly wasn't me.

"Is that—" Gem started, but I cut her off as I opened the bathroom door, holding the wrapper out with a straight arm, pinching it between the tip of my thumb and index finger.

"Bobby."

"Yeah?" My boyfriend lifted his head from the garish gold pillows he'd insisted on buying when we moved in here last year. When I flicked the offending foil packet at him, his smile vanished immediately.

"I found it in the garbage."

He stood up slowly, his eyes drifting around our condo, and I could see it all crumbling at my feet. The last three years, the amazing job I'd left to work with this man because he'd begged me to, the time and energy I'd put into this relationship. It was all gone.

"I can explain."

An indignant guffaw burst out of me. "Yeah?"

"It's not what you think, joey."

"Don't call me that," I snapped, hating the cute nickname I ordinarily loved. He couldn't be cute. Not now.

"I'm sorry," he said like he was calming a wild animal. I felt wild. Maybe even a little rabid. "Please, love, let's talk about—"

"Laney," Gem said, interrupting us, one hand on her stomach, the other holding out the test.

The answer was right there. In clear blue letters. Pregnant.

And then Gem vomited at Bobby's feet.

I sighed. "Happy twenty-eighth birthday to me."

CHAPTER TWO

Ethan

"So, what's going on?" I studied the faces of my family members—my parents, brother, and sister-in-law—all seated around the dining room table. I hadn't had a good feeling when my brother texted me to meet at our parents' house, and now that I was here, I knew it was going to be bad. I felt it in my bones.

Mom and Dad both appeared as nervous as I felt, and the three of us patiently stared at Justin, who glanced at his wife, Leah, wrapping his fingers around hers.

I was stuck on her red-rimmed eyes. This was *really* bad.

"I got the test results back today," Justin said in his usual halting cadence. "It's Huntington's disease."

My breath caught in my throat, my mind tripping over the vaguely familiar term. "Huntington's? What is that?"

Justin cleared his throat, swiping a knuckle over one eye, and I could count the number of times I'd seen my older brother cry on one hand.

Fuck.

"It's progressive, and there's no cure." He gazed at our parents, and Mom gasped out a little breath that quickly morphed into tears. Dad reached for Justin's hand, silent and stoic.

Progressive. No cure. I stared at the space above Justin's head. My older brother, who was the strongest person I knew, had a terminal disease. Memories flashed in my mind. The two of us playing basketball in the driveway as kids. Wrestling in the living room and breaking an antique lamp handed down from our great-grandmother. Hugging each other on the day Justin left for college and later on when I graduated with my master's. Me giving the toast at Justin and Leah's wedding a few years ago.

"It's, uh, it's a genetic disorder," Justin said, and I swiped my clammy palms down my jeans, blinking back to the present.

"Genetic," I repeated in a quiet tone. Meaning my brother inherited this disease from his biological parents, and guilt swept over me that he would have to suffer with this genetic disorder, but I wouldn't.

"We didn't know," our dad said. "If we did…"

Mom grabbed a tissue, dabbing under her nose. "If we knew, we would have gotten you help, and I'm so sorry. We love you," she said, swiping at tears on her cheeks. "We love you. We love you."

Justin and I had both been adopted, and even though Justin had tried to find his biological parents at one time, it was a dead end.

"There was nothing in the medical records," Dad went on. "Maybe they didn't know."

Justin lifted a resigned shoulder, the barest hint of a smile on his face before he turned to his wife. "But at least I have an answer now. It's better than having to keep living in limbo."

I shot out my arm. "So what? What the fuck was all that shit about the gluten intolerance and ataxia?"

"Ethan," Mom murmured, a subtle reminder to watch my language.

Leah placed her hand on the dark wood of the table, smiling through her tears. "A misdiagnosis. Since it's genetic, and obviously no one else in your family would have had symptoms or a previous diagnosis, they didn't think to test for it until now."

"There's a clinic at Penn," Justin explained, "but I have to wait for my insurance to preapprove it."

"Fucking insurance," our dad mumbled, and Mom tossed her hands up.

"Can everybody calm down with the goddamn language, please?"

That earned a relieved laugh from everyone. Rita Marrero did not curse. Until now.

"You know it's bad if Mom is cursing," Justin stage-whispered to me, and I nodded theatrically.

"What can we do, honey?" she asked, and I removed my glasses to rub the heels of my hands over my eyes, willing my brain to connect the dots, to figure out a solution.

"There's nothing to do," Justin said, and I slid my glasses back on before thumping my fist on the table.

"No. No. We have to do something."

Justin met my gaze, for what seemed like the first time since he'd arrived, and I shriveled under the defeated look in my brother's eyes. I couldn't—didn't want to—believe there was nothing to be done.

"There are two medications out there right now," Leah said. "They'll help the symptoms, hopefully slow the progression of them."

Justin swallowed, his jaw working, as he smiled at Leah. His wife was forever patient and kind, and I had to glance away from their private moment. After a few seconds, Justin said,

"I'll have a team at the clinic. Neurologists, therapists, social workers."

"We'll get through this," Leah finished, smiling at everyone in turn before gazing back at Justin.

Our parents nodded, but my chest burned. We were going to get through this? No, there had to be a way to *stop* this.

Justin was only thirty-four. He was the dad to a four-year-old. There was no way this should be happening to him. Then again, another thought halted my train of thought. "Wait. If…" I rolled my index fingers over each other in a circle. "If this is genetic, then Trace is…"

Justin sucked his lower lip between his teeth and dropped his chin to his chest, offering a faint nod.

"There is a fifty percent chance he's inherited it," Leah said quietly.

I thought of my perfect little nephew, and my heart broke all over again.

Dad let out a low breath. "Okay, let's not get ahead of ourselves with this. We will take this one step at a time, all right?"

Everyone nodded except for me. I crossed my arms, forcing my father to repeat himself with a firm snap in his voice. "All right?"

"Yeah," I mumbled then stood up, and Mom reached out to me.

"Where are you going?"

"I…" I slung on my coat. I didn't know. I just needed to get out. I shook my head and walked over to the other end of the table to hug my brother. "I'm sorry. I'm so sorry."

Justin didn't answer, only patted my back, returning the embrace.

I felt like shit for leaving, but I couldn't stay and cry, or be weak-willed when my brother needed support and strength. I had to pull myself together before I could give that to Justin, so I waved to my parents and walked out their front door, straight to my car, where I promptly Googled Huntington's disease. After a quick read of three different websites, confirming what I thought I knew about it, I texted my best friend.

Are you home? I'm coming over.

Ten minutes later, I pulled up to Dean's house. All the lights were on and the front door open, so I knocked once on the storm door before heading in. "Hey, yo!"

Led Zeppelin blasted from upstairs, accompanied by a couple of loud bangs. On the second floor, I found Dean in the bathroom, safety goggles on, demolishing the countertop. After he put the sledgehammer down, I slapped the doorframe to get his attention.

He whipped around to me. "Oh hey, man. Didn't know you were here."

"I texted you."

He removed his goggles and grabbed his cell phone from where it sat on the windowsill. "Sorry. Didn't hear it." Then he wiped his hands on his T-shirt and grabbed a bottle of water. He chugged a few gulps before asking, "What's up?"

I shook my head, staring down at my shoes.

"What?"

"My brother."

Dean kicked something out of the way to stand right in front of me, thumping my arm. "What's going on?"

When I finally lifted my gaze to him, I found concern etched all over my friend's face, and I lost it. I took my glasses off, giving in to the tears that had been threatening to spill out since I'd sat down at my parents' table.

"Hey, hey, what's going on?" Dean asked again, this time throwing an arm around me.

"It's not ataxia or a gluten intolerance. It's Huntington's."

"Huntington's? I don't know what that is."

"It's like a mix of Parkinson's and dementia, a progressive neurological disease. It's..." I cleared my throat, moving away from Dean to wipe my eyes and put my glasses back on. "It's going to get worse."

He patted my shoulder. "That really sucks. I'm sorry to hear that. How's he doing?"

I shrugged. "He found out earlier today and texted me to meet him and Leah at Mom and Dad's, and I..." I blew out a breath. "I freaked out. I couldn't stay there, you know?"

Dean pursed his lips and nodded. "What can I do?"

I tipped my chin at the broken pieces of the counter, a door hanging off its hinges. "You mind if I take some swings?"

Wordlessly, he handed over the safety goggles and sledge-hammer, and I went to work. I smashed my frustration and worry out on the wood, and then when Dean gestured to the yellow-tiled shower, I went after that too. I needed this destruction, to be able to throw my anger and fear at something.

After a minute, I set down the hammer and removed the goggles to run the back of my hand over my forehead and the thin sheet of sweat there.

"Feel better?" Dean asked.

"Yeah." I inhaled deeply. "Yeah. Thanks."

"You know you cou—" His phone buzzed, interrupting him, and he grabbed it to check the screen, his brow furrowing. He answered with one hand on his hip. "Hey, what's up?" He kicked some pieces of broken tile with the toe of his boot as he listened and then dropped his hand, his voice rising. "He *what?*"

I leaned against the wall, watching my friend tug at his hair.

"Why didn't you call me yesterday?" Dean darted his gaze around as if looking for something. "I don't give a shit that it was our birthday, you should have called me." He let out an indignant laugh at the person on the other end of the phone call. "To do what? To kill him, that's what."

I pushed off the wall, aiming to get closer and hear the other side of the conversation. There was only one person who had the same birthday as Dean, and that was his twin sister, Delaney Hargrove. Even the mere thought of her had my pulse beating in a funny staccato.

"I could kill him," Dean sneered. "Yes, I could—why are you laughing? Are you high right now?"

I chewed on the inside of my cheek, my curiosity about this phone call off the charts. So much so that Justin was no longer in the forefront of my mind. If something happened to Laney, I might kill someone too.

"You're with Gem? Which one is she? Uh-huh." Dean walked in a tight circle, his attention on the ceiling, his jaw tight. "Yeah, uh-huh... Of course you can... Okay, text me later. And no more edibles." With a shake of his head, he pocketed his cell phone.

"What was that about?" I asked as evenly as possible.

Even though there was nothing left to destroy, he picked up the sledgehammer and dropped it straight down on a pile of wood like Thor.

"Laney's boyfriend cheated on her."

My jaw dropped, and I blinked up to the old, ugly light-bulbs above the mirror. "Laney's boyfriend cheated? On her?"

Dean bent to toss the debris into a big black bag with a nod.

"On your sister?" I asked, still confounded. "Delaney?"

"Uh-huh."

"What the fuck?"

The squeaky question got Dean's attention, and he quirked his head up at me. "Yeah, you all right?"

I readjusted my glasses. No, I wasn't all right. First my brother and now Laney. "How is she? Is she okay?"

Dean shrugged. "Her friend was out there visiting with her, and I don't know... I couldn't get much out of her. Apparently they got a pot brownie, but her friend is pregnant, so Laney ate the whole thing herself."

I bit back a smile, digging my finger into loose grout.

"She packed up all her stuff. Guess she's moving back here for a bit," he said, gesturing to the pile of wood. "You want to grab that? Gotta take it all out to the trash." Then he laughed to himself. "Laney'll be so pissed when she finds out the bathroom is in the middle of a renovation."

I grinned too. Laney had never been vain, but she did own a lot of products. At least, that's what I remembered. After grabbing as much as I could carry for the first load, I followed Dean downstairs, right out the front door to a waiting trash bin at the curb. We both wiped off our hands and turned back for more.

"Hey, you let me know if there's anything I can do for your brother," Dean said, and I lightly elbowed my best friend, one of the first people I'd met when my family had first moved to West Chester a little over ten years ago.

"Yeah, you too. With Laney, I mean."

He nodded and headed back inside. I followed but paused at one of the only photos in the house, a framed picture of Dean and Delaney, in their high school caps and gowns, the same height, same wheat-colored hair, and blue eyes.

I closed my eyes, remembering so much about our senior year of high school, and the girl I'd been in love with.

"Hey, Marrero, what're you doing?" Dean called from the second floor. "You better not be drinking my beer. You gotta help me with this shit first!"

I shook off my reverie and took the stairs two at a time, saying, "Maybe *you* need an edible."

CHAPTER THREE

Laney

The thing about going to a small Catholic school is that everybody knows everybody. And everybody knows everybody's business. And everybody talks about everybody's business.

From kindergarten through twelfth grade, the same kids are together every day for 180 days a year. That's a lot of time to spend with Fred Whately, who peed his pants in second grade, and Molly McMann, who was the first girl to get her period in fourth grade. It was horrific because it was all over her yellow uniform gym shorts. Totally mortifying.

Holy Redeemer's graduating class was about 250 people, and almost all of them were part of a Facebook group, in theory to stay in touch about reunions, but really it was to keep up-to-date with gossip. Unfortunately, I was the gossip now.

Back then, I was the class vice president, star athlete, and prom queen. Now, people were DMing me across all my socials with things like *OMG heard about you and Bobby. So sad.* Or *He seemed like a douche canoe anyway.* Or my personal favorite from a frenemy, whom I hadn't spoken to in years, *Guess not even a hot, rich, Australian chef is good enough for you? LOL!*

With a perturbed flick of my thumb, I deleted the app, and

—surprise, surprise—the world didn't end. No sense in reliving the trauma over and over for people I hadn't spoken to or cared about in years.

Although before I could toss my phone down, it buzzed with a message from one of my best friends.

BRONTE

How are you doing? You want to get together
for dinner?

Sweet, sweet Bronte. It almost made me want to cry. But I didn't cry. Ever.

I smiled and put on a good show. I'd been doing it for so long, I didn't know how not to be *the show* even when I was alone.

I'm all right.

I coasted my gaze around my brother's living room. He'd bought the house last year for cheap, a real fixer-upper, but the living room was completely finished and furnished straight from the Wayfair home page.

Bingeing Netflix documentaries.

BRONTE

Naturally.

BRONTE

What about dinner? I could come to you.

Allentown was over an hour from West Chester.

No, we can meet halfway.

A couple of side-eye emojis appeared.

> **BRONTE**
>
> Chris has to go to New York next weekend, so
> it's no big deal. You pick the place.

> Twist my arm.

Bronte sent a GIF of Winnie the Pooh eating and dancing in his seat, and I smiled as I put down my phone to stretch out along the couch. Dean wouldn't be home for a couple of hours, so I could watch TV in peace.

I had been back in my hometown for a little over two weeks and hadn't done much besides eat junk food, watch movies, and engage in an occasional treadmill run at the local Y. But Dean didn't seem to mind me loafing around.

My brother, older by six minutes, was really saving my ass. If there was such a thing as twin telekinesis, Dean and I didn't have it, but there was still some special connection. I wouldn't and couldn't stay in San Francisco. Not after I'd moved out of the condo that was under Bobby's name and quit my job at the Magnate Company. There was nothing left for me in the Bay Area, so until I knew what to do next, I had to go somewhere.

Each of my girls offered their couch, but I wouldn't impose on them. And my parents were completely out of the question. I might have been desperate but not *that* desperate. Dean, though, I didn't hesitate to call and let him know I needed somewhere to stay.

Reaching for another Cool Ranch Dorito, I settled back against the cushions to get more comfortable, but as I opened my mouth to chomp on my snack, the front door flew open. Dean stood in the doorway, juggling a few grocery bags as he tried to close the door behind him.

I got up to do it for him. "What're you doing home?"

Among his many good qualities, Dean had a couple of bad ones, including his anal-retentive cleanliness, and he threw me a look when he spotted my drink without a coaster. He huffed and grabbed one, sliding it under my water glass. "It's poker night."

I grimaced. He had mentioned monthly poker nights at his house, but I'd forgotten. When he moved the ottoman to the corner and pushed the coffee table closer to the couch, I realized that I'd have to sulk somewhere else.

"You want to stick around?" Dean asked, grabbing a folding table from the back of the coat closet in the hall. "It's just Nadir, Seth, Hank, and Ethan."

I went over those names in my head one by one. Nadir, Seth, Hank, and "Ethan?"

He nodded and then moved the black folding chairs.

"Ethan who?" I asked, even though there was only one Ethan I'd ever known in my entire life.

My brother raised an eyebrow as if I'd lost my mind. It was possible I had. "Marrero."

My heart sank clear through my body, and I checked the floor to see if it was flopping around by my feet like a fish.

"I didn't know you guys still talked," I said, my voice only slightly hysterical. Of course I knew they still talked. They had been best friends since Ethan's family moved to West Chester right before our senior year of high school and he transferred to Holy Redeemer.

Back then, Ethan was like a big puppy dog, all loose limbs and big ears, with a matching personality. He was the one person who didn't see me as the *it girl*. Maybe it was because he was the new kid in town that I didn't feel the need to keep up the perfect veneer. Or that he simply didn't care about my popularity or reputation. Whatever it was, it led me to fall for him. As much as an eighteen-year-old girl could.

But we were practically babies.

It was puppy love. Nothing special, really.

At least that was the story I'd kept up after all these years.

Because sometimes when I couldn't sleep, I'd sink into those memories of Ethan. Of when life wasn't complicated. Of when I wasn't pretending. Of when I wanted to remember being excited about life and love.

And now with the lingering memory of my recent dream about the man and my best friends' reaction to it, I couldn't help but think that the universe was trying to tell me something.

Or maybe I was overthinking this.

Trojan-gate was messing with my head.

At Dean's bemused chuckle, I refocused my attention to the present and my brother's narrowed eyes. "What?"

"I said, are you gonna play with us?"

"Oh, uh, no. No, you guys go ahead. I'm, uh..." I jerked my thumb over my shoulder and trotted to the kitchen, where I grabbed a water bottle and banana, planning on spending my evening at the Y. I could go there, maybe run a few miles and hang out with the old guy at the front desk. Poker night would be over by ten, right?

I could totally avoid my ancient history with Ethan and hopefully try to right my jumbled-up brain.

But then a few male voices floated in from the living room, with one standing out above all the rest. Though Ethan and I followed each other on social media, staying vaguely in contact with a *like* button, we hadn't seen each other in years. Since that one Thanksgiving, when I had been home and we'd run into each other outside of the grocery store. He'd been walking in while I'd been walking out from an emergency tampon run and couldn't spare more than a quick hello. I supposed I was in for a lot more run-ins with Ethan and his smooth yet slightly playful voice, like an Americanized version of Disney's cartoon fox Robin Hood.

Seeing as how that was my first crush, I really never stood a chance against the gangly teenager with dark eyes.

Now, though, I was in a different place in my life. There would be no falling for a smooth talker. If only I could get upstairs without going through the living room. Damn turn-of-the-century townhouse architecture. I contemplated the odds of finding an invisibility cloak in the kitchen cupboards when Dean called out, "Hey, Laney, come say hi."

With a deep breath, I set my shoulders, although there was no help for the decades-old Maroon 5 T-shirt and yoga pants which were a tad too tight with a big turquoise paint stain by my knee. Another reminder of Bobby.

When we'd moved in to the condo, we had argued over what color to paint our bedroom. I wanted something more neutral, but Bobby was all about color. He had said that since he paid the mortgage, he should be able to choose. I had given in on that one, and while he had been out filming a segment for some morning talk show, I'd been home painting our bedroom Tiffany blue.

Forgetting him and my life in California, I ventured forward, trying on my most confident smile as I entered the living room.

"There she is," Dean said. "Seth, Nadir, this is my sister, Laney. And Laney, you already know Hank and Ethan."

I looked down to where Hank sat at the table. He grinned up at me. "Lookin' good, Laney."

I rolled my eyes at his silly green visor. "Hey, Hank."

Hank Lau had started hanging around the Hargrove house freshman year of high school. Both of his parents were doctors, so he was often there because of their long hours. Hank was a great guy but a total dimwit. Like Zach Galifianakis's character in *The Hangover*.

"Nice to meet you," I said to Seth and Nadir then finally lifted my gaze to the man slipping off his coat.

With his back to me, I had a moment to compose myself before he turned around.

Then he did, and my internal organs rearranged themselves, my heart in my throat and my stomach up somewhere behind my ribs.

Ethan looked exactly like Ethan but different. While he was still long and lean, he wasn't a gangly kid anymore, with broad shoulders visible even through his zip-up hoodie. Ethan had been adopted as a baby and looked nothing like his parents with his dark hair and richly tanned skin, but he still had that cowlick. Clearly, he'd grown into himself, even his ears which held a pair of dark tortoiseshell glasses over ever-aware eyes that zeroed in right on me.

"Hi, Laney."

And it was like I was eighteen all over again. "Hi."

Dean looped an arm around me, and I took shelter in him, sagging into his side. "What were you doing in there?"

"Grabbing water and a snack."

Hank opened up the box of poker chips. "You playing?"

"No, I'm going to go out."

"Are you sure?" Dean's eyes narrowed, silently asking if I was *really* sure.

I nodded, trying to ignore the gaze I sensed on me. But when it became too much, I shifted my eyes to Ethan, finding him watching me. And I immediately blinked away. "You guys have fun. I'm gonna go change, and then I'll be out of your hair."

I sprinted upstairs two at a time, needing to get out of the house and away from Ethan until I could compose myself. Possibly even act like a proper grown woman. After changing into workout gear, I laced up my sneakers before heading back downstairs, intent on slipping out the back door in the kitchen. With barely a glance to the guys, I raced past them. "Have fun! I'll see you later!"

But I stopped short in the kitchen. Ethan had his hands around a couple of pint glasses, and I froze, hoping maybe he wouldn't notice the statue.

Portrait of a shamed woman returned home.

"Hey," he said, and my shoulders sagged.

"Uh, hi there." There was a weird air between us—so weird —and I winced, trying again. "Hey."

He assessed me with a teasing raise of his brow that showed he knew how twisted up I was, but I didn't want to consider how it was possible he could still read me so well after all these years. Instead of answering that question or focusing on my sudden social ineptitude, I plastered on a smile. "It's nice to see you."

He put the glasses down on the counter and gave me his full attention. "Yeah, how are you? How've you been?"

I didn't know how to respond. Did he mean recently or in the last ten years? Because I was...not great. I contemplated what or how much to say, overanalyzing that normally easy question of *How've you been?* as the gerbil spun uselessly on the wheel in my mind.

Then Ethan stepped closer, close enough that I could see the tiny specks of brown, amber, gold, and coffee that made up his irises, and the gerbil fell off. "I heard what happened."

With that punch to the ovaries, my hackles rose in defense. My life might have been a Greek tragedy playing out for what felt like the whole world to see—the downside of being a social media maven—but I didn't want Ethan to be a part of the chorus.

I folded my arms over my chest. "Yeah?"

"Dean told me," he said, officially leaning into my space,

and I averted my eyes to the floor. "Are you okay?" When I didn't answer, he whispered, "Hey," drawing my gaze back up to him, and I instantly regretted it.

He was staring at me exactly like he used to. Like he was trying to crack open my head to take a peek inside.

If he looked hard enough, he'd see ten-year-old memories buried deep inside. Memories of first love, first heartache, first *everything*. Waiting patiently for an answer, he tilted his head, squinting the tiniest bit, and that familiar move had me saying, "I guess I'm doing okay."

"You guess?"

"I'm not sure what you want me to say." The anger-tinged words were unexpected, even to me, and a flash of sadness crossed his features before he fixed that easygoing smile back on his face.

Though we were adults now, and I thought I was over whatever it was we'd had, it was impossible to stand here with him and not have those ancient feelings surface. The hurt that I'd buried long ago had found its way back to the top.

He stuffed his hands into his pockets. "I just want to know that you're all right. You're my friend. I care about you."

I closed my eyes at his sweet tone and how it walloped my chest. "We haven't been friends for a very long time, Ethan."

When I opened my eyes back up to his face, that fact sat heavy between us. So much had happened to me, probably to him as well, and we weren't the kids we used to be.

"I'm sorry," he said, although I didn't know what he was apologizing for. Tonight, the Bobby situation, our history, maybe all of it—I didn't know.

He opened his mouth to say something, but with a stiff shake of my head, I stopped our mini-reunion. I needed to get out. My wound from Bobby was still fresh, and with how I knew Ethan could affect me, I was liable to say anything. "I gotta go."

I took wide steps to get around him, and as my fingertips touched the door handle, he said, "Hey, Laney." When I glanced over my shoulder at him, his smile wavered. "It's good to see you."

The air rushed out of my lungs because, yeah. "It's good to see you too."

CHAPTER FOUR

Ethan

I had moved around a lot as a kid, with a mother who worked as a United States Foreign Service officer and a father who had a PhD in economics. We'd lived in DC, San Diego, Canberra, Australia, and Rome, Italy before finally landing here, and I was happy to know my parents were well and truly settled. Even though I still loved to travel and had gone away for school, home was now West Chester, Pennsylvania.

Sitting at the card table with my friends, including Dean and Hank, my buddies from high school, my mind reeled with memories.

"Hey, where're the glasses?" Nadir asked.

"Oh." I shook my head. "Yeah. Sorry."

Hank snorted a laugh. "That's the reason you went to the kitchen in the first place."

I stood back up to grab the pint glasses I'd left on the counter when Laney had walked into the kitchen. I'd seen her, and my mind had gone blank for what felt like a century. I shouldn't have been surprised to see her. Dean had told me she would be staying at his house for a while, or at least until she got back on her feet. Yet actually seeing her in the flesh, I felt it was like I was a kid all over again.

By the time my family had settled in West Chester, Justin had already graduated college and had been living with Leah in New York City, so I had started senior year at the new school by myself. My only saving grace had been the marching band. I'd met Dean, Hank, Gabe, and Patrick, and they'd all taken me right under their wings, so the first day of school wasn't bad. Especially once I'd spotted Laney, right there in front of the Jesus statue, arguing with Dean. Her huge mass of curls had been piled up on the top of her head with a pencil sticking out. Her uniform skirt had been short, definitely against dress code, with one of her knee-high socks drooping down her endlessly long legs. Her voice carried as she'd threatened to murder her brother by running him over with the car they'd shared and that he'd apparently taken to school on his own so she'd had to ride the bus.

Eventually the argument died out, and Dean had introduced his twin sister to me. She'd turned around, hit me with those baby blues and a smile that made me feel as if I could fly, and I'd been smitten.

Seeing her again tonight, I was smitten all over again. Even if her smile was fake and there were light purple bruises under her eyes like she hadn't been sleeping well.

With the pint glasses in hand this time, I made my way back down the hall to the living room, where Hank held up his growler of home brew. He was saying something about the hops, but I didn't pay attention. Instead, I grabbed a handful of pretzels and a napkin. God forbid, I got crumbs anywhere. Dean was a stickler about keeping his house pristine.

Once everyone had a pint full of beer, Seth dealt the cards, but with my mind still lost in a fog of history, I had trouble concentrating.

"What's with you tonight?" Dean asked after I had lost yet another hand.

I chewed on the inside of my cheek. "Just...got my mind on other stuff, I guess."

"Your brother?" Hank asked, and I nodded. Because it was true. Since my brother's diagnosis, I'd been able to think of little else.

Until tonight.

After a few minutes of quiet play, Seth drained the last of his beer then tapped a poker chip on the table, his eyes on Dean. "So, your sister..."

"Don't," was all Dean said.

"Don't what?" Seth went on, poking the bear.

"Don't, Seth."

Nadir pointedly kept his eyes on his cards but sucked air through his teeth when Seth continued to push.

"How do you even know what I'm going—"

Dean thumped his fist on the table. "I don't want to hear whatever it is you're about to say. My sister got cheated on by an asshat, so no, I don't think she wants to go out with you. And no, I won't give you her number. And no, I especially don't want to hear how hot you think she is."

Seth worked with Dean, and I never had a problem with him before. Besides this once-a-month poker night, we didn't know each other well, but I had a strong urge to hurl my pint glass at his face now.

"Hey, whoa, all right. Just saying," he said, holding his hands up in surrender.

"Well, don't," Dean snapped.

Dean had always been protective of Laney, even though they'd tended to fight like cats and dogs when they were younger. With her being the girl everyone wanted in high school, I supposed Dean had felt some kind of innate responsibility to make sure she wasn't hurt. Which was part of the reason why Laney and I hadn't told anyone about our...*thing*.

We met up in secret, kissed in the dark, and for sure had never told Dean. In school, we'd run in different circles. Dean and I were in the band, took AP classes, dated the dance team girls, while Laney was an athlete and went to parties with the football players. Sure, everyone had been friendly, but there were still cliques, and the prom queen didn't go together with a bando.

Throughout history, there had been the caste system, the feudal system, and the social politics of the modern-day educational system. Surely robots would study it one day when they eventually took over the world.

Plus, Laney was Dean's sister. That was a line better left uncrossed.

"Your turn to deal," I said, changing the subject as I tossed the deck of cards to Seth. Obviously, that line was *still* better left uncrossed.

If only I could forget about those few weeks when that line hadn't existed.

Nadir tapped on the table, calling everyone's attention back to thc game. "Come on, ante up."

With that, we all got back to playing. And I lost fifty bucks.

CHAPTER FIVE

I parked my car back in front of Dean's house. The lights were off, but I peered through the blinds of the front window to make sure everyone was gone. The few miles on the treadmill and subsequent aimless driving did nothing to calm my nerves. It was as if I were adrift in the ocean, still struggling to come up for air from the Bobby Magnate wave, only to get knocked back down by the presence of Ethan.

Making my way into the house, I kept the lights off and crept upstairs. The walls were paper-thin, and I could hear Dean snoring in his room, yet instead of going to my bedroom —or rather, the guest room I'd been borrowing—I tip-toed to the middle of the hall, wincing when the wooden floorboards creaked.

Holding my breath, as if that would make opening the door quieter, I snuck into the small room which was apparently of no use to Dean except for storage, including some boxes from my previous life. They were stacked up, still unopened and wrapped with packing tape. Keeping sound to a minimum, I moved them around to get to the one at the bottom labeled *Miscellaneous* in my sloppy handwriting. Inside were random mementos, framed photos, a raggedy stuffed Thumper almost as old as me, and a few books, including the Holy Redeemer High School yearbook from my senior year.

With the tiny lamp on in the corner, I flipped through the thick pages, scanning the little notes and signatures written in every color, in every direction. A lot said *Call me sometime!* with a phone number. Cash, the resident class pothead, had drawn a marijuana leaf, while somebody sketched a big penis with no name. Nice.

The pages held black-and-white photos of every team and activity in the school. I was in a lot of them: the volleyball and softball team photos, standing on the stage at the homecoming dance with a court sash, making announcements as school vice president, dancing with JT as prom king and queen. Then there were those with Dean in the marching band, along with his best friends, Patrick, Gabe, Hank, and Ethan. They'd had their own jam band too. They called themselves the Anchormen, and a bunch of photos of them were included as well, all the boys in various states of shaggy hair and shirts untucked, against school dress code.

Stopping on a page about Religious Education, I skimmed my finger down to a picture of the whole school at mass in the gymnasium. It was Ash Wednesday, marked by the dark crosses on everybody's foreheads, but besides that, my eyes tripped over a detail I didn't think I'd ever noticed before. In the photo, Ethan was turned around to look back at me a few rows behind, my hand raised a little as if I might have been waving to him. I didn't recall that particular moment, but I did remember the big fight Ethan had gotten in with his girlfriend, Madison, that day. He hadn't sat next to her during mass, and she'd found him afterward in the main hall, hissing at him in that way she used to do so everyone knew they were fighting.

I pressed my fingers to my mouth now, holding back a laugh at how dramatic we all were back then. Everything was the absolute best and worst, highest of highs and lowest of lows. If only I knew then what I knew now, maybe I would've done everything differently.

Skipping ahead to the pages with the formal senior portraits, I found what I'd been looking for, the tiny writing—Ethan had always written so small—next to his picture with his wavy hair combed to the side, save for that cowlick. The smooth bronze color of his skin was done no justice by the photo, but the quirk to his lips was perfectly captured.

Lane,

Getting to know you this year has been great. The only thing I regret is not having more time with you. I hope we can change that this summer. –Ethan

Pangs of melancholy shot through me as I thought about how we had danced around each other that year. He'd started going out with Madison, a dance team girl, and I had whatever it was with JT, so that by the time we figured it out, we'd barely had any time together.

Though by then, I knew how I felt about Ethan. I knew from all the hours we'd spent talking throughout the year. I knew what his goals and aspirations were, and he knew that my greatest fear was disappointing people. And he'd been the only person I cried in front of.

When he'd found me in the hall that late winter afternoon, and he asked me what was wrong, I broke down. Because he had been the one to ask me. I had told him how stressed I was, feeling pressured about college and my grades and everything going on at school. I had always felt guilty for feeling frustration over my circumstances—why should the popular, pretty, rich girl have problems?—which led me to hide behind my mask of perfection, but Ethan knew. And he'd held me and let me soak his shirt with tears.

That was the day I realized I loved Ethan.

I read his note three more times before I closed the year-book and tucked it away, unable to put my finger on the reason for this late-night archaeology dig. Something about being heartbroken and home and longing for comfort. All of it together had me trying to imagine what might have become of us, of myself, if things had been different between me and Ethan. I wouldn't have been afraid to run into him on break and might not have taken that summer marketing internship with the Triple-A baseball team, which led to the next intern-ship and the next and the next, until I'd graduated with a job offer in hand. If Ethan hadn't moved on with his life, with other girls, I might not have learned how to curate my social media to make it seem like I was living it up. Maybe I wouldn't have tried so hard to stay with men who didn't respect me. Maybe I wouldn't be twenty-eight years old with no job and living with my brother, no husband or boyfriend. Not even a dog.

At this point, I'd even take a goldfish, but Dean didn't like animals of any kind. He always said if he wanted to live with animals, he'd move out into the wild. Last week when I'd brought up adopting a cat, he'd told me to go to the Phil-adelphia Zoo if I wanted to see some cats.

The idea of buying a fish clung to me as I showered and changed, but as I crawled into bed, the heavy loneliness I'd become friendly with lately snuggled in next to me. The self-doubt and insecurity had been paralyzing at times, but I'd been good at keeping myself secluded from everyone and everything so they couldn't witness me struggling with it. I'd even shut my parents out as much as possible, turning down my father's offer to work in his office and blatantly ignoring my mom's texts and voice mails about dinner or getting a pedicure together.

It felt impossible to face people sometimes, to put on a

brave face and gather enough pieces of myself to not be a scattered puzzle. And now, on top of everything, Ethan—the one person who'd always seemed to know what to say to put me back together—would be around. It was hard enough to work through everything going on in my life. I didn't know how to do it under the shadow of our past.

———

After yet another text message from Bobby, this one saying he needed me, I had turned my cell phone off and grabbed my laptop, updating my résumé on different job recruiting sites. However, nothing quite struck my fancy. I'd majored in marketing and communications, graduating at the height of when companies across the globe were expanding their digital footprints with social media directors. The role was a perfect fit for me, but with the 180 my life had taken, I wasn't sure I was interested in spending so much of my life online anymore. I'd given everything I'd had to Bobby and his growing food conglomerate. I hadn't been afraid to post photos and updates of us together, and he basked in the attention of strangers from around the world.

Bobby Magnate was a magnet for the spotlight, not unlike me. Although, while he craved it, I didn't much care either way. The number of followers I had didn't matter. The people I kept around me were the most important, and that was why I found myself down a Google rabbit hole.

Dean opened the front door of his house and shook off some snowflakes from his hair, a few shades darker than mine since I paid top dollar for my balayage. "Why aren't you answering your phone? Mom won't leave me alone because she can't get a hold of you."

I snorted a breath and rolled my eyes.

He removed his shoes and put them on the little rack by the door. "What's going on?"

"Nothing."

He knocked the top of my computer down on his way to hang up his coat in the closet. "Liar."

"Bobby keeps texting me," I said once he plopped down next to me.

"For what?"

I shrugged, and he threw his arm around me, quiet for a few moments. Then he met my eyes, the exact same as mine. "I know you're feeling pretty low right now, but he's going to suffer the rest of his life knowing he lost you. He'll be old and wrinkly on his deathbed, wishing he wasn't such an asshole. You are worth fighting for. He doesn't deserve you."

That was the thing, though. Bobby *was* fighting for me, at least a little bit, and that was what kept me from blocking him. Maybe I wanted to see him suffer, to know he was struggling. Or, maybe, a tiny piece of me still wanted to feel wanted.

"But seriously," Dean said, breaking up my thoughts. "You need to call Mom."

He tapped the screen of his cell phone a few times and held it out, speaker on. Our mother picked up right away. "Are you home?"

"Yeah, I'm with Laney."

"Hi, Mom," I said when he poked me in the arm.

"Delaney, why aren't you answering your phone? You have me nervous. I'm ready to get in my car to make sure you're still alive over there."

"I'm alive."

"Then answer your phone!"

"All right," I said, dragging the words out like I was thirteen again. "I've got a lot going on."

"Yeah? Like what?"

Dean sucked his lips between his teeth, so they disappeared in his short beard, and I elbowed him.

"I was looking up jobs today."

"Really? How did that go?" Mom asked.

Dean removed his arm from around my shoulders to study my laptop screen, but I moved it away. "Um, okay."

"Why do you sound unsure?"

I blew out a silent breath. Katherine Hargrove was not an overly demonstrative person, but she thrived on making sure her kids succeeded. "Because I'm not exactly sure what I want to do anymore."

Mom let out a curious sound on the other end. "What are you doing for money? You have some in savings, right?"

Dean and I both laughed. Our father had drilled assets and interest into us since we were kids.

"Yes, I have a bit stored away."

"And a benevolent brother who is letting her stay rent-free," Dean added.

"Laney, you can't take too long to decide what you're going to do. It's hard to explain away gaps on your résumé. You know you could still work with your father for a few hours a week, something down on paper so it doesn't look like you had a mental breakdown for a year."

"I am having a mental breakdown," I mumbled, and Dean shifted, pulling the phone closer to him.

"She's good, Mom. She needs a little time, that's all," he said, because when push came to shove, the Hargrove twins would go down together.

"Well, remember that we love you. Both of you. And the best way to get revenge is to just be you, Delaney. Be the best version of you and live your life."

"Thanks, Mom," I said at the same time Dean told her, "Talk later, Mom."

He hit the end button and pocketed his phone before looking me up and down in my hoodie, leggings, and green socks. "Mom's right. We gotta get you out of this house more often."

I made a face and repositioned my laptop on my thighs, making sure all evidence of my Ethan Marrero stalking was gone.

"What's for dinner?" Dean asked, lightly smacking my arm as he stood.

"I don't know. You don't have much in the fridge."

He crossed to the steps. "Seems like you need to go to the grocery store, then."

"Or," I said, holding my finger up, "we could order Thai."

"Great." He headed upstairs. "You're buying."

CHAPTER SIX

Laney

I loved my brother, but I hated his bathroom. Especially that it was only half finished.

Dean was a particular guy. He didn't like strangers in his house, so he refused to call anyone for help, which meant that when he'd bought this run-down townhouse last year, he'd decided he was going to completely renovate it himself. When we had talked about it, he'd said, "It can't be any harder than the bar exam."

According to him, working on the house was a way to de-stress from his job at the law firm. Every night, he'd come home and hammer some stuff, which was cool, if only he could hammer a little faster.

I'd been applying my makeup and completing my multi-step hair care routine in a shell of a shower and with a tiny mirror. My array of products were in Tupperware containers on the floor under the sink, and my makeup sat on the back of the toilet. One compact had already been lost to the sewer system—my favorite cream eye shadow—and I said a prayer over the watery grave every time I picked up my case.

Just as I finished my hair, the doorbell rang, and two

distinctly feminine voices carried upstairs. Dean had become a player in recent years, ever since his friend had died a few years ago. He struggled with his grief and seemed to substitute his real emotions with a steady rotation of women. His latest conquest was a nurse...or medical assistant...or maybe a vet tech.

I couldn't remember, except for the fact that she wore scrubs. I only knew that because I'd found them in the hallway one morning.

"Hey."

My hand jerked and broke the black line I'd been drawing with liquid eyeliner. "Damn."

"Sorry, didn't mean to scare you," Ethan said.

My heart pounded like it was attempting to get out of my chest. "You can't give me a warning or something?" I said as my eyes took on a mind of their own to survey him up and down in dark jeans and a thin pullover on top of a button-down. "How long have you been standing there?"

"Long enough to know you still stick the tip of your tongue out when you concentrate."

If there had been anything other than sweet familiarity in his voice, I might've been embarrassed. I'd never been able to break the habit.

"Did I mess you up?" he asked, tipping his chin toward the eyeliner wand in my hand, and I closed my eyes so he could view the damage. "Looks like a tiny inkblot test."

I opened my eyes again to his slanted smile. "You're a tiny inkblot test."

"Oh yeah?" He crossed his arms and tilted his head. "What do you see?"

What did I see?

Lots of things.

I saw my old friend. I saw traces of a teenage boy's smirk grown into a man's smile. I saw years of memories faded yet alive in front of me. Mostly, I saw a ghost of what could have been.

"That's a loaded question," I said after a few seconds, and he bent his head toward me in acquiescence. "Do you need to get in here?"

"Finish up. I'll wait."

"Sure?" When he nodded, I rounded back to the mirror and wiped my eyelid clean, starting all over again. "What're you doing here?"

Although he stayed in the hall, I knew he was watching me. "Dean has someone for me to meet."

With a sudden flashback to high school, I recalled Dean and Ethan going out with Kayla and Madison, who were best friends and on the dance team together, and something that felt an awful lot like jealousy bit into me. But that was stupid. There was nothing going on between me and Ethan. I didn't even know him anymore.

He could and should go out with whomever he wanted to.

"Where are you headed tonight?" he asked.

I cut him a glance. "I'm meeting one of my best friends for dinner. She lives in Allentown but is coming down for a few hours."

He skimmed his hand over his jaw, a few days' worth of stubble on it, and I couldn't believe that the loping puppy dog of a boy I used to know had grown up into this gorgeous man.

"We're getting tapas," I went on, tossing my mascara back into the bag. "Rather, we're getting two-for-one margaritas with tapas on the side." As his gaze raked over me, I tugged on an oversized sweater. "How do I look?"

His eyes softened behind his glasses. "Perfect. Except for the hair."

"What's wrong with my hair?" I whirled back to the mirror.

"It's straight. You used to have all that hair, bouncing all over."

I refused to laugh. "I still wear it curly sometimes. On a rare occasion."

"Yeah?" He drifted his attention off over my shoulder for a few moments before meeting my gaze again. "I remember when we went to the beach, and you were so annoyed at me when I got your hair wet."

My cheeks flamed that he would remember that small detail, or even bring up senior week. It was when we'd finally gotten together. Lost our virginity to each other down at the shore. Earlier, we had gone swimming together, and he'd splashed me with water, pointedly getting my hair wet even after I explained how hard it was to control. But then he'd snaked his arm around my waist under the water and pulled me close so that I'd forgotten why I even cared. I'd pressed my hand to the center of his chest and said, "I feel your heart beating."

Ethan had done the same, his long fingers spreading across the space between my breasts. While most boys only cared about how big my cup size was, he had never made me feel like that was all I was worth. "I feel yours too," he'd said. "It's beating so fast."

My heart was still beating fast. Ethan had always done that to me, made me feel both exhilarated, like the high from a run, and safe, like I could be my honest self with him. Even now.

"It takes a lot of time and energy to put this together," I said, aiming for nonchalance while images of our night on the beach flashed through my mind. With his furrowed expression, I assumed he might have been thinking of the same things too.

"Lane…"

My pulse stuttered and then galloped away. "I haven't heard that name in years."

"Really?"

"You're the only one who's ever called me that."

He shifted ever so slightly toward me, lowering his voice. "Is it totally clichéd to say you haven't changed?"

I swallowed the giant rock in my throat. "Totally."

He accepted that with a gracious bow of his head. "Then I am a cliché, and you haven't changed."

As he stared at me, my lips parted, and his eyes settled on them for a long moment, but when a laugh echoed downstairs, Ethan looked over toward the steps. He'd come to the bathroom for a reason, and I shuffled out to allow him inside, accidentally brushing his side on the way.

"Sorry," we both said at the same time, exchanging fractious smiles before I walked to my bedroom. By the time I'd picked a pair of boots from the closet, I met Ethan back in the hall as he pushed up his sleeves, showing off his forearms.

He had once joked with me that he had "drum muscles." He was well over six feet, even in high school, and built like a twig, although he had definition from the hours he spent behind his drum kit. I had liked his forearms then and even more now. Curling my fingers into fists, I resisted the urge to reach out and trace the lines of muscle and veins running between his elbows and hands. Hands that once knew me intimately.

When he leaned against the wall, I followed suit opposite him. "So, you're big-time now, huh? Vice president."

His lips turned down the slightest bit, the tops of his cheeks darkening. I didn't know much about his work, except for the random bits and pieces I'd heard from Dean.

"I'm assistant vice president," he corrected. "Of one department of the company, not the whole thing."

"What do you do exactly?"

"I'm a quantitative analyst."

I raised my brows for more.

"My department is responsible for developing, testing, and implementing quantitative models for risk management of traded assets."

"Right," I said, not comprehending the language.

He wrinkled his nose and pushed his glasses back with the tip of his finger. "I basically make financial models with math."

I kept my face blank. "Of course."

"Sounds like my tutoring did you a lot of good," he said, and a laugh burst out of me because when I had been hanging on to a D minus by my fingernails in precalculus in high school, he had tutored me to bring it up to a B.

A slow smile unfurled across his face as he slowly shook his head, and I was desperate to know what he was thinking. "What?"

He clucked his tongue, making me wait for his answer. Wait so long that I began to sweat.

"Your laugh. That's still the same too," he said eventually, his eyes never leaving mine.

"Loud and obnoxious?" I'd long gotten used to the side-eyes in public. "I know."

"No." He straightened and lifted his foot as if he wanted to step closer but only readjusted his stance. "Not at all."

I ignored my own automatic response to move toward him and instead asked, "How's everyone? How's your family?"

Ethan quirked his lips to the side before running a hand through his hair, and I recognized the habit. The lip twitch almost always preceded the hair tug. He was nervous about something. "My brother moved back home a few years ago because he and his wife had a baby."

I smiled. "Oh, congratulations."

But he didn't accept my felicitations. "They moved back because her parents unfortunately both passed away, and they needed help with the baby when my brother started having weird symptoms." He sniffed once and dropped his eyes to the floor. "He started talking funny, like he was drunk or couldn't find his words, and he's never been clumsy, ever in his whole life, but he began to drop things and..." He sniffed again, and I didn't think when I wrapped my hand around his elbow, offering support with a light squeeze. Then he raised his gaze to mine. "He's been forgetful, and in the last two years or so, he's started having these seizure-like movements. He can't control them. The doctors have had trouble diagnosing it. Turns out it's Huntington's."

"Oh god, Ethan. I'm so sorry. How is he?"

Ethan toggled his head back and forth. "Justin's good, for now. I think he's relieved he has an answer. Not the one he wanted, but now he can focus on the right therapies."

I stepped closer to him, smoothing my hand up his arm to his shoulder. "How are *you*?"

"I'm..." He let out an audible exhale. "I'm fine."

I gave him a sad smile. "I know you're lying because I've been saying the same thing lately."

He pursed his lips, sweeping his eyes over my face. "I hate that you're not fine."

"Same," I said with a fragile laugh. "I'm so sorry, Ethan. I know you're really close to your brother."

He nodded, and the shine of tears in his eyes stung like a scab breaking open, the decade-old heartbreak seeping through. Unable to keep my affection for him at bay, I wound my arms around his waist, resting my head against his shoulder, and after a short moment, he locked his arms around me too, settling his hands together at my lower back.

"Your shampoo is different," he said against my head.

"How do you even know that?" When he shrugged, I pretended not to understand the significance of his silence. "Guess that means I have changed."

"Not really." His fingers pressed into me a little tighter than before. "But for the record, I like this version of you just as much." His nose ruffled my hair. "I remember it used to smell orange, like a creamsicle. Now it smells flowery."

I shouldn't have cared that he remembered that insignificant detail, but the mixture of his honesty and his breath against my ear had my own eyes prickling, and I clung to him, burying my nose into his neck to hide the emotion. I didn't know if the tears were for him, me, or all of it.

"Hey! Marrero, what're you doing up there?"

A surprised huff rumbled in Ethan's chest, and he rubbed a few soft circles on my back before letting go. His lips tipped up in a half smile. "I better go."

I cleared my throat, mindlessly twirling my hair up in a bun then let it drop. "Yeah, sure. Sorry I held you up."

"Never." He shook his head, slow to turn around. "See you later, Lane."

I sagged against the wall and listened to a short exchange between my brother and Ethan and then a few giggles from the girls.

"Laney! We're leaving! See you later!" Dean called up, and I nodded to myself. I had somewhere to be too, and by the time I got to the restaurant, Bronte was already there.

We greeted each other with a hug.

"Look at you with your cute little bob," I said, gesturing to my friend's recent haircut.

She smiled and preened then pointed to the margaritas on the table. "I ordered you blood orange."

"Perfect, thanks. Sorry I'm late."

"Everything okay?" she asked, sitting back down, ever concerned.

"Yeah, yeah." I removed my coat and scarf. "I got caught up. Ethan was over."

She froze with her drink halfway to her mouth. "The high school heartbreaker?"

"Yes, but it was no big thing." Laney reached for my own drink. "He and Dean hang out a lot, and we were talking, that's all."

At Bronte's suspicious eyebrow, I rambled on. "He has an older brother he's really close to, Justin, who was diagnosed with Huntington's disease recently, and..." I paused for a sip of my margarita, avoiding my friend's gaze. "When we saw each other last week, it felt weird."

"Wait." She held her hand up. "First of all, that's really sad for Ethan's brother and their family. Second of all, you didn't tell us you saw him last week. I find it funny that you haven't mentioned any of this."

"Because there's nothing to mention."

Bronte pinned me with her teacher stare. "No, only that you've been like a zombie since you left Bobby except for that little twinkle in your eye when you mentioned Ethan."

I rolled said eyes. "I do not twinkle."

"All right." She held out her hand. "Let me see a photo of him."

With nothing to hide, I grabbed my cell phone and opened up my Instagram app. Bronte had shunned all social media and was even more vigilant since she had married Chris "CJ" Cunningham, an A-list actor whom she'd met on a plane ride home from one of our girls' trips, oddly enough. Since they'd gotten together, he'd gone from a Hollywood train wreck to a Pennsylvania homebody, filming small projects and working on his own production house. He and Bronte were sacred about their privacy, but at this point, he was really more of a stay-at-home husband with acting as a side gig.

Bronte scrolled through Ethan's profile. "There aren't many photos of him on here," she said, noting the majority of nature pictures. "Is this him and his brother? They don't look anything alike."

I took in the photo. Ethan with his wide grin, stretching ear to ear, and his brother, who was much paler with sandy hair. "They're both adopted."

She nodded and found another photo. "Aww, this one's cute. Who's this?"

I smiled at what had to be a picture from a few years ago, of Ethan holding a baby with a tiny afro. "That's Justin's kid, I think."

Bronte went back to scrolling for a moment before tapping her thumbs a few times. She stuck her straw in her mouth, humming thoughtfully.

"What?"

"I'm reading his LinkedIn profile. He went to Princeton and studied abroad for two semesters in Germany and Argentina then earned his master's in statistics." She glanced up at me with a laugh. "He'd get along well with Jason."

I ignored her implied meaning that Ethan would somehow be invited into our couple group, and that he'd have something in common with Jason since they were both in the STEM field. But there was no way that was happening. "I just broke up with Bobby. Let's slow your roll, okay?"

"Okay." Bronte lifted one hand in innocence and handed my phone back with the other. "So, how are you doing? And don't say fine," she said, beating me to the punch.

"I'm..." I cleared my throat, playing with my utensils. "I'm a little lost. I don't know what I'm doing or where I'm going."

She pursed her lips. If any of the girls could understand that sentiment, it was Bronte, who had her life planned out in milliseconds and was thrown off by the tiniest of changes. "That's okay, though. Take some time for yourself."

I grimaced at the thought. I came from a family of people who didn't know what taking "time for yourself" meant. My father was a locally renowned orthodontist, my mother was the director of human resources for a national consulting firm, and my brother's idea of a good time was coming home from his day job to renovate his house. Success was measured in money and title promotions in the Hargrove family.

I already felt like a leech staying at my brother's house, but I didn't know what else to do. Finding that condom in my trash had thrown me for quite a loop. All of my confidence had gone down the drain, along with my motivation.

"He keeps texting me," I said, swirling my straw around my glass.

"Bobby?" Bronte's normally low voice squeaked out her indignation. "About what?"

"Apologies. Saying that it's the worst mistake of his life."

"Laney..."

When I lifted my gaze, I was appalled at myself to feel a well of tears in my eyes. For the second time today.

"Tell me honestly," Bronte said, "what's going on in your head?"

"I'm not sure. That's the whole problem." I felt like an asshole admitting it, but... "Everything has always been kind of easy for me. I worked hard, but I got lucky with privilege and opportunity. One connection led to another, and now that I've quit the Magnate Company, I don't know where to go. I don't even know what I want to do anymore."

She squinted at me. "What about Bobby? Are you done with him? For good?"

"I mean…" I shrugged. People always said never say never, but I couldn't imagine being able to overcome him cheating on me. "That night, he said it was a one-time thing, and I feel like that almost makes it worse. Like, if it meant something to him, if he wanted to be with her, I could understand it more. But he did that for what? If being with another woman meant nothing to him, then what did *I* mean to him?"

Bronte dabbed at her own eye with her cloth napkin. No one cried alone in her presence. "It's terrible. You don't deserve it. No one should ever feel disrespected like that."

I was about to tell her how when I packed up my bags, Bobby literally clung to me so I wouldn't leave our bedroom, but my cell phone buzzed with an alert. A pathetic laugh bubbled up as I showed her my phone and subsequent text message.

BOBBY

We need to talk. Please. I love you, joey.

Bronte shook her head. "What are you going to say back?"

"Nothing." I tossed my phone into my purse. "Let's forget about him for now. You want the shrimp flatbread?"

"Yes." She clapped once, her eyes on her menu. "We're getting the cheese board, right?"

"Of course. My stomach will hate me tomorrow, but we're no amateurs here."

She laughed and ordered a few plates of food so that by the time tapas arrived, we were both done with our first round of drinks. As I was about to order more, a man sidled up to our table with a friendly wave.

"Delaney? I thought that was you."

I smiled up at him. Although I didn't recollect who he was, I was nothing if not good when I couldn't remember people's names. "Hi! How are you?"

"Great, great," he said, leaning toward our table, and I racked my brain for the reason I knew him. He was so familiar with that big grin and bit of gray at the temples, even though something told me he wasn't more than early thirties. "I haven't seen you in a while."

I inclined my head. "I just moved back from San Francisco."

"Oh?" He tilted his head, his smile momentarily lost. "You're home?"

"For the time being. I'm having drinks with one of my best friends, Bronte." I gestured to Bronte, and he extended his hand to shake hers.

"Hi," he said, "I'm George."

I barely held back from snapping my fingers in recognition. "George works with my dad."

Bronte nodded politely. "Nice to meet you."

"Well, ladies, I don't want to take up any more of your night," George said, his hand on the back of my chair. "I only wanted to come over and say hi." He pointed to our empty glasses. "What're you drinking? Can I buy you the next round?"

"Oh no, you don't have to do that," I said, admiring his perfectly white smile against his honey-brown skin. Of course, I knew who George Ataya was. I'd met him on multiple occasions, always sweet.

"Please. It's my pleasure." He raised his dark brows. "You doing the specialty margarita? I can't resist it either." Then he rapped his knuckles once on the table. "It was great seeing you again, Delaney, and nice meeting you, Bronte. Enjoy the rest of your night."

A few minutes later, our drinks arrived, courtesy of George, and we both turned toward the bar. George was facing us, and when I raised my glass to him in a thank-you, he winked before shifting back to the two men he was with.

"Nice guy, that George," Bronte said.

"Mm-hmm."

"You're so popular you don't even know all your fans."

"He's not a fan," I said into my drink.

Bronte pointed a slice of Manchego cheese at me. "We'll see."

CHAPTER SEVEN

Ethan

"Come on, buddy. Why don't you come with me?" I offered my hand to my nephew, so he'd leave his mom alone, and Leah sent me a grateful smile.

"I'm hungry," Trace said, tugging on my fingers. "Like a lion." Then he roared, and I bent down, roaring right back.

"Dinner will be ready soon, but you gotta be a little patient. Look." I pointed to a couple of coloring books haphazardly thrown on the kitchen table. "Let's color for a bit." I sat Trace on the chair next to me and spread out the animal-themed coloring books and crayons between us while Justin and Leah finished dinner.

It'd been a few weeks since the diagnosis, and my brother had begun a regimen of medications to help the symptoms, but he still had a long road ahead of him. Watching him wrap an arm around Leah's waist, peering over her shoulder as she fiddled with a pan on the stove, I felt that familiar brick land in my stomach again. My brother and sister-in-law had already been through so much, with Leah's parents passing within months of each other, and now this. They didn't deserve it.

But god, they'd made a cute little kid. Rubbing my hand

over Trace's short curls, I kissed the side of his head. I'd do whatever I could to help my brother's family, although at the moment, I didn't know what else to do besides make sure my nephew was well taken care of, taking some of the load off Justin and Leah.

"How's school?" I asked, and Trace exchanged a green crayon for a yellow, scribbling in the trees behind a leopard.

"Good. I was line leader today."

"Yeah? You like that job?"

"Uh-huh." Trace swiped at his nose with his sleeve. "And doing the weafer." Then he started mumbling some song about what's the weather today, and I laughed, happy that Trace was still too young to understand the full weight of his father's situation and, unfortunately, his own possible future.

I tried not to dwell on the bad stuff, but sometimes it seeped into my thinking, and all of this had made me curious about my own health, family, and identity. Even though my parents had never kept information from me, I never felt the need to contact my biological parents. After seeing the anguish my brother had gone through when he couldn't find his own, I hadn't been interested in following the same path. Yet now, I'd been reconsidering that stance.

Trace held his paper up to me. "For you! You hafta hang it on your fridge."

"You got it, my man." I took it and blew out a low whistle. "A masterpiece like this might need to be framed. Put on the mantel."

"Mantel?" He hopped from his seat onto my lap. "What's a mantel?"

"It's usually a big piece of wood that goes over a fireplace, and you put important stuff on it, like pictures of people you love."

"Like that?" He pointed to the half wall separating the kitchen from the dining room, where a picture of Leah's mom and dad sat, and I nodded.

"Kind of like that."

"Papa and Granny are in heaven," Trace told me as if he didn't remind everyone at least once a week. The kid was obsessed with death and heaven and the stars in the sky being those people who had passed. Incidentally, Trace was also obsessed with *The Lion King*.

"I know, buddy."

"Hey, by the way," Leah said, turning around. "My cousin's birthday is coming up, and we wanted to go up to the city for the night. Have a little date night away from the gorilla over there."

Trace puffed out a couple of gorilla sounds, banging at his chest.

"We asked Mom and Dad to watch him, but they already had plans," Justin added, his head ticking to the side, another of those uncontrollable movements.

I shrugged. "I'll watch him. No problem. When is it?"

"End of the month," Leah said, setting a fork down and clicking the burner off. "We'd be staying over. Is that okay?"

"Yeah, of course." I held my hand out to Trace for a high five. "You're coming to stay with Uncle Ethan for a night."

"Really?" He shot his arms up, cheering. "Woo-hoo!"

Justin grabbed a few dishes from a cabinet and walked around to set the table. "All right, kiddo. Have a seat. It's time for dinner."

Trace reached out for his special plastic plate so his food didn't touch and smacked the table with his fork a few times.

"Uh-uh, no, sir." Leah eyed him so that the four-year-old immediately froze, though he still shot her his best grin. "You think you're so cute."

"Like his dad," Justin said, having a seat, and Leah clucked her tongue at them both before setting the chicken, green beans, and potatoes on the table.

We all dug in, except for Trace, who played with his food more than he ate it.

"This is delicious, babe," Justin said, and I agreed.

"Yeah, thanks for having me over."

Leah pointed at me with a green bean on her fork. "You know you're welcome any time you want."

I chewed and swallowed a bite of chicken. "I don't want to inconvenience you. I don't want to add more pressure to everything you guys are dealing with."

Justin held up his water glass, the liquid trembling from his unsteady hold. "You're not an inconvenience," he said, meeting my gaze. "I want you here. We want you here."

I nodded and dropped my attention back down to my food, pushing away the emotion in my throat to finish my dinner. Afterward, Trace and I cleared the table to earn his ice cream with sprinkles, and I helped myself to a few scoops too.

"Like this," Trace said, showing me how to shake the container of sprinkles to get the optimal amount. "When I stay at your house, can we have a sprinkle party?"

"Obviously."

"That's all he's going to talk about now," Leah said, leaning back in her chair. "Sleeping over at Uncle Ethan's house."

Trace danced in his seat. "I can't wait! I go tomorrow?"

"Not for another two weeks, buddy."

Trace pouted, and Justin tapped on the table a few times. "When you finish your ice cream, I'll give you a bath, okay?"

"Okay," he said, then shoved a big spoonful in his mouth. "I bring my animals in. Lobster and octopus and whale, they're all sea creatures," he told me. "Sea creatures!"

We all laughed at Trace's never-ending energy and animal

fascination, and when he finally finished his ice cream, Justin held his hand to take him upstairs. "Night, night, Uncle Efan!"

"Night, buddy!"

When I moved to stand up and put our bowls in the sink, Leah stayed me with her hand on my wrist. "Don't worry about it. I'll do it later."

I sat back down, resting my elbows on the table, taking note of the lines at her eyes that seemed to appear overnight. "How're you doing?"

Her shoulders rose on an inhale. "Taking it day by day."

"You wouldn't tell me if it were any different," I said, because I knew she shouldered her burdens with a smile.

Like she did now. "You can't fix everything, you know."

"I know." I swiped my palm over my mouth. "God, I know."

She patted my arm, exchanging an encouraging smile with me. "This is a tall mountain to climb, and it's going to take a long time. We can't give in to sadness so early, huh?"

I nodded at Leah's suggestion, feeling a little ashamed at how upset I'd been when it was my brother who was sick. I liked to solve problems. In my work life, that's what I did, but I couldn't solve this one, and that kept me up at night. Burying my guilt, I inclined my head, trying on a slick smile. "You aren't gonna, by any chance, be bringing home some leftovers when you go?"

She laughed, a high, tinkling sound. "You want some?"

Leah's family was Jamaican, and if I could, I'd dislodge my jaw and pour their oxtail down my throat. "Only if it's not a hassle."

"I think I could find a couple of takeaway boxes for you."

"You're the best. Truly," I said, standing to kiss her cheek. "Thanks again for dinner."

She squeezed my side. "Don't forget your picture."

"Oh, yeah." I grabbed Trace's leopard and waved behind my head on the way out the door. "Love you."

59

CHAPTER EIGHT

Ethan

Saturday morning, Dean texted to ask if I could come over and help him finish up the bathroom. I was happy to oblige since I needed to talk out some stuff anyway. Mid-February in Pennsylvania was cold, and with a sudden snow squall, I hustled up to Dean's house before my face froze off in the bitter wind. "Goddamn," I mumbled with a tip of my chin to my friend. "It's like ten degrees out."

From his place on the couch, Dean lifted a mug. "You want some coffee?"

I removed my hat and coat and kicked off my shoes. "Yeah, thanks." I helped myself in the kitchen before making my way back to the living room, noting how quiet the house was. "Where's Laney?"

"Running errands. I told her I'd have the bathroom finished before she got back. Get her off my ass about it."

I held the coffee between my palms to warm up. "What's left?"

"Install the vanity and lighting. Finish the grout."

"Shouldn't take long, then."

"Two hours, tops," Dean said, and I took a seat on the leather recliner in the corner.

"So, listen, I wanted your opinion on something."

Dean carefully set his coffee cup down and leaned forward, his elbows on his knees, his hands knitted together. "Yeah?"

"If I wanted to start a charity, what would that entail?"

"Charity? For what?"

I tugged at the hair at the back of my head. "Something for Huntington's."

He rubbed his hands together. "Sure, yeah. Okay. We can do that. You'll need a registered agent." He pointed to himself. "We'll open a 501(c)(3), get an EIN and all the tax stuff registered and sorted. Are you going to want a board?"

"I, uh, I don't know. I haven't thought that far ahead, really. I figured I'd run the idea by you first to see what you thought."

"I think it's a great idea." His eyes lit up. "How big are you thinking?"

I pushed my glasses up my nose. "I mean...right now, I was thinking to do a local fundraiser. See how it goes and expand from there, but I'm not sure where to start."

Dean snapped his fingers. "You know who you should talk to? Laney. I know she's got experience with fundraising. Plus, she's got all kinds of connections."

As if I needed another reason to talk to Laney. I only slurped my coffee, hoping my best friend couldn't see how the prospect of working with his sister excited me.

"I know you've felt kinda helpless with all this," Dean said after a minute. "I think this is a great idea. We got you."

"Thanks." I finished the rest of my coffee then slapped my thighs. "I guess we should get started, huh?"

We worked for the next hour, drilling white cabinetry into place under the sink and hanging the fancy lighting fixtures above the huge mirror before finishing the grouting around the new tile Dean had installed.

Stepping back to admire it, he nodded. "Looks good, right?"

"Yeah, man, if you ever want to leave your career, I think you've got another one in home renovation."

Before he could say anything else, the front door opened downstairs, and he ducked his head out into the hall. "Laney, get up here! Come look!"

A couple of thuds sounded before, "What?"

"We finished the bathroom."

She hightailed it upstairs, her footsteps echoing through the house, and when she reached the top step, a grin broke out across her face. "You finished?"

Dean gestured for her to come inside, and I took two steps back, offering her a smile of hello. She still wore her coat and scarf wrapped around her neck, but her nose and cheeks were tinged red, and I had trouble not reaching out to curl my palm around the curve of her jaw, feel how cold her skin was, and warm her up.

"Oh my god." She gasped, reaching out for the new sink. "It's gorgeous." Her smile was blinding as she turned in a circle. "Look at you, even got a little hanging plant in the corner. Great job, boys."

She high-fived her brother and gave my bicep a friendly squeeze. There was no reason for me to flush with heat. But I couldn't take my eyes off her. Whatever made her happy made me happy.

"I've got to put groceries away downstairs," she said, and I glanced at Dean.

"I'll clean this up." He tipped his chin to the tools scattered on the floor, so I followed Laney back downstairs, where she hung her outerwear in the closet, revealing a matching athletic outfit, like she'd been at the gym, and *fuck*.

Laney was tall, barely shy of six feet, but when we were in

high school, she didn't have the curves she did now, like an old-school pinup. My attention drifted down to her ass as she sauntered to the kitchen, and I physically shook my head, attempting to refocus. And not on the sliver of golden skin revealed between her top and leggings. With how the material clung to her, she might as well have been wearing nothing.

At her laugh, I blinked back into the reality that I was supposed to be helping her empty grocery bags. "I'm sorry, what?"

With the raise of her eyebrow, I'd obviously been caught ogling her, although she didn't seem to mind. "I said, how long have you been here?"

"Since about ten."

She effortlessly reached up to the cabinet above her head to put away a box of cereal, and that didn't help my gawking. She'd been a good athlete, into volleyball and even received a scholarship for softball, but not long into her first season at Pitt, she'd gotten a compound fracture in a game, on a bad slide—according to her brother—and had to have surgery. After a MCL tear in high school, the new injury was career ending for her. I knew she would have been devastated but was afraid to reach out. Even though we hadn't stayed in touch directly, I had kept tabs on her from afar, always asking for updates from Dean, making sure she was all right. I assumed she still had that athletic inclination, but sweet lord, I appreciated how soft and plush her hips looked now.

"Good friend you are," she said, pivoting around to open another bag. This one of small heart-wrapped chocolates and a bouquet of flowers. "I thought maybe you'd have plans today."

"Valentine's Day," I said, filling in the blanks. I'd forgotten, not caring all that much about it. I placed a loaf of bread on the counter, followed by a carton of eggs. "You have plans?"

She held up the chocolates. "If by plans you mean eating

these and watching a true crime documentary, then yes. What about you? Going out again with...what was her name?"

I tipped my head to the side, swearing I heard a hint of jealousy in her voice. "Who?"

She put away a couple cans of soup. "The girl you went out with on your double date."

"Gretchen." I shook my head. "Not for me."

She slanted her eyes to me for a moment before folding up the reusable bags and sliding them into a spot underneath the sink. "Well, you never were one for Valentine's Day."

I huffed a laugh as I passed her the eggs to put in the refrigerator. "No."

"I honestly thought Madison was going to break up with you for that."

I scrubbed my hand over my jaw, biting back a smile as I recalled how my high school girlfriend had been mad at me because I'd told her I hadn't planned anything special. So, the next day, I'd put a bunch of rose petals in her locker, thinking it was romantic, but by the time she'd opened it, they had all shriveled up. A waterfall of browned and wilted flower carcasses landed at her feet. We'd gotten into another argument, and I had spent my Valentine's Day at the Hargrove house, tutoring Laney in math.

"I'm more of a spoil her every day kind of guy," I said, stepping toward Laney with the bread.

She only pursed her lips in thought, so full and pink, and I had to force my eyes up to hers, the same color blue of a summer's day. She cleared her throat and turned to put the bread away, her back to me.

"I wanted to talk to you about something," I started, leaning my hip on the counter. "I had a chat with Dean about it, and he said you might be able to help me."

That had her peeking over her shoulder, but from my position, all I could see was the slight tilt of her lips and the tiny mole by her nose. "What's up?"

"I want to start a nonprofit, dedicated to raising money for Huntington's research. Dean's going to help me set it up, but I was wondering if you'd help me figure out how to go about putting an actual fundraiser together. Throw a party or something."

She folded her arms across her chest and spun slowly toward me. "I don't know."

The answer honestly surprised me. I assumed this would be right up her alley.

"I'm not sure how long I'll be here."

"Well, that's okay," I said, taking another step toward her. "I'd appreciate any help you could give me."

She nodded, shifting her weight back and forth as she considered this. Her hair was pulled back in a low ponytail at the nape of her neck, but a few loose strands floated by her ears, and I had to curl my fingers into my palm to keep from toying with them.

"I don't know," she repeated after a while.

One more step closer to her, and I placed my hand on the counter, right next to her hip. "You don't know?"

She lifted her gaze to my face, settling somewhere below my eyes before drifting over my shoulder. "You know I was working with Bobby, right?"

I nodded but didn't understand what that had to do with anything.

"I could send you some resources, but I don't think it's a good idea for me to work with you on this."

"Why?"

She met my eyes, the corner of her lip between her teeth, one slim eyebrow raised as if I should know.

"I don't get it."

"You're really going to make me spell it out for you?"

I lifted my hand up. "Please."

"Ethan." She sighed. "You and me, we have history, and I don't know if…"

With the way she dropped my gaze again, I thought our history wasn't so much history. It felt very present.

"Lane," I said, waiting until she flicked her eyes to me. "I—"

Her phone buzzed, and we both looked at it on the counter. She brushed past me, our forearms grazing as she picked it up. "Hello?"

I couldn't hear who was on the other end, but from the momentary crimp in her brow, maybe she wasn't sure either.

"Oh yes. Hi, George," she said, smiling at nothing as she spun away from me as if to hide the conversation. I didn't know who George was, but I didn't like him. "Oh, really?" she asked with a laugh. "No, that's okay. I don't mind. My father has been known to give my number out to lots of people. How can I help you?"

I mumbled a curse in frustration. She was willing to help out this George guy, but not me? The guy she'd known since high school?

"Oh." Laney's voice flitted higher, and she played with her ponytail. "Um, I guess that's okay." I got a funny feeling about this phone call, especially when she said, "This Friday? That sounds good."

I placed my hand on my neck. It was hot, and I blew out a breath.

"No, that's all right. We can meet there. Seven o'clock? Sure."

I really didn't like the sound of that. I'd been about to bring up our sordid so-called past when this George person had ostensibly called to make plans with Laney. Perfect timing.

"Okay. See you later," she said and signed off, dropping her cell phone to her side.

"Who was that?" My question came out more hostile than I meant it to.

She rigidly turned on her heel, cocking her head to the side. "Someone who works with my dad. We're... He's taking me out."

"On a date?" I ran both of my hands through my hair a few times, this whole situation like déjà vu. "I thought that..." My sentence broke on a mirthless laugh, my hands on my hips.

"What?" She crossed her arms, glaring when I didn't answer. "What, Ethan?"

"This," I said, giving her what she wanted. "It feels exactly like it did back then."

"I don't..." She shook her head, and I could see her throat working on a swallow. "What are you talking about?"

"You and me."

"You and me?" she echoed almost incredulously, which was nonsensical because not even five minutes ago, she explained how she couldn't work with me *because* of our past.

"Yeah." I lowered my voice, once again invading her space. I knew I should have waited for an invitation, but the way her pupils dilated and her chest rose and fell at a quicker pace was invitation enough. "You and me."

"What about you and me?" She released her arms from their stiff hold to immediately backtrack, holding her hands up. "Never mind."

"No, not never mind. You wanted to know what I'm thinking, so let's get it out there." I lifted my chin in a challenge because Delaney Hargrove never backed down from a challenge.

"Fine." She stood taller. "Let's hear it, then."

I let out an audible breath. "Lane, you had to have known how I felt about you then."

She huffed. "Need I remind you, you were the one to leave?"

"Jesus, Laney, you…you were the 'it girl,' everybody loved you. You had so many friends, guys fell at your feet." I threw my hands out to her cell phone, evidence of my point. "They still do. And I was no one. I felt like—" I peered off into the distance of ten years ago "—I felt like I didn't deserve you. You had everything and everyone at your fingertips."

She flinched. "I'm sorry. I didn't mean—"

"No." I grabbed her hands. "I don't mean that in a negative way. Everyone loved you because you had an energy around you. You were sweet and smiling and never made anyone feel like they weren't the center of your world when you talked to them. At least, that's how you made me feel."

She closed her eyes at that last bit and twisted out of my light grasp, but I went on, undeterred. "I sat back all those months, waiting, hoping for something to happen. I wasted time, thinking the differences between us mattered. I thought there was no way you'd want me, a band nerd."

A strangled laugh left her mouth, and when she finally looked up at me with what appeared to be regret crisscrossing her familiar features, I had to tell her everything. She had to know. "When I finally had my chance, the timing wasn't right, and I'm so sorry I hurt you." I reached for her again, this time to skim my knuckle down her cheek. "I hated how we left things. I hated that every time I came home from college, I never saw you. I hated that when I went to your house, you conveniently weren't there."

"Don't make me cry," she whispered, the space between her eyebrows pinching. "You know I hate to cry."

Wrapping my hand around her neck, I leaned down to her.

"I lived in so many places, all over the world, but my home is here, and when I heard what happened between you and that Australian chef, I was furious. I was mad because if I'd been the man I wanted to be back then, if I'd done what I wanted to do, maybe you wouldn't have been with him in the first place. Maybe you'd have been with me instead."

"That's a lot of 'maybe's." She whirled away from me. "But it was a long time ago. We were kids—"

"We were kids," I said, cutting her off. "And I know what I felt for you was real." With my hand on her elbow, I spun her back around to me, halting whatever argument she had on those bee-stung lips of hers. "I need you to know how I felt because my reaction to that—" I motioned to the air next to her ear "—phone call is jealousy. Laney, I was hesitant back then because I didn't think you could feel about me the way I felt about you. But I know better now. I'm not going to stand by and let you go without telling you how I feel."

I hadn't realized that she'd curled her hands into my shirt until she was tugging on it, silently inviting me to take what I wanted. And what I wanted was a kiss. With one hand around her waist and the other on her jaw, I bent to her.

Her lips were soft, and she tasted exactly like I remembered, and I pulled her closer, sweeping my tongue into her mouth. Ten years—ten long years—and she still had the ability to melt me into a puddle at her feet.

With a light pull at her bottom lip, I backed away, and a quiet groan of protest sounded from the back of her throat. A few seconds passed before she opened her eyes to me.

I grinned down at her. "Happy Valentine's Day."

She bobbed her head, a little like a rag doll, as if I had kissed all her words away. And it was possible I had, because she silently circled away from me and made her way upstairs.

Let her think about *that* on her date.

CHAPTER NINE

Laney

Friday night, I contemplated my reasons for canceling my date with George and staying home instead. One hour, twenty-seven minutes, and counting until I had to meet him at the Mediterranean place downtown, and I was already sweating. Starfished out on my bed, I texted an **SOS** the girls.

A few minutes later, Gem, Bronte, and Sam were all on my screen. FaceTime was a miracle.

"I don't want to go," I said without preamble.

"Why not?" Sam asked, lifting a water bottle to her lips.

"I don't know what to do. I haven't been on a first date in…" I did the quick mental math. "Four years."

Gem flicked her hand. "It hasn't changed since then. You go out, you eat, you talk."

I huffed. "How would you know? You haven't been on a first date in almost as long."

"Yeah, and I'm paying for it now." Gem held up an orange popsicle, one of the few things that didn't make her nauseous while pregnant. She'd been sick almost her whole first pregnancy, and this second one was turning out the same way.

"I think this is a good idea," Bronte said. "George seemed like a really nice guy for you to rebound with."

"I don't need a rebound."

Gem pointed the popsicle at her screen. "Yes, you do. You can't hide forever."

Even though Gem was exactly right, I didn't want to admit it. Yes, I was aware I had to leave my hermit life behind at some point, but I wasn't prepared to do anything other than crawl out of the shell I'd come to find comfort in. "I'm not hiding," I muttered. "I'm...gestating on what I want to do with my life."

Gem snorted. "You're gestating some cobwebs between your legs is what you're doing."

Bronte and Sam laughed like the traitors they were.

I flipped them all the bird.

"Come on," Sam said. "You deserve to be taken out on a nice date, and according to Bronte, this guy can ease you back into it."

Bronte nodded enthusiastically, and I groaned. "I don't even know what to wear."

"You have a closet full of clothes," Sam said, "I'm sure you'll find something."

"Make sure your underwear is cute."

I rolled my eyes at Bronte's suggestion. "They're a nice pair of high-waisted cotton."

"You're twenty-eight, not eighty-eight." Gem polished off the rest of her popsicle. "And that's exactly why you need to have sex again. You're aging too early."

"That's not a thing," I grumbled, rolling off my bed to slink to the closet, one hand holding my phone while I flipped through my clothes with the other.

"Well," Sam started, the brain of the group. "Orgasms are proven to keep your stress level low. There was a small study done that found if you have sex at least once a week, it could delay the effects of aging because it keeps up your physical and mental health."

"Is that a fact?" I propped my hand on my hip.

Gem smiled. "It's science."

"I know you barely passed chemistry in college." I aimed an accusing finger at the phone.

Gem shrugged. "Yes, but my struggle with covalent bonds has nothing do to with your sex life. Unless, of course, you're going to do some covalent bonding with George."

I squinted at her. "If you can tell me what covalent even means, maybe I'll consider it."

"Jason!"

Bronte, Sam, and I all snickered when Gem's husband appeared behind her, their daughter, Willow, in his arms.

"What's a covalent bond?"

"You do know what Google is, right?" he asked her then waved to the screen, and their toddler followed suit. "What's up, girls?"

"What's a covalent bond?" Gem repeated.

"It's when atoms share electrons. Everybody knows that," he said to her, and then to Willow, "Right, even you know that?"

Gem plopped her chin in her hands, explaining to the us, "He's bought this entire series of science for babies books."

"We're really into quantum physics lately," Jason said, and Willow shouted out, "Dis a ball!"

Jason kissed his daughter's head. "Right. That's the first line of every book."

"Laney has a date," Gem told him, and he pumped his fist.

"Yeah? Did we vet this one?"

Bronte raised her hand. "I did."

"Good." Then he wiggled Willow's hand at the screen. "We're going to have dinner. Hope you have a good time, Laney. Me, Chris, and Mike have our date night too."

The three boys got together a couple times a month to play

online video games, and even though Bobby had been invited to be part of their little group, he'd never accepted. He was either too busy or said that he didn't want to take my friends away from me. At the time, I thought it was okay Bobby wanted to keep his friends separate from mine, but now I realized he never wanted to share our lives. No matter how many times he'd told me he loved me, it was surface level.

"Okay, I have to get going anyway," I whined.

Sam waved. "Let us know how it goes."

"And make sure you wear something cute underneath," Bronte said. "At least for a confidence booster."

"Or don't wear anything at all," Gem suggested.

I heaved out a sigh. "Bye!"

After my primping and pruning, I was ready but not so raring to go and made my way downstairs to find Dean and Hank on the couch, watching some sci-fi movie.

I swatted Hank's socked foot, a big hole on the bottom. "Why're you always here? You *are* married, right?"

He munched on a chip. "She says she likes me better when I'm not around bugging her."

I snorted a laugh.

"She's into scrapbooking and does it pretty much every weekend. Tonight, all these women came over with stamps and construction paper and..." He blew a raspberry.

"So, now we get him." Dean gestured to me as I zipped up my booties. "You look nice."

I tugged on my long-sleeved wrap dress. "I have a date."

"Yeah?" He picked up his phone when it buzzed, typing as he asked, "Where're you going?"

"To that new Mediterranean place."

"Are you driving?"

When I didn't answer, my brother lifted his attention, shooting me a stare. "Text me if you aren't coming home."

"Yes, Dad."

His annoyed glare faded into a reluctant smile. "Don't be dumb."

Sliding my arms into my brown pea coat, I stalked to the door, and Hank clapped a few times. "Go get 'em, killer."

Behind me, Dean told Hank, "Ethan says he'll be here in ten. He's picking up the food."

I blew out a breath that fogged in the cold air and closed the door on that particular piece of information. I hadn't seen Ethan since our conversation last week, and after that kiss—that tease of a kiss—I definitely didn't want to think about it before my date with another man.

But since it was in my head now, it was all I could think of. The warmth of his hands, the press of his lips against mine, his stupid, perfect smile. And I shoved it all in a box in the back of my mind as I parked the car, locking it away.

Inside the restaurant, I spotted George at the bar, sipping a dark drink, dressed in a striped shirt, perfectly fitted pants, and sports coat. When I tapped him on the shoulder, he twisted toward me, smiling. "Hello, Delaney."

I placed my clutch on the bar. "Hi, how are you?"

"I'm fantastic. Would you care for a drink? It'll be a few more minutes for our table."

I put on a smile, concentrating on unclenching my jaw and relaxing my shoulders, which he seemed to notice.

"Maybe a shot of ouzo?"

"No, no." I laughed, relieved that he was, like Bronte said, a very nice guy to dip my toe back into the dating pool with. "I'll take a glass of red wine, please."

When the bartender slid me the glass of wine, George raised his own drink. "Cheers."

"Cheers," I echoed, clinking his glass. I didn't shy away from his eye contact. They were so dark, almost black, yet the dark honey color of Ethan's steady gaze invaded my mind, and I blinked away to the mural on the wall.

George called my focus back to him. "I have to tell you, Delaney, I'm really glad we're finally doing this."

I touched my collarbone, genuinely heartened. "Yeah?"

"You know you're kind of famous around the office." He chuckled, and I covered my frown with a sip of my drink, those genuine feelings depleting faster than my wine.

I had worn braces as a kid and, of course, got the best of care because it was my own father doing the work. So, when those suckers were finally popped off, I was left with a picture perfect smile. A few professional photos later, and I was the face of Hargrove and Associates Orthodontics and their regional *Smile with us!* campaign. A huge poster of my face still hung behind the check-in desk.

"Your smile is beautiful," he said.

"Ah, well," I started, aspiring for a level of playfulness I didn't feel. "You should've seen me before. Like Bugs Bunny."

"I highly doubt that," he said, and I refused to look away from him, desperately struggling to keep the image of Ethan out of my head. But then the hostess appeared, and George stood up to escort me with a hand on my back. The small touch was enough to anchor me to the moment, and I hoped the bumpy start was only nerves.

Once seated, we exchanged small talk while looking over the menu. After we put in our orders, we got into our histories with the usual *where'd you go to school?* and *tell me what you do for fun* stuff. It was all rather boring, and I was glad to move on when the waitress arrived with the hummus platter.

George shifted forward in his chair, helping himself to a piece of pita and scooping up a bit of roasted red pepper hummus before holding it out to me. I hesitated, momentarily confused at what was going on, but he held it up higher, waiting for me to open my mouth to him.

That wasn't happening. Instead, I took it out of his hand and popped it into my mouth, pretending it wasn't the most awkward moment in all of dating history.

"Good," I mumbled around the mouthful.

It wasn't until the entrees arrived that George asked me about why I was back home in West Chester. Rather than explain anything to him, I babbled on and on about god knows what until his eyes practically rolled to the back of his head in boredom.

"Would you like to go somewhere for a cocktail?" he asked when the check arrived.

"Thank you, but no. I have an early morning tomorrow." I hoped he couldn't see through the lie. I only wanted the torture to end, and I gathered my purse and coat before standing. "Thank you for dinner."

"It's my pleasure." He walked me to my car, where he hovered close, and when I started to say goodbye, he cut me off with his hand on mine.

"How about a goodnight kiss?"

I appreciated that he asked, and with my friends' advice still in my ears, I nodded, giving the whole night one last chance.

The kiss wasn't bad, except that I could taste the faint flavor of garlic on his lips, and my mind wandered to my stuffed chicken entrée and how good it was. When George moved his hands to my hair, I realized my brain and mouth were on two different wavelengths.

I was kissing the man as an automatic response and stepped away from him to prevent it from going any further. "Thanks for dinner."

"I'll call you," he told me as I shut my car door, but I was pretty sure he wouldn't be following through on that promise. The conversation had been stilted, the kiss was weird at best, and I was totally out of my depth when it came to dating.

Arriving back at Dean's house, I plodded inside to find the living room empty except for Ethan, who was sprawled out on the couch. A few empty bottles of Yuengling sat on the coffee table.

"Where is everybody?" I tossed my coat and purse on the nearby chair and slipped out of my shoes before I noticed him studying me.

"Hank left a while ago, and your brother—" he glanced at his watch "—went upstairs about fifteen minutes ago. Has yet to come back down. I suspect he's passed out."

Dean had been pulling long hours at work, and most likely, it had finally caught up to him.

"Where were you tonight?" Ethan asked, dragging his gaze up from my legs to my eyes. His stare warmed me.

"I had that date."

"Oh yeah. I forgot." Although his deadpan face told me otherwise. "How was it?"

I sank down on the arm of the sofa next to his feet. "Terrible."

His eyebrows narrowed in question.

I flapped my hand near my temple. "The date was fine. He was fine. I was terrible."

"I find that hard to believe."

"Believe it." I relaxed against the cushion, watching people run around on what looked to be a spaceship on TV. "I went on and on about this cheerleading documentary and how there are no professional jobs for collegiate cheerleaders after college, except for, like, Dallas Cowboys cheerleaders, and then that led into me talking about the one time I went to Texas and got food poisoning. I spent the weekend in the hotel room, watching *Real Housewives*, and I remembered the episode with the fight between LeeAnne and Tiffany, which ended with LeeAnne running into traffic like she was in *Frogger* or something. It was crazy."

Ethan picked up his head, regarding me with wide, mocking eyes. "Crazy."

I tried to offer him a smile, but I was tired, over it, and ready for bed.

"Hey." He sat up. "What's wrong?" When I didn't answer, he scooted closer, grazing the side of my knee with his finger. "It couldn't have been that bad."

He was so earnest that long-ago memories once again bubbled to the surface. Someone somewhere once said the person you were in school shaped the person you grew to be, and in school, I was the girl who'd been in love with her brother's best friend. I was a girl who learned even the nicest of guys could break your heart.

Yet, here I was, facing those first inklings of possibility again, like I had ten years ago. The thing was, that same girl was even more afraid now. Even more broken. And I wasn't sure if I wanted to show Ethan those pieces of myself.

CHAPTER TEN

Ethan

With what looked like watery eyes, Laney pulled her gaze up to me, and I never thought of myself as a violent guy, but I wanted to hurt everyone who'd ever hurt her. This George person or that dickbag Bobby Magnate or anyone else who would dare make Delaney Hargrove cry.

"I feel like I'm broken," she murmured. "Like something is broken inside me, and I don't know how to fix it."

"Hey, no." I gently pulled her to the couch, next to me. I wrapped a hand around the back of her neck, my lips brushing against her ear when I whispered, "You are not broken."

"I can't even act normal on a date," she said, falling against me like it was the most natural thing in the world. Because maybe it was. "I was so uncomfortable."

"That's the problem."

"What's the problem?" she asked, shifting slightly to meet my gaze.

"You were uncomfortable. You babble when you're uncomfortable." I stroked circles on the nape of her neck, eliciting goose bumps along her soft skin, and I craved a kiss there. But, more than that, I needed for her to hear me.

"I do not," she argued weakly, her pouty lips tipping into

an infinitesimal smile. It was one of my favorite things about her, the nervous babbling because it didn't happen very often. But nervous Laney was a delightful mess.

I skimmed my hand down her arm. "This date of yours should have recognized that about you. He should have tried to make you more comfortable." She opened her mouth like she might defend him, and I stopped her with a stare down my nose. "Did he kiss you?"

She blinked twice slowly as if she didn't comprehend.

"Did he kiss you?" I repeated, leaning in close to make sure she could grasp the seriousness of the question, and her eyes blazed with something I hadn't seen from her in a long time.

Desire.

She nodded, her cheeks flushing, and I dragged my index finger along her jaw. "What? Are you embarrassed?"

"No." She swallowed, and I wanted to kiss her throat too. I would. Eventually. After I got through to her. "I just don't understand why you care so much," she said, all haughty-like.

I readjusted my glasses then stood up. I'd make this real plain. "I told you, Laney, now that I have you, I'm not going to let you go this time."

That made her spine stiffen, her words sharp. "You don't have me, Ethan. You never had me."

She didn't fight me when I took both of her hands in mine and towed her up to stand in front of me. With fire in her eyes, she clearly wanted this challenge. To be chased. Or simply given proof she was worth it.

No question. She was worth everything.

"Is that really how you feel?" I asked, and she let out an irritated snort, attempting to wiggle out of my grasp. I hauled her closer to me, her back to my chest, with one hand around her waist, the other spanning across her collarbone. "I've never forgotten about you. All these years, you were always on my mind."

For a moment, she dropped her head back to my shoulder, and I nuzzled her neck. "I know your heart." I drifted my palm lower, to where her dress opened in a V, revealing the most perfect cleavage I'd ever seen. Underneath my fingers, her heart beat wildly. Like mine. "You can't pretend you don't feel something for me."

"It doesn't matter." She suddenly pushed off me and turned away, crossing her arms.

"It does," I said a little peevishly, before I stopped and took a breath to measure my next words. "If you don't feel something for me, then tell me what you do feel. Did you like kissing that guy tonight?"

She tipped a stubborn chin up, avoiding my gaze and the question. "I'm not talking about this with you."

"You didn't mind talking about it with me a few minutes ago." I held on to her arms, my fingers circling her biceps, trying again. "Did you like kissing him?"

"I don't know." Her bland tone gave her away.

I stepped close enough that the skirt of her dress brushed along my jeans. "How can you not know if you like kissing someone or not?" She didn't answer, so I traced her lips with my index finger. "I remember you used to wear that ChapStick. It was a skinny tube, berry-flavored."

Her mouth opened, her breath coming out in little puffs against my fingers.

"Do you still use it?" I asked, and at her nod, I had to control the urge to throw her down on the couch. "Do you have it on now?"

She licked her lips, her pink tongue teasing me before her question came out, low and raspy. "How 'bout you find out?"

I didn't waste another moment. I curved my hands around

her cheeks and jaw and devoured her, sucking on her top then bottom lip, following the same path her tongue made with my own. She moaned, and I swallowed that too, wanting—needing—to inhale every part of her. Every sound and breath.

"Berry," I said, confirming that, yes, she did indeed still wear that ChapStick. Then I slid my hands down to her hips. "Can you tell me you're not sure if you liked that kiss or not?"

"No." She swayed into me. "I liked it." She reached up to wrap her arms around my neck, but I stopped her, stepping back.

"Am I making you uncomfortable?" I asked.

She shook her head, no more signs of nerves or rejection. "No."

"I used to think of you all the time, dream of you," I said because it was the truth. "You can't imagine what it's like for me to be standing here in front of you."

She smiled at that. "I think I can, actually."

She could imagine? Meaning she'd dreamed of me too?

With that emboldening thought, I closed the distance between us again and touched the sleeve of her dress, rubbing the luxurious material between my thumb and forefinger. "I thought about what I might say, what I might do if I ever got the chance."

I curled my right hand over her shoulder, and she kept her eyes on me, unblinking, as I eased my fingertips down to her collarbone. I toyed with the small gold charm on her necklace before walking behind her, letting my fingers drag along her throat. I pressed my chest against her back, and this time, she was fully relaxed. We took one, two, three breaths together.

With the curve of her ass pressing right up against me, my body responded reflexively, grinding my quickly hardening length against her. "You're beautiful, Lane."

I nipped at her ear, and when she stretched her neck to the

side, I opened my mouth against her pulse, licking and sucking at her throat. She groaned, and I smiled into her skin. "Still like that, huh?" I didn't give her a chance to answer, going back to the spot she'd always loved. "Of course you do."

Then I let my hand sink below the neckline of her dress to her breast, so full and soft. Her nipple pebbled beneath the lace of her bra, and I had to see it. I untied the bow at her waist, and her dress listed open. I lifted my head to take in her body in the matching dark pink set. She turned her head to meet my gaze, the corner of her lip trapped between her teeth, and I tugged it out with my thumb then dragged the pad of it along her lower lip. "Did you wear this for him?"

She shook her head, inhaling deeply, so my hand on her belly shadowed the movement. The tip of my middle finger dipped below the top of her panties on her exhale. "I wore it for me. To feel confident. It didn't work."

I growled out my approval into her neck. "It's working for me."

She laughed, deep and full, and I sought more of it. More of her laugh, more of her mouth, more of *her*. When I kissed her again, she arched into me, inviting my hands to wander over the landscape of her body, relearning every tender and ticklish spot until she was writhing against me.

I would have liked to continue, to slip my hand into her underwear and show her exactly how much and how often I dreamed of making her scream my name, but Dean was upstairs, and I wasn't much into him finding us this way. So instead of curling my fingers between her legs, I forced my hand back up to her shoulder and followed the lines of her shoulder blades with my knuckle as I circled back in front of her.

Her skin was flushed all over, and she was breathing heavily, her thighs pressed tight together.

"I'm not some needle-dick kid," I told her, tying the belt of her dress together so her lovely lace was completely covered up once again. "I *know* you, and I know what you *need*."

Then I grabbed her waist and offered her one more kiss. One that proved we weren't eighteen years old anymore. She clung to me, gripping the cotton of my shirt in her fists like she might fall over, and I held her tighter. The feel of her fingertips on me, the taste of her lips, the smell of her perfume, it was all familiar yet new at the same time.

"See?" I said against her lips, finally loosening my hold on her, and she leaned back in my arms to gaze up at me. She blinked. Blinked again. And I made sure my glasses weren't crooked before smiling. "You're completely comfortable with me. That other guy is the problem." I kissed her forehead, cheek, and then mouth one last time. "Don't let that asshole ex of yours affect who you are. You are *not* broken, Lane. You're perfect."

Then I picked up my coat and stepped into my shoes. "See you later."

She only lifted her hand, her cheeks pink and lips kiss-swollen. Gorgeous.

———

I removed my glasses to rub at my eyes with the heels of my hands before slumping back in my chair. It was almost five, but I'd been hoping to finish this report before quitting time. Although with the way my mind cycled back to Friday night with Laney in my arms, I'd been useless all day. Hell, all weekend.

The Anchormen had practice Saturday morning, but I'd been all over the place, screwing up songs I'd been playing since high school. Once a month, we had a standing gig at a local bar. Dean, Hank, and I had formed our jam band in high school with two other friends, but since we'd reformed, we'd recruited two other guys, Tony and Jerry, on keyboard and bass guitar. The money wasn't great, but it was fun to do something we all loved, and we got a night of free food and drink on the third Thursday of every month.

Twisting my pen between my fingers, I briefly wondered if Laney knew about the gig coming up and if she'd be there. In high school, she'd attended any performance we had. Even though Dean and Laney ran in different circles, they had always shown up for each other. I had known some siblings to be competitive, but with them, they were so different, I thought it might have been impossible to have any competition between them.

Like what I had with my own brother. With six years between us, I had basically worshiped Justin as a kid. The guy could do no wrong, and my analytical brain couldn't let go of the fact that I hadn't been able to fix this yet. When Laney had turned me down for help with my nonprofit, I'd spent a few hours Googling what to do or where to go for advice on fundraising, but I wasn't confident enough in my schmoozing skills to pull a big event together. Sure, I was good with a small group, easily befriending people, but I didn't know how to host a fundraiser.

With a sigh, I put my glasses back on and combed my fingers through my hair before picking up my phone. I'd had Laney's cell phone number for a long time but hadn't used it since high school. No better time than the present, I supposed.

You coming to Walt's on Thursday?

I tried not to overthink it when she didn't immediately respond. At five of five, I shut off my computer, slung my coat on, and waved goodbye to the department's administrative assistant before heading out to my car, checking my cell phone on the way.

LANEY

That's my hair-wash day.

I grunted a laugh.

You could've said no. You don't need to give me an excuse.

LANEY

It's not an excuse.

I tossed my messenger bag in the passenger seat when I dropped behind the steering wheel.

LANEY

It's serious business.

She sent a photo of a few hair products lined up along the vanity for proof.

So, that's a no?

LANEY

That's an IDK.

Biting into my cheek, I tapped out one last message.

I'd like to see you there.

I didn't expect her to respond and plugged in my phone before I turned the ignition over, calling Leah on the speaker.

"Hey, Ethan," she said when she picked up.

"Hi. I was calling to see if you'd had time to look over the email I sent you yesterday."

"I gave it a quick glance during my lunch break, but I was so busy I didn't really get to read it."

"I don't want to move forward without getting your opinion."

She laughed. "What about your brother's?"

"I already talked to him about it, but I was hoping you would sit on the board." Dean had gotten all the necessary paperwork together and was ready to submit everything. I only had to form the backbone of the nonprofit to make sure it could function appropriately.

"I don't know anything about that."

"Neither do I," I said. "But you're being directly affected by what we're going to try to raise money for. I think you'd be perfect to help steer this thing in the right direction."

She hummed a thoughtful sound on the other end of the phone call.

"Right now, I'm focused on putting one event together. One big fundraising campaign, and then, depending on how it goes, we could make it annual and maybe expand it to other locations to raise money and awareness for Huntington's."

"As long as I don't have to do any planning of anything," Leah said eventually. "I don't have the energy for that."

"All you need to do is give things a thumbs-up or thumbs-down."

"That's it?"

I raised my hand like I was on trial, even though no one else was in the car with me. "How about this? What kind of fundraiser do you think is better, a race or a party?"

"Party. Obviously."

"Great, we'll do some kind of party."

"All right, all right," she said in a singsong voice. "You got me. I'll be on the board."

I thrust my fist in the air. "So, I'm going to file the papers, then. Let me know if you think of anyone else who might be good to add to our team."

"Who's on the team so far?"

"Me and you."

"Oh Jesus." It sounded like she had smacked something. Maybe her own forehead. "I gotta get going. We're still on for next weekend?"

"Yeah. I've got a whole *Jurassic Park* marathon planned."

"That's why you're his favorite uncle."

"I'm his only uncle," I said, and Leah laughed.

"Exactly."

We hung up, and I smiled out into the setting sun outside of my windshield. Finally, I felt like I had gained some control back. With the wheels in motion on this nonprofit, the pit in my stomach had begun to dissolve. Now if only I could relieve the tightness in my chest.

Though I knew that wouldn't be happening until I had Laney in front of me once again. She was the only relief for this heartburn.

CHAPTER ELEVEN

Laney

By the time I had shown up to the bar, the Anchormen had already started their set and were in the middle of a cover of "Learn to Fly" by the Foo Fighters with Hank on the microphone, Dean on guitar, Ethan on drums, and two other guys I'd never seen before playing the keyboards and bass guitar. Dean tipped his head in acknowledgment of me, while Ethan grinned, his hair flopping onto his forehead as he banged out his rhythms. I ignored how my heart leaped and twirled like a teenager.

It was a good crowd, and I grabbed a seat at the corner of the bar, ordering a beer. I didn't drink it often, but at a dive bar with sticky floors, I wasn't about to order a glass of wine. With a glance around, I spotted Hank's wife, Angela, a pretty dark-haired woman whom I'd met once or twice before, and we exchanged waves.

Hank, in a Tommy Bahama shirt, dedicated the next song to her, and she clapped as the first couple of notes of "...Baby One More Time" rang out. They slowed it down and added a slight alternative edge, but I sang right along with Hank, laughing when he tried some of Britney's dance moves. After that, Hank introduced "Sunday Morning" by Maroon 5, one of my favorite songs, and from Ethan's eyebrow waggle, I knew he must have made them learn it specifically for me. Hank made a joke about how he, much like Adam Levine, had women throwing themselves at him because of his voice and his body, to which Ethan hit the drums *ba-dum-tss*. Then he readjusted his glasses and twirled the stick in his right hand, staring straight at me.

Honestly, this man. *So annoying.*

They played through a couple more songs, some from our high school days, some newer, some from the 80s. They even played "Waterfalls" by TLC, and I raised my hand in the air, rapping right along with Hank during Left Eye's verse. By the time they had finished their set, I had barely drunk any of my beer, but the bartender leaned his elbows on the bar in front of me.

"How we doing over here?"

"Good, thanks."

"You need anything from me?"

I shook my head, and he offered me a crooked smile. He was handsome with gauges in his ears and a scruffy beard.

With a glance over my shoulder to see the guys in the band packing up their stuff, I didn't know how long I'd be staying, if at all. "No, I think I'm—"

"Yo, Laney!" Dean had a couple pieces of Ethan's drum kit in his hand as he headed toward the door. "Order me some nachos."

I lifted my hand to show I'd heard his order then turned to the bartender. "Nachos, please."

"Your boyfriend is kinda rude to yell at you like that."

"That's my brother."

He smiled. "Oh, sorry. I assumed. There's no way you're sitting here by yourself."

I chanced another peek over my shoulder. Ethan was in the

middle of zipping up some equipment. Sure, we'd kissed last weekend, and he'd left me in such a state of worked-up nerves that I'd raced upstairs for my vibrator. And, yes, I did spend ten minutes searching through my clothes for something to wear tonight that looked like I wasn't trying, and I only came because he asked me to even *after* I'd already told Dean I wasn't planning on it.

But still. I was currently sitting at the bar by myself with Bobby's betrayal still lingering beneath my ribs and the embarrassment of my date with George fresh in my mind.

"For right now, I am," I told the bartender, and he gazed at me from under thick eyelashes. That expression probably worked on lots of people. It didn't work for me.

"You staying here awhile?" he asked.

"Not sure."

"Well, if you're planning on it, I'd love to treat you to another drink on me."

I'd been hit on a lot in my life, starting when I was barely even thirteen. I had the stereotypical looks of American beauty standards and was often mistaken for being older than I was. That early education led me to focus on sports and not worry about boys and men. Nevertheless, they were hard to avoid, and I quickly learned that no matter how hard I tried to be "nice" when I turned men down, they could still be intimidating and relentless in their pursuit.

Which was why I breathed out a tiny sigh of relief when Ethan appeared next to me, one hand on the back of my stool. "You're here."

"Despite it being hair-wash day."

The bartender toggled his eyes between us before finally saying to him, "Can I get you anything?"

"Nah." Ethan picked up my glass and kept his gaze on the bartender as he drank from it. A clear sign. "We're good."

After the bartender circled around to help other patrons, Ethan leaned in close to me. "You okay?" When I nodded, he narrowed his brows. "I have to finish up taking my kit out to my car, but I wanted to come over here," he said, evidently having caught onto the exchange between me and the bartender. "You had your shoulders hiked up by your ears, and I thought maybe…"

"Thank you," I said, and he grazed my shoulder with his fingertips before helping the rest of the band clean up the small stage in the corner.

A few minutes later, Dean grabbed the open seat next to me when a trio of patrons left, and the bartender set down the nachos in front of him without casting even a glance in my direction. Then Ethan was back on my other side, introducing Tony and Jerry, the other two guys in the band. Hank and Angela rounded out our little group too, her baby bump protruding under her sweater.

We all chatted for a bit, but I had trouble concentrating on Hank and Angela's story about how she knew the gender of the baby while he didn't because Ethan was still drinking from my beer. Friends shared food and drinks all the time, but I didn't know the significance of idly sharing a drink after one person had recently turned the other into a puddle of human flesh.

It had to mean something.

Or maybe nothing.

But more than likely something.

Right?

I didn't want to give in to this pull toward him. I was still working on crawling out from the crater Bobby had left in my life, and falling into Ethan's orbit would disrupt everything.

But then Hank and Angela left, followed by Tony and Jerry, and Dean was off flirting with some woman at the opposite corner of the bar, so I was alone with Ethan. And I took that as my cue, fishing my keys from my purse.

Ethan slid into the seat next to me, beckoning me to sit back down with a crook of his head. "Leaving so soon?"

"I figured…"

He made a show of checking his watch. "You turn into a pumpkin soon or something?"

I shot him a look but slipped my keys into my purse and planted myself back down anyway.

Ethan pulled Dean's leftover nachos toward him and stuffed a chip into his mouth, gesturing for me to do the same, but I shook my head. "No. My insides are starting to hate me. Dean plies me with too much junk food. I need to eat more vegetables."

Ethan popped a bean into his mouth. "He's got the diet of a third grader, huh?"

"Dinosaur nuggets and soda. All day long."

"The breakfast of champions." Ethan knocked his shoulder into mine. "Well, I'm a pretty decent cook, you know."

I did not know that, but *of course* he was.

"I try to eat mostly vegetarian," he said, sipping on my beer. "I make a mean spinach, mushroom, and feta burger. You could come over whenever you want."

I fell so easily back into his trap with that smile and smooth voice, but I held my ground. "No."

"Why not?"

I arched an eyebrow, and he turned his smile up to eleven, scooting closer to me, his hand on the outside of my thigh, stirring up butterflies deep in my belly. "I know my brother is not the only one going out with lots of girls. I know you do too."

"Not really," he said, and when I cocked my head to the side, he huffed. "You going to hold it against me? You went out with other guys. How long were you with Bobby?"

I pressed my fingers to my warming cheeks. I didn't know how many more excuses I could come up with. "I don't care that you date around and hook up with whoever. I'm only saying that I'm not interested in getting into a relationship with anyone, especially with someone who I know isn't interested in settling down."

"Delaney," he said, and I knew it was serious because he *never* used my given name. "For the last ten years, I've been looking for someone who could live up to you. That's why I've gone out with so many different women. I've been hoping I'd be able to find someone who makes me feel the way you do."

I pulled my hair up, wrapping it around my wrist to air off the back of my neck. It was hot in here all of a sudden.

"I have a really good time hanging out with you," he told me as if he couldn't see I was having a mild panic attack. "I always did, and now that I get to do it again, I can't get enough."

Letting my hair settle against my back, I felt a blush start to rise up my neck, and I attempted to cover it with my hand.

He smiled. "Let's go out tomorrow."

"No."

"Why not?"

His eyes were almost too tender to meet, and I barely kept the truth from slipping out.

Because I was afraid.

Because I was still broken.

Because he was my brother's best friend.

Because it was complicated.

Because we were complicated.

But I kept it all inside, under lock and key.

"I'm busy."

"Doing what? Your hair?"

I snarled at him, earning a laugh. "You know if I didn't do it, it'd be all over the place."

He shrugged. "I like it all over the place."

"Ethan," I warned, and he sat back, his *Goonies* T-shirt clinging to his chest, his arms still thin but defined with muscle. *Goonies* was his favorite movie. In fact, I'd bought him a T-shirt with Chunk on it for Christmas senior year. He'd loved it so much he'd lifted me up, laughing against my ear. Dean had seen us and scowled, so we'd pretended it wasn't anything. It hadn't been.

Not really.

Kind of like when I stood up now, taking a moment to search for my keys, and he pressed the advantage to get up and pull me toward him. I'd like to say his kiss was a surprise, but it wasn't. And if I pretended I didn't want it, I'd be lying.

This time when his tongue stroked mine, I didn't hesitate to wrap a hand around his neck to deepen the kiss. I felt more than heard the groan he let out, and even though we were in public, it was hard to stop. But we did. Barely.

"Go out with me," he said, and I flicked my eyes over to where my brother was still chatting up some woman.

"No."

He kissed the corner of my mouth. "Go out with me."

I nudged my nose against his once before stepping away, finally able to take a good, clearing breath.

"Then will you help me with my fundraiser?"

I laughed, a great big cackle. "I told you, besides some resources and advice, no."

He dropped his head back in exasperation, speaking to the ceiling. "Lord, why have you forsaken me with this stubborn woman?"

"I am not!" I caught myself in the middle of my offended rant and lowered my voice, my car keys between my fingers as I tapped them against his side. I hated that he was so tall because I loved that he was so tall. "I am not stubborn. I'm just not going to work with you when we..." I circled my hand in the space between us, indicating how we'd kissed not even a minute ago. And last weekend before that.

"Then go out with me."

I shook my head and slipped on my coat. "No." When he pursed his lips as if trying not to laugh at me and my weak refusal, I pointed a stern finger at him. "Goodbye, Ethan."

"Bye, Lane." I turned and lifted a hand behind me, but as I reached the door, he called out, "Goonies never say die."

Code words: I'm not giving up.

CHAPTER TWELVE

Ethan

I generally wasn't a liar, but it wasn't beneath me to tell an occasional white lie. That was why I texted Laney.

> Can you come over? I have an emergency.

She texted back almost immediately. As I knew she would.

LANEY

What's wrong? Are you okay?

> I'm having an animal problem.

LANEY

Animal problem?!!

> Please come over. Quick.

Then I added my address, laughing to myself. Did it make me an asshole to worry her? Maybe. But all was fair in love and war.

Not even fifteen minutes later, she was at my door, windblown and red-cheeked. "What is it?" she asked, her eyes darting over my shoulder, into my place. I lived on the first floor of my apartment complex, and my door opened up to a closet so she couldn't see anything. It was a terrible choice in design, although it made her face of shock even better when Trace growled from the living room. "What is that? A raccoon? Why did you want me? I can't do anything about a raccoon!"

I laughed, towing her inside with my hand on her wrist. "I have never been in close contact with a raccoon, but I don't think they growl." I lifted my hand out to my nephew, currently crouched down on all fours, his head thrown back as he growled again. "My animal problem."

Laney guffawed and unraveled her scarf from around her neck. "I thought something was really wrong. A bear attack or, or..." She flopped her hands down at her sides, glowering at me. "You're awful, you know that?"

I apologized, completely unrepentant, and then beckoned Trace over. "Hey, T-rex, come here."

Trace raised his arms to his sides and stomped over to us, letting out a low rumble. "I'm a brachiosaurus."

"Excuse me," I said with my hands up then tipped my chin to Laney. "This is my friend."

Laney squatted down to Trace's eye level. "I'm Laney. Should I call you brachiosaurus, or do you go by another name?"

"Trace," he said then stomped away, roaring. "We're playing Jurassic Park. Wanna play?"

When Laney tossed me a look, I grinned. "Wanna play?"

She hung her purse, scarf, and coat on the rack and tugged on her loose long-sleeved shirt. She must have run right out of the house because her socks were mismatched when she took her shoes off. "Don't think you're cute."

I pressed my thumb and index finger together. "A little?"

She pointed to Trace. "He's cute."

"I thought you'd think so."

She elbowed me on her way to the living room, where she

sat on the floor with Trace, who had a variety of jungle animals and dinosaurs lined up. "Quite an emergency."

Trace bellowed like a siren, echoing, "Emergency! Emergency!" Then he growled and bowled over an elephant with a dinosaur. "Here." He handed Laney a tiger. "T-rex and Tiger fight a lot."

Laney and Trace faced off with their plastic toys, and I slid down on the floor next to her, extending my legs and propping my back against the sofa. "You eat already?"

She shook her head and wound her hair up in a messy knot. It wasn't as straight as it'd been when I'd seen her at the bar, the beginnings of curls taking root, a few flyaways waving by her cheek.

"I have veggie lasagna," I said in a whisper so Trace didn't hear. If my nephew knew how many vegetables I had hidden away in the sauce, he'd never eat it. "Will you stay?"

Trace pumped his hands in the air. "Uncle Efan said we can have a sprinkle party later!"

"What's a sprinkle party?" Laney asked him.

"We have ice cream with sprinkles and dance. Woo-hoo! Sprinkle party!" Then he stood up and waggled his butt side to side like an excited puppy.

"I guess I can't say no to a sprinkle party." She slanted her gaze to me, leaning back against the couch, right against my side, and she dug her fingertip into my thigh. I deserved an Oscar for acting as if the tingle didn't shoot straight to my dick. "Don't smile."

"I'd never," I said and cleared my throat. "Should we start the movie now?"

"Yes!" Trace passed the remote to me, so I could cue up *Jurassic Park*. It wasn't exactly G-rated, but the kid really liked dinosaurs, and I fast-forwarded through any scary parts.

Once the movie had started and my nephew was

entranced, I slipped my hand behind Laney, along the edge of the couch cushions. She narrowed her eyes at me. "I'm onto your game."

"This isn't a game."

"Then what is it?"

I shrugged. "A Saturday night with my nephew, and I thought you might enjoy it."

"You can't charm me into saying yes to a date with you."

"But—" I grabbed Trace, pushing my fingers around his mouth to purse his lips, earning a laugh from the kid "—could you say no to this face?"

Trace walked a dinosaur up Laney's arm, letting it graze on her hoodie, and she smiled at him. "Depends."

"I need your help," I said, this time not taking advantage of Laney's enduring love for her friends but because I truly needed her expertise. "I don't know anything about raising money or putting an event together. I know how to make lists and analyze figures, but I'm sh—" I glanced at my nephew to make sure he didn't catch my almost curse "—bad at what I need to know to throw a big party." I patted Trace's back, repositioning the dinosaur off Laney and down to the floor, despite her patience with letting it roam all over her, roaring and biting.

"I don't think I can. I—"

I cut her off, expecting her argument. "I don't want to know the details of you and Bobby. I hate him as it is." Then I lowered my mouth to her ear. "If you really don't want to do it, I'll stop asking, but I wanted you to meet my nephew. He has a fifty-percent chance that he inherited the Huntington's gene. If I can do anything to stop it or help him, then I'm going to."

Laney watched Trace play for a minute. She kept her attention on him as she said, "I worked with Bobby for three years. My whole life revolved around him and his business."

If there was another word for something more than hate, I didn't know it, but that's what I felt for him.

"So, I left not only him but my whole life. He ruined everything for me. My livelihood, my work, my confidence." Then she lifted one shoulder and moved her eyes to me. "Or, I guess I let him. I let myself be swept up, and I..." She blinked, her eyes darkening with sadness, and her throat worked on a swallow.

I couldn't help bending forward, kissing her jaw. "I'm sorry. Do you want me to kill him?"

She laughed, shifting back, forcing me to look her in the eyes. "You're about the same height, but he definitely weighs more than a matchstick. I don't think you could take him. Sorry."

"Lane." I pressed my hand to my heart. "My god, how you have the ability to hurt me. I've put on a couple of pounds since high school. At least two." But then I licked my lips, letting my smile slip at her guileless expression.

"You can hurt me too, you know," she confessed quietly. "Which is why I don't want to say yes."

I couldn't fault her for that, for protecting herself after everything she'd been through.

"You can trust me," I said, reaching for her hands that sat in her lap. I tangled my fingers with hers. "We can take it one step at a time."

"Take what one step at a time? The fundraiser or..." She pointedly regarded our linked fingers.

"Let's start with the fundraiser, okay? We'll see where the rest goes." Although if it were up to me, I had *the rest* already mapped out.

Laney nodded to herself a few times then shook off my hand to stand up.

"Where are you going?" I asked, my voice all squeaky and unmanly.

She dug in her purse for her phone and held it up. "Nowhere."

Relief washed over me. "Good." Then I stood up too. "Dinner's almost ready."

Leaving Trace in the living room, we made our way to the kitchen where she peppered me with questions, taking notes on her phone. As we talked, she made a list of things to start with: a website, social media pages, contacts, sponsors.

"When were you thinking of having this?"

"I don't know." I placed the lasagna on the stove top to set and grabbed bagged salad from the fridge to toss into a bowl. "I was thinking spring sometime, but you'd know better than I would about how long it takes to put something together."

"Well, how big do you want it?"

"Uh." I threw some Italian dressing on the lettuce and mixed it up with tongs. "As big as it can be, I suppose. The more people, the more money, right?"

She bent over, methodically tapping her fingernails on the counter, talking to herself. "Let's see, it's the end of February now. Six weeks would take us to mid-April." She stuck her tongue out of the corner of her mouth, studying the dates on her calendar app. "I'm thinking beginning of May would be good since Passover and Easter are in April, and those who celebrate may not be available. We want to hold the event at a time when as many people as possible could come." She typed something in her phone then lifted her gaze to me. "Remember when you were Jesus in living Stations?"

I shook my head at the memory of acting out the Stations of the Cross, a weekly prayer that Catholics did on Fridays during Lent that commemorated Jesus's death. "Kinda hard to forget."

She snorted, lightly slapping the countertop. "That red paint."

"Don't remind me." I took plates down from the cabinet, thinking of how it took days to wash the paint out of my hair and from under my fingernails. They had really gone all out to make the passion of the Christ look believable.

"Catholic school is wild, man," she mumbled, and I dragged my hand down her back to get her attention.

"Dinner's ready." Although my Catholic education was strict, with all its arbitrary rules and awful priests, I'd also met my best friends there. I'd met Laney. So I couldn't discount it as a whole.

I paused the movie and ushered Trace into the kitchen so the three of us could sit at the small table to eat. Trace chowed down on the lasagna, happy to play with the red sauce as he regaled Laney with the gossip from preschool. Apparently, Emery did not like Preston, and Charlie forgot his show-and-tell yesterday so he cried.

"What did you bring for show-and-tell?" Laney asked, smiling so warmly at Trace that I had trouble eating. I couldn't keep my eyes off her.

"A saber-toof tiger." Trace pawed at the air in her direction. "It is a prehistoric animal!"

"What's your favorite animal?"

He tilted his head to the side. "Favorite?"

"Yeah, the one you love the most."

"Oh." He moved to his knees. "Um. Ah. Ah." He tapped his finger on his chin, ever the showman. "Woolly mammof!"

"Woolly mammoth? You have one of those?"

"Yeah, at home. Uncle Efan doesn't have one."

I rolled my eyes because this was not the first time he mentioned it today. "I'll work on it for next time you stay over, buddy."

"Okay. Is it sprinkle party time?" He folded his hands in front of him. "Pleeeeease."

"Are you finished eating?"

Trace had made a pretty good dent in his lasagna and licked a piece of lettuce, at least. "Yeah! Time for sprinkle party!"

"Okay, let me clean this stuff up first."

After I got the leftovers put away, I pulled out the tub of chocolate and vanilla ice cream from the freezer. I dished some out for my nephew and looked to Laney, who was helping to make sure Trace didn't spill any of the rainbow sprinkles. "None for me. Dairy doesn't always agree with me."

"I saw a video somewhere saying that if a girl has GI problems, you gotta wife her up."

She flattened her growing smile. "I don't know if you'd like my GI problems."

Trace twirled his spoon in the air. "G.I. Joe! G.I. Joe! Oooh! Laney, look." He held up a blue sprinkle. "Blue like your eyes. Here, you have it."

"Thanks, Trace. You're very sweet."

That little bugger was scoring more points with her tonight than I was. "Now, time to dance!" He jumped down from the chair and grabbed her hand. "Play da music, Uncle Efan!"

I played a random song from the music on my phone, "Dance With me" by Shockley, apropos, and Trace twisted under Laney's arm, swinging his spoon in the air. I nodded my head to the beat, not a great dancer but loving the show Laney and Trace put on, bopping around together. When she grinned over at me, I reached for her hand, tugging her close as Trace jigged off on his own.

She tossed her head back, laughing as I spun her in a circle before dipping her backward. Despite my nephew being only a foot away, I bent to place a quick kiss on her throat then stood her back upright. Out of breath and eyes alight, she was the most beautiful woman I had ever seen, ever would see.

The song changed to something slower, and I looped my arms around her waist to leisurely sway in a circle.

"Hey, me too!" Trace held his arms in the air, bouncing up and down, and I picked him up so all three of us could slow dance together.

And I was completely incapable of keeping my imagination from running wild. I saw a future with Laney, of marriage and babies and dancing in the kitchen every night. But then Trace wiggled to get down, and Laney dropped her gaze to the floor.

"I think I should head out."

"You don't have to."

She showed me the time on her phone, almost eight. "I'm assuming it's bedtime soon."

"We didn't finish the movie yet," I said, although I'd have to somehow trick Trace into taking a bath to get him asleep before nine, at the latest. Leah would murder me if I allowed him to stay up later than that.

"I'm going to go home and get started on my new job." She smiled, and if nothing else came out of this, at least I could give Laney some of her glow back. Though if it was up to me, that would be the very least. I had a lot more in mind.

"I'll get an outline to you by tomorrow night. Rough ideas and numbers. By the end of next week, we should have a direction to go in so that I can start making calls and appointments. Okay?"

"I'm following your lead."

She held her palm up to Trace for a high five. "See ya later."

I followed her to the front door, where she wrapped up in her scarf and coat then stepped back into her boots. "You're the boy who cried wolf now. So, next time you have a raccoon or bear attack, I won't be there."

I stuffed my hands into my pockets to keep them to myself, although I did allow a moment to lean into her, getting a good whiff of her shampoo. "Thanks for coming over anyway."

She breathed deep enough that I could see her shoulders rise under her thick coat, like she was afraid to admit it. "I had fun."

"Good. That's all I want." I held the door open for her, and she gave me one last smile over her shoulder that was an arrow straight to my heart.

By agreeing to put the fundraiser together, I subsequently made myself part of the board, and since no one else—meaning Ethan or his sister-in-law—had any experience with charity work, I took charge. I held a Zoom meeting to go over the details of what would hopefully become the first annual fundraising event for Research and Awareness of Huntington's Disease, otherwise known as RAHD. Ethan and Dean thought it was good because you could pronounce it like "rad."

I would definitely be working on the name.

But in the meantime, I had outreach to do, beginning with making connections with the local vendor community. With printed and digital outlines and proposals for the event, I'd driven all over West Chester, introducing myself to business owners who might've been able to donate time, resources, or money. The last stop of the day was a shoe boutique owned by a woman who'd graduated from Holy Redeemer a few years before I did, and I hoped to pull in some goodwill with our alma mater.

When I stepped out of my car, my heel caught on a broken piece of macadam, and my ankle turned in my boot with the heel still stuck in the ground. My ankle was fine, but the left heel of my favorite taupe booties was not. I hissed out a low curse. "Ah, fuck!"

A laugh sounded from behind me. "The call of the Laney bird out in the wild."

I held on to my car door, still open, and hobbled against the side, eyeing Ethan. "What are you doing here?"

He pointed to the optometrist two doors down. "I had an appointment. What are *you* doing here?"

"Soliciting donations," I said, as he reached out to my elbow, helping me balance. "I broke my heel."

"Is your foot okay?"

I shook it out, the heel dangling on a literal thread, to make sure. "Yeah, fine. But these were my favorite."

"Here, hold on to me," he said and bent down to rip off the heel. He inspected it from his kneeled position then gazed up at me, frowning. "Maybe it's fixable."

"I don't even know where I'd send it. Elves in a tree?"

He laughed, still in front of me, and as if we both realized his head was at crotch level at the same time, the tops of his cheeks flamed, and I licked my suddenly dry lips. "Come on, off the ground. It's freezing."

Upright once again, he held on to the lapels of my coat, keeping me steady as I stood unevenly. "Can I help you?"

"I've got one more stop." I tilted my head toward Seraphina's, the huge sign on a storefront in simple but elegant cursive. "A shoe store."

"Well, that's convenient," he said, holding on to my waist as we walked to the door. He held it open for me, and I limped inside. Seraphina Bianco stood behind the counter, trinkets and small pieces of jewelry set out in cases.

"Hello, welcome to Seraphina's. How can I help you today?"

With Ethan at my elbow, I hobbled over to introduce

myself. "Hi, Seraphina. My name is Delaney Hargrove, and this is Ethan Marrero. We both graduated from Holy Redeemer, three years after you."

Seraphina shook her head, smiling. "Fellow survivors, huh?"

"Yeah. I wanted to stop by today to introduce myself and tell you a little bit about a fundraising event we're having at the beginning of May." I passed Seraphina a folder filled with a few papers. "We're raising money for research and awareness of Huntington's disease." I glanced at Ethan then, who nodded and took over.

"My brother was recently diagnosed with it. Before then, I didn't really know anything about it, but I've been learning as much as I can, and I felt like I needed to do something to help families like mine, who may be struggling with the diagnosis."

Seraphina flipped through the papers. "I'd love to help you any way I can." She gave us each a wide, fake grin, raising her fist in a limp cheer. "Crusader pride."

"Wonderful," I said. "You can find information about the nonprofit in the packet as well as the event in May. We have sponsorship opportunities, but we are also in need of silent auction donations."

"Fantastic. I'll look through everything in the next day or two."

"Perfect." I pointed to my business card paper-clipped on the front of the folder. "My contact information is here, and you can also find all of the printed information on the website listed. Thank you so much for your time."

"My pleasure." Seraphina sauntered around the counter as if to walk us back out, but I put my hand on Ethan again to pick up my left foot.

"I have one more thing. I need new shoes."

Seraphina tossed her head back, amused, and even though

I hadn't known Seraphina at all while we were in school, I thought we could've been friends with her laid-back laugh. "You've come to the right place! Come on, have a seat. I'll get you fixed up."

I followed her farther into the store, where a small sitting area contained two comfy love seats with a table between them. A few clothing racks were draped in upscale athleisure wear along the wall, and Ethan surveyed the items as he helped himself to a seat.

"Why don't you take your shoes off?" Seraphina said to me. "And I'll take them to the back. In the meantime, you can look around, see what you like."

I removed my shoes and passed them off before perusing the shelves.

"Found 'em."

"What?"

When I turned to Ethan behind me, he pointed to a pair of black heels, not at all suited for cold weather. "What size are you?"

"I'm not getting those."

"Why not?" He stood up to grab them, showing them off as if they were a prized fortune.

They were shiny patent leather with a heel that had to be six inches, at least. The back was full, but the front was nonexistent except for straps that crisscrossed from the toes up the shin, creating a half boot, half stiletto. "I think they're best used for stripping."

"First of all," Ethan said, putting the shoe back down, "that's a stereotype, and second of all, everybody's got to make a living."

"I need a new pair of boots. Save those shoes for your next girlfriend." I shoved at his side so he'd sit back down, but he only hooked an arm around my waist.

"Well, then, you're in luck. These shoes are yours."

I edged away from him, unwinding my scarf from my neck before taking off my jacket, too hot under the fluorescent lights. Not to mention Ethan's penetrative stare. "I am not going to be your girlfriend, Ethan."

"Think what you like, but those shoes are going to be your Christmas present. And if you happen to only wear them in the bedroom, so be it." He shrugged and stepped over to another shelf of shoes.

"I'm looking for another pair of short boots, brown or taupe."

"What's the difference?" he asked, showing me a pair of brown boots that were nothing like my old booties.

"Too tall."

He pursed his lips, holding them up. "I like them."

I absolutely refused to laugh and shifted over as one of Seraphina's workers carried out a stack of boxes for another customer.

"Did you find anything you like?" Seraphina asked, returning from the back.

I pointed to a beige suede pair with a chunky, low heel.

"Love those," Seraphina said. "Really comfortable because of the wide toes. What size are you?"

"Nine and a half."

Seraphina held her finger up. "Be right back."

"Nine and a half, eh?" Ethan licked an imaginary pen and pretended to write it down on an imaginary pad of paper.

"You're too much," I said as I accepted the box from Seraphina. I tried them on and walked to the mirror, checking them out, side to side. "What do you think?" I asked Ethan, eyeing him in the reflection of the mirror. "Of the boots, I mean."

He lifted his attention from my butt. "Love 'em." He waved

his hands up and down the length of me. "Love the whole package."

I rolled my eyes. I only wore skinny jeans and a thin cream sweater, nothing spectacular, but with how he had that silly tongue-hanging-out-of-his-mouth expression, I might as well have been wearing nothing.

"Getting them?"

"Yeah."

"Good, they make your legs look..." He gave me the OK sign, not even bothering to finish his sentence. I may not have been ready to make this a "thing," but I couldn't deny I liked that goofy face and how easy it was between us.

I paid for the shoes and wore them out of the store with a promise that Seraphina would be in touch soon. Back outside, Ethan tucked his hands into his pockets, elbowing me lightly. "Are you hungry?"

It was almost six. "I can eat."

"Anything in particular?"

I spotted a red-and-white sign lit up at the end of the strip mall. "Pizza?"

He seemed like he wanted to suggest somewhere else but held his arm out, allowing me to step ahead of him to the pizza joint. After ordering, Ethan carried our tray to open seats by the window.

"Thanks for paying," I said, grabbing my soda from the tray.

He handed me a few napkins from the dispenser in the middle of the table. "I have to admit, this isn't the place I imagined our first date would be."

I knew he was trying to goad me, charm me. But it wouldn't work. "We've been out plenty of times before."

"Sure, we hung out a lot when we were in high school, but I never got to take you out on a real date."

I thought back on it. He was correct, yet this right here wasn't a date, and I told him so.

"How do you suppose it's not?" he asked in between munching on a bite of his pizza. "We're out, having dinner at Big Slice, and I paid. Grade A date, if I do say so myself."

I choked on the sip of my soda when I snorted a laugh. "Yes, the seventeen-year-old in me is swooning."

"I hope so. I'm looking forward to my goodnight kiss."

I clenched every muscle in my body to keep from responding with "me too" because this wasn't a date.

It wasn't a date.

It *wasn't* a date.

"Awfully arrogant of you to assume you're going to get one."

"Not arrogant." He wiped off his hands, lounging back in his seat, the corner of his mouth kicked up. "Confident."

"We'll see about that."

I ignored the flutter in my belly that had become a constant whenever I was with Ethan anymore as we chatted about his job—I still didn't get it—and how I was excited to work on the fundraiser—the first of many reasons why this was *not* a date. When we finished our food, Ethan dumped the garbage and held the door open for me.

At my car, he stepped into my space, tugging my scarf farther up my neck. "Warm enough?"

"For right this second, I'm okay."

He darted his eyes behind me, as if checking to see if anyone was around, then crowded my space even more, heat radiating off his body. "You know I planned on asking you out."

"Huh?"

He loosened my arms from where they were across my middle to wrap them around his torso, trapping them between his sweater and coat, sharing his heat. I curled my hands in the soft material.

"In school," he said, dropping his attention briefly to my lips, and I didn't dare make any noise to stop him or interject. I wanted to hear his version of our history.

He tucked a loose strand of hair that had fallen out of of bun behind my ear. Even his fingertips were warm, and I cuddled closer to him. "We were talking after school one day. The three of us—me, you, and Jenna—were in the basement before a football game, and she said Madison and I would be good together. You know, bando and dance team girl."

Jenna was a friend of mine from the softball team. We used to be close friends but grew apart when we went to different colleges, though we stayed in semi-touch through social media. Jenna was now married to her wife, Brittney, and lived out in Jersey.

"Then I saw you and JT before the homecoming game," he went on, those amber-colored eyes illuminating with emotion that seemed centuries old. That was what it felt like for me. Like we were brushing the dust off some ancient text. It was both exciting and a little nauseating. Like this feeling could crumble to ash at any moment.

Ethan swallowed, his Adam's apple bobbing, and I was tempted to tuck my head against his throat, but I didn't want to miss anything he said. "So, I asked Madison out instead. I was jealous. And then it sort of..."

"I know," I finished for him. We were stupid kids. Stupid being the key word. If we had been honest with each other from the beginning, maybe it would've been different between us. Or maybe even right now. "If you would've asked me out, I would've said yes."

He nodded, his eyes far away for a long moment before

they slanted back to me. "Yet I can't get you to admit this is a date now."

"I've changed," was all I said as a slight breeze picked up, causing a shiver to run down my spine, and he wrapped his hands around my cheeks and jaw.

He dropped his lips to brush along my temple as he spoke. "You think you have, but you haven't. At least, not in the ways that matter."

Then I tipped my mouth up to his, unable to resist any longer. With my hands around his waist, and his fingers curving along the back of my neck and up into my hair, pieces of myself I thought I lost clicked into place. A page of our history book turned as new words were written.

I smoothed my tongue along his in what was now a familiar dance, and he tasted both tangy and sweet. He pulled back slightly, licking his own lips, and I wondered what he tasted. I wanted to be the only thing he tasted. To be the only thing he wanted. Though when he gently pushed me back against my car, his thigh moving between mine, I *felt* I was the only thing he wanted.

As he ground his hard length against my hip, I threaded my fingers through his hair, pulling his mouth back to mine when he started to kiss down my throat. He laughed against my lips, nipping at them as if he was frustrated I stopped him, but I murmured a dissent. We had to stop. We were making out in a public parking lot.

"That's one helluva good-night kiss," I said, fixing my hair back into its bun.

He gave me one more quick kiss to the corner of my mouth and cheek. "That's one helluva first date."

Opening my car door, I tossed him a playful glower. "This wasn't a first date."

He closed the door after me, and I started the ignition to

lower the window. He leaned down so we were nose to nose. "High school date trifecta says otherwise. Shopping mall, pizza, kiss. It's a date."

I shook my head at him, refusing to admit I was so far gone already. He only hit me with a goofy smile as I rolled the window back up and reversed out of my parking spot.

At home, I found Dean in the living room with his feet up on the ottoman.

"Hey." I took off my jacket and scarf.

"Hey." He saluted me with a sandwich that he ate over a plate. "You hungry?"

"I already ate."

I sat on the chair to collect my thoughts and turned my attention to the television.

"What's on your neck?"

I whipped my head to him. "Hmm?"

"Your neck is red. Are you breaking out in hives or something?"

"It's probably from my scarf." I covered my neck and prattled on. "I was shopping, and you know how it is when you're in a store, trying stuff on. You get warm and the wool rubs." I stood up, retrieving my very comfortable, non-rubbing scarf, and pointed to my new shoes as evidence that I had shopped and had not kissed Ethan for ten minutes against my car.

Dean shrugged and went back to watching TV, so I scurried back upstairs with my new boots to Google how to get rid of a hickey.

CHAPTER FOURTEEN

Laney

I had fallen back into my groove as if I'd never left the dance floor, taking meetings and checking off my daily to-do list with ease. I'd already secured multiple sponsors for the RAHD—I still hadn't been able to convince Ethan the nonprofit needed a new name—event and was racking up views, shares, and likes on all the social media platforms I'd set up.

Seraphina Bianco had thrown all her weight behind the project and even offered to introduce me to friends who might be interested, which was why I'd agreed to go to this "Mom's Night Out" party. Although I was neither a mom nor needed a night out, I did like a good party. And if Gem was any indication, moms were a good time when they got to stretch their legs.

After stepping into my new booties, I checked myself out in the mirror one last time and headed downstairs. It was poker night again, and I waved to all the guys—Dean, Nadir, Hank, Seth, and Ethan—scattered on chairs as the doorbell rang. Since I was closest, I answered the door, and the pizza delivery guy, probably in college, smiled at me. "Hey, what's up?"

Ethan appeared behind me, thrusting bills into the kid's hand and grabbing the boxes from him. "Not you, my man. See ya later." When he closed the door and whirled around to me, I shook my head in laughter. "What?"

"I told you not to be cute," I whispered, but he only shrugged.

"Can't help it."

He may have been cute, but there was no reason for him to be jealous. A couple of make-out sessions didn't change anything. Especially when we were working together.

I was invested in making sure this fundraiser went off without a hitch. I wouldn't jeopardize the success of it because I didn't know how to draw lines in the sand.

What was that Dean liked to say? Don't shit where you eat.

Gross but effective in its purpose.

Hank and Dean took the boxes from Ethan as Nadir offered me a plate.

"No, thanks. I'm going out, trying to drum up more interest in the fundraiser."

"Thirsty Thursday?" Hank asked around a mouth full of pepperoni pizza.

"No, I graduated college a few years ago, but thanks for reminding me you didn't." I patted his head, and he nuzzled into my touch like a cat.

Dean leaned his chair on its back two legs, considering me. "What time are you going to be home?"

"I don't know. It's a school night, so not late."

Hank moved away from me, shimmying his shoulder in a quasi-imitation of me in a high voice. "It's a school night."

Then I felt long fingers wrap around my leg a moment before Ethan's question. "You're going to Seraphina's house?"

With his hand below the table, no one else could see how he stroked the inside of my knee, and I pressed my thighs together, trapping his hand so it couldn't travel any higher.

Though that wasn't the best idea because having his hand there made my insides melt and all my muscles tighten.

"Mm-hmm. She called it a mom's night out party."

Seth snorted, obviously unimpressed, while Nadir nodded.

"You're not a mom," Dean pointed out.

"So? I like to have fun," I said. "And besides, this is for work. Right, Ethan?"

He perked up, smiling at me, and the rest of the guys went back to eating and shuffling cards, except for Ethan, who skimmed his fingertips down the back of my calf.

"You look nice," he said quietly as his hand journeyed back up my leg on the next stroke. Awfully adventurous when everybody sat mere inches away.

I stepped back and stuck out my foot, modeling the boots. "Like these? I got them last weekend."

He ran his hand through his hair, lips pursing, undoubtedly holding back whatever he wanted to say. By the time his studious gaze traveled up my body to meet my eyes, they were narrowed and dark. "They're very nice."

He readjusted his glasses, and it had a Superman kind of effect, where I could swear he saw through my clothes. Especially when the corner of his mouth quirked up.

I pivoted away from the table. "You boys have fun now."

"More than you," Seth said to her back.

"Don't be dumb," Dean told me.

"I won't."

Then I closed the door on Ethan's lingering stare and stepped out into the chilly night air, helping to cool my heated skin. I was dangerously close to being caught in our little cat-and-mouse game, my rapid heartbeat evidence of how much I enjoyed being hunted. But there was no way I could allow myself to give in, and I ran to my car like my ass was on fire. The farther away from Ethan, the better.

Fifteen minutes later, I arrived at Seraphina's house, where I spied a group of women through the big bay window. The hostess answered the door with a bright smile, as usual. "Laney! I'm so glad you came...or maybe I should say *you* will be glad you *came*."

"Huh?"

She only laughed and raised her glass of wine higher, ushering me inside and to the back of the house. A dozen women were spread throughout the kitchen and living room, drinking wine and eating charcuterie. My favorite things. After a few minutes of introductions, a woman named Maylin lifted her hands to the group. "Should we get started?"

"What is this?" I whispered to the woman next to me, noting boxes in the living room. "Pampered Chef party or something?"

"No." She sniffed a laugh, covering it with the side of her hand. "Didn't Seraphina tell you? It's a sex toy party."

"*What?*" My booming voice carried across the whole house, and the entire party shot their heads to me. I offered a chagrined smile. "I just need to..." I grabbed my cell phone from my purse. "...make a quick call."

They all headed into the living room, and I could barely contain my glee as I took a good look at the different pink and pastel boxes, a few stacks of what appeared to be lotions. Small pouches containing suspiciously large *things*.

I texted the girls.

ALERT. ALERT.

I am at a sex toy party with a bunch of moms. What does everyone want for Christmas?

GEM

Is there an online catalogue?

Sam sent a couple of laughing emojis.

BRONTE

What's it like? I never even knew that was a thing.

SAM

How did you get roped into that?

Trying to make connections for the fundraiser.

GEM

WHAT A CONNECTION

BRONTE

I thought it was supposed to be a family affair.

Do you want a sex toy or not, B?

A minute passed before she answered.

BRONTE

Yes.

The other girls threw up some skulls.

Look out for covertly wrapped packages from your sex Santa Claus.

Then I tucked my phone away and took a seat in the living room, right on time for the clitoral stimulation segment of the party.

CHAPTER FIFTEEN

Ethan

Nadir had already left by the time Laney arrived home, her eyes bright.

"Looks like you had a good time," Dean said, tossing the cards on the table after boxing them up.

"Was it fun?" Hank asked, throwing some napkins into an empty pizza box.

She cleared her throat and tamped down a smile as she hung up her coat. "Yeah. A lot of fun."

Seth snorted. "A party with a bunch of moms was fun?"

Giving in to her laugh, she nodded. "Yeah. It was a sex toy party."

The room fell silent. A record might have scratched.

"A *what* party?" Hank croaked.

"A sex toy party."

I couldn't take my eyes off Laney, her cheeks rosy, a smile so wide, I couldn't help my own from growing. She looked downright giddy.

"That's a thing?" Hank asked, pulling out his phone. "I'm texting Angela."

Seth backhanded him. "You missing out?"

"Fuck, yeah, I am." He got up from his chair in a huff and grabbed his coat. "See you guys later."

"So, Laney," Seth said, "find anything there you liked?"

Dean pressed his hands against his ears. "Nope, nope, nope. Do not like."

She only clucked her tongue. "Even if I knew you well enough, Seth, I wouldn't tell you."

He inclined his head, and she sashayed upstairs, barely sparing me a glance. If she was worked up from this party, I had to know.

I cleaned up the empty pizza boxes then used the excuse of needing the bathroom to hightail it upstairs. I knocked on Laney's door at the end of the hall. She opened it, already having changed from her jeans into cotton pajama bottoms and a T-shirt.

"Hey," I said, leaning against the doorjamb, attempting to keep the desperation out of my voice.

She held up her hand, blinking a few times. "I'm having a déjà vu moment."

"Yeah?" I was too. With her face washed of makeup and her hair all tied up on the top of her head, she looked younger. More like her eighteen-year-old self.

Back then, I had often sneaked away to Laney's room to talk whenever I was at the Hargrove house. I remembered one time sitting on her bed while she put her laundry away, and I'd seen a pair of her panties with pineapples all over them. She'd tried to cover them but hadn't been quick enough. Her whole face had flamed, and I'd thought of her in those underwear for weeks on end. Even when I'd still been dating Madison.

Similar to years ago, I stepped into her bedroom and sat down on the mattress, the pale green comforter all twisted up on one side. "So, tell me the truth. Was this really a sex toy party, or are you giving us shit?"

She sat next to me, laughing. "I swear."

My eyes widened. "You can't give out information like that to a guy and then not explain."

"What do you want to know?"

I laid back on the bed, my arms forming a pillow under my head, and she followed, staring up at the ceiling. I turned to stare at her profile. She was gorgeous. Her full lips, the little mole by her nose, the arch of her brows. When I was a kid, not yet fully grown into my body, I didn't think she'd ever look at me with desire in her eyes, so it was a fantasy come to life when I'd finally been able to touch and kiss her. And now?

Now, I thought there might be a chance of death by asphyxiation for how my blood roiled for her, up from my groin to my stomach and throat.

"What do you do?" I asked her. "Test them out?"

She shifted to her side, her cheek in her hand, grinning. "Not there. The woman who ran it talked about some products, demonstrated how they worked. We were allowed to try a few items, lotions and oils, stuff like that."

I nearly swallowed my tongue. "What, uh... Did you end up purchasing anything?"

She bit the corner of her lip, nodding.

"What?"

"Ethan!" When she shoved at me, I caught her hand, bringing it to my lips.

"Laney." I kissed her pulse. It fluttered like a bird's wings. "What did you get?"

Her eyes darted away toward the closet as color rose from her neck, and I started to get suspicious.

"Have you used one before?"

She met my eyes. "A toy? Of course. I think most women do."

"When was the last time?"

She tugged her hand out of my grasp. "I'm not telling you that."

I leaned up on my elbow. "Why not?"

"It's personal."

I eyed her critically. We couldn't get more personal than we had been in the past, and I wanted to get back there. With a little more finesse this time around.

When her sizzling blue gaze landed on my mouth, I rolled on top of her, lifting both of her arms above her head to hold her wrists in one of my hands, and she gasped out my name. My favorite sound was my name on her tongue, and I kissed her, consuming that sound for my own greedy self, as I let my other hand drift down her side until she arched into me, whimpering. "You're torturing me here," I said. "I think it's only fair I get to torture you, too."

Then I kissed her again, sucking and nibbling at her lips, pulling at her tongue, claiming her mouth until she raised her hips up off the mattress, pressing against me. I lifted my head away two inches, basking in her needy little mewls. "Stay like this. Don't move."

She nodded, breathing rapidly through parted lips, her nipples hard through the material of her shirt.

"That's my girl," I rasped, dragging the tip of my nose down hers before focusing my attention on her neck. I teased my fingers under her shirt, over her ribs, brushing the under-sides of her breasts, and she jerked her arms up at the contact, looping them around my neck, but I immediately stopped.

"I said don't move, Delaney."

I unlatched her hands from around my neck and pushed them back into the mattress, holding them there for a few seconds. Her eyes roamed all over my face, and she let out a breath. It smelled like mint, and I kissed her again. She tasted like memories.

"You're killing me," she said into the crook of my shoulder when I licked at her throat.

"I'll take care of you. Don't worry."

I slipped my hands under the waistband of her pants, teasing my knuckles against her skin, my fingertips barely edging into her underwear, and she panted underneath me. I continued to kiss her, but only when she was frantic and writhing did I shift off her with one last peck to her jaw.

She picked her head up off the bed. She was beautifully out of breath. "Wha-what are you doing?"

I stayed silent, searching. I opened random drawers, peeked under the bed frame, checked inside bags at the bottom of her closet.

"What are you looking for?"

I stopped, glancing over my shoulder to find her sitting up now. "I told you to stay put."

She crossed her arms. "I'm not a puppy."

"No," I said with a shake of my head, taking the three steps back to the foot of the bed. With a knee between her legs, I guided her back down until I could grind my hard cock against the cleft between her thighs. She moaned, and I gripped her hip, giving it a good squeeze. She was thick and soft, and I wanted to bite her there, but right now I settled for nipping at her throat. "Where do you keep them?"

"What?" she gasped.

"Your toys."

She laughed into a kiss then tilted her chin toward her closet. "Top shelf. With the towels."

I got up immediately and followed her directions, locating the small, zippered bag, and I opened it carefully like it was buried treasure. I found two, a dark multifunctional thing that was a bit intimidating, but she also had a small pastel-pink wand. With a simple press of a button, it buzzed to life, and I lifted a brow at Laney, still laid out on the bed.

Lowering myself next to her, I kissed her roughly, and I had to pause to rein myself in. Or else I'd lose it like I was a kid. And I sure as shit was not going to waste this time with Laney.

"Keep your hands where they are," I reminded her and lifted her shirt a few inches, revealing her stomach, softly rounded and perfectly smooth. I dragged the vibrator in a straight line, from the bottom of her ribs to the top of her pants. When she spasmed, I pulled it away. "We just started, and already, you're losing the game."

She narrowed her eyes. "You're not making it very easy."

I bent my head, licking below her ear. "That's the fun of it."

She growled and gripped the comforter in her fists, and I hummed in approval. "You've always been in control of everything, the center of attention. I like to see you doing what I say. It's like harnessing the sun."

She wrinkled her nose but stayed silent. Until I pressed the vibrator against her again, this time on her inner thigh. Then she licked her lips and groaned, yet stayed as still as possible, and God, she was perfect. I teased her, dragging the wand up her sides, over her ribs, around her belly button, then finally to her breast.

Dragging her T-shirt up higher, I sucked at her peach-colored nipple as I pressed the vibrator against the other. She arched into me, biting into her bottom lip, and I switched, moving the vibrator to her other breast, alternating until she once again lifted her hips toward me.

"Please, Ethan."

I nearly came in my pants just from hearing her moan my name like that.

I could see her arms practically shaking with tension, and I relented, kissing down her throat as I moved the vibrator below her waist. I rested it between her legs, over her pants. "Feel good?"

She nodded, her eyes closed, and I tugged down the elastic waistband an inch to get my hand in her underwear. She squirmed as I changed the pulse setting then pressed it gently to her clit. She sucked in a breath. "Oh god, Ethan.

"I'm here," I said against her neck. "You make me lose my mind, you know that? What you do to me. What you've always done to me."

She whimpered, and I switched the setting again to make it go faster. She opened her eyes to me, wide and shining. "You're the one doing *this* to *me*."

"And you love it. Tell me you love it."

"I love it," she whispered, and I rewarded her with circles of the wand. She spread her legs, arched her back up, and I sucked a nipple into my mouth, earning a loud moan. So loud, I briefly thought of her brother downstairs, so I silenced her with a kiss, swallowing all of her sweet sounds down. It was only another few seconds of the vibrator on her until she threw her head back and her skin flushed.

"You're so beautiful," I told her and shut off the wand, reluctantly dragging it out from her panties. I sat up and adjusted myself beneath my jeans. I'd have to go home and take a cold shower immediately.

She was breathing hard, and I took my time righting her pants, lowering her shirt back into place. She was still so sensitive, any small brush of my finger over her, even on her stomach, caused a slight tremble, yet still, she didn't move. Only letting me finish my ministrations of tucking her hair behind her ears, rubbing my hands along her arms, and bringing them down to her sides.

"You know it's Redeemer's anniversary of something in two weeks."

"I know," she said after a moment and sat up.

"They're having some big thing, some kind of capital campaign."

She nodded, eyeing me. "*I know.*"

Of course she knew. She had undoubtedly received the same alumni letters and pledge requests that I did.

"JT is being inducted into the hall of fame."

That was new information, and I rolled my eyes petulantly. "That's so stupid. Having a high school hall of fame."

"He was all-state." She shrugged. "Played all four years at Penn State."

"Anyway." I lifted one shoulder. "I was thinking we could go and schmooze people."

She grimaced. "Really?"

"Yeah. What better way to market this event than with our old pals?" I said with barely restrained sarcasm. "Is Seraphina going?"

"Yes." Laney probably knew what I was getting at. West Chester was not a cheap place to live, and most families who sent their kids to Holy Redeemer had deep pockets. "But I'm…"

"What?"

She combed her fingers through her hair toward her bun yet only succeeded in letting more tendrils loose. "I don't really want to see those people."

"Why not? It'll be like a reunion."

"Yeah." She met my gaze head on. "Exactly why I don't want to go."

I drummed my fingers on my knee, staring out into space. "Okay. Well, what if we skip that shindig at the school, but go to Al's. I'm sure everyone will be there."

Al's was an Italian restaurant with two floors, the bottom acting more like a recreation area with a bar and tables scattered around. The place was packed every weekend. It was the hangout for Redeemer kids. If they weren't sharing a basket of breadsticks, then they were downstairs, playing foosball or darts. Al's two children had gone to Redeemer, a while before Laney and I graduated, and he often turned a blind eye to kids stealing a sip of beer from their parents when they ordered a one. Or even grabbing a pitcher by themselves.

"I don't know," Laney said, pulling my attention back to her pursed lips.

"It'll be fun."

"I very much doubt that."

"*We* can have fun," I said.

She scrunched up her nose.

"Delaney Hargrove doesn't hide."

She leaned back on her hands, brows arched. "Don't be a jerk. I haven't been hiding. I've been working. For you."

"And you've been running everything like a boss." I stood and skimmed my fingertip across her cheek. "Don't back down now."

She turned her face away, evidently really mad at me.

"I'm sorry." When she didn't acknowledge my apology, I stepped over into her view. "Lane, I'm sorry. I didn't mean to make you feel bad. That's clearly—" I gestured to the bed, where I'd brought her to orgasm a few minutes ago "—not what I wanted to do."

Her shoulders slumped, and I bent over, forcing her to meet my eyes once more. "I know you said you lost your confidence, but those people are the last ones you should be afraid of. Come on, Laney." I curved my palms around her cheeks and gave her one chaste kiss. "Say yes." Then another one. "Yes."

"Fine," she mumbled against my mouth. "You owe me for this."

"I owe you for a lot of things." I straightened and backed

away to the door. "I can't wait to see what you ordered from the party."

That earned me the hint of a smile. But with her hair askew and the shadow of red along her throat and chin from my scruff, I didn't believe she was even really angry with me. Then again, maybe I'd have to work my way back into her good graces, and I looked forward to it. "Night, Lane."

She lifted her hand. "Night, Ethan."

CHAPTER SIXTEEN

Laney

I had kept in touch with who I wanted to from high school, which was to say, not very many people. There were, of course, my brother and his friends, plus a couple of girls from my sports teams, but other than that, I didn't care to talk to anyone. Heavy was the head that wore the prom queen crown, and most of the people who were my "friends" back then didn't sincerely care about me. The girls wanted to be around me for attention from guys, and the guys wanted to be around me because they were always trying to get in my pants.

Since sixth grade, when my father ran his stupid campaign with my face on billboards and city buses, I'd earned a little local celebrity in school. That same year, I'd also sprouted huge boobs, and high school boys had been suddenly staring at me. Even grown men.

That was why I'd learned to be the center of attention, at a distance. To smile and wave like some pageant contestant, give of myself without giving everything. I locked up my true self for the people I loved. So, I really wasn't looking forward to going to Al's tonight, but I'd promised Ethan I'd go.

Although, really, after that orgasm, I didn't think it was fair. Underneath him and his eyes that burned gold with craving and his steady hands and mouth torturing me, he could have asked me for a kidney, and I would have said yes.

Dean agreed to go with me, and by the time we got to Al's, people spilled out onto the small porch on the side and every table was taken, bodies jammed in next to one another. Clutching my arm, Dean led me through the crowd, down to the basement, where lots of familiar faces roamed.

"You want something to drink?" Dean asked, over the noise of the crowd.

"Yeah, grab me a red wine. Whatever it is, I'll take it."

He nodded and squeezed his way to the bar, leaving me in the middle of the floor with a group of guys not too far away. They were a bunch of football and basketball players, some of them more familiar than others. When JT Rowan spotted me, he ambled away from the group and opened his arms for a hug. "Holy shit! Delaney Hargrove!"

I wrapped my arms around him, and he bear-hugged me.

"It's been forever," he said with a laugh and turned over his shoulder, pointing at the group of men with his beer. "Hey, yo, it's Laney!"

Three of them broke off to greet me in the same enthusiastic way as JT. Kevin Lopez, Matty Bell, and Antonio Roberts. They passed me around like a rag doll before settling me between them. At one time, these guys were all my buddies, my go-to good-time pals, former lost boys and perpetually immature. They told stupid "yo mama" jokes, thought it was funny to hit one another in the balls, and were obsessed with dance-offs in the cafeteria, embarrassing underclassmen by forcing them to join in.

Now, they were dads, accountants, and teachers. They wore pleated pants, for god's sake. They showed me baby pictures, exchanged business cards, and made me promise to keep in touch.

JT, with a slightly rounder belly than the last time I'd seen him, introduced me to his wife, Mel, and we chatted about his high school coaching career, but the conversation inevitably boomeranged back to me.

"JT tells me how you guys were good friends in school," Mel said. "Prom king and queen, that's so cute." She gazed up at him proudly. JT *would* marry the type of woman who thought prom king looked good on a résumé.

"How's everything going with you?" he asked.

"Everything's good." I smiled. Maybe a little too brightly, according to his slight frown.

"Really?"

"Uh-huh."

I hadn't posted anything publicly on my social media about my breakup with Bobby, but according to my sudden erasure of a lot of my history after I'd had so much about us together and the LinkedIn update about me leaving the Magnate Company, it was probably easy to put two and two together. Plus, Dean knew the story, and he'd apparently told Hank, which was basically like telling the *New York Times*.

I didn't mind people knowing I'd broken up with Bobby because he cheated on me, but I did mind their sad eyes.

"I'm sorry about what happened," JT said. "That's a real shit thing to do to someone. Especially you."

I accepted his words with a pat to his arm then made an excuse to move toward the bar, not even getting five feet before I was stopped by more people. They all wanted to talk to me, reminiscence about our high school years, and get the gossip. Kylie Fallstaff, who reintroduced herself to me—and thank god because I didn't remember—said, "I can't believe that happened to you. You were always so popular."

As if popularity checked off some kind of get out of jail free card in life.

The only good thing about so many people wanting to speak to me was that I could talk up RAHD, even though I hadn't yet spotted Ethan.

I would murder him if he ditched me here in this lion's den.

At the bar, I accepted a glass of wine from Dean, my throat like sandpaper from all the conversation, but before I could take a sip, Kayla Levy and Madison Gallagher showed up, arm in arm.

Dean gave Kayla a quick once-over. They'd been hot and heavy in school, and everywhere Kayla had gone, so did Madison. Easy path for Madison and Ethan to get together.

"How've you been, Kayla?" Dean asked congenially, and she smiled.

"Great. I'm getting married next month."

"Yeah?" Dean raised his glass to her. "Congratulations."

"Maddie's the matron of honor," she said, and Madison performed a little curtsy, always one to put on a show.

She was thin with a long neck, like a swan, and ten years ago, the dark-haired girl practically spewed fire from her eyes whenever she looked at me. Not much had changed in that regard.

"How's it going, Madison?" I finally got a sip of her wine. "I heard you own a ballet studio now?"

"That's right." Madison pressed her long fingers against her collarbone, her smile laced with a menacing lilt like Malefi-cent. "You keeping tabs on me?"

"Well, I've been researching local businesses to help out a friend. I'm not sure if you know, but Ethan Marrero has started a nonprofit to raise money for Huntington's disease."

At the mention of his name, Madison's eyebrow ticked up infinitesimally.

"He asked me to head up the first fundraising event, and

I'm looking for sponsors." I fished a business card out of my purse. "Maybe you'd be interested."

Madison took the card though she stayed silent while Kayla held out her hand. "Can I have one too? I couldn't sponsor, but are you taking cash donations?"

I nodded. "You can head to the website listed here and donate right through the link. We appreciate anything you can give."

Madison let out a short laugh. "So, you're back in town for, what? A few weeks? And already you slid right back in with Ethan."

"Madison," Kayla hissed under her breath as Dean held up his hand.

"Hey, whoa, we're all friends here, right? My sister's just helping him out."

"Right," Madison sneered at me. "Same game, different decade." She tugged on Kayla's arm. "Come on, I need to go call my husband. Check in on him." She backed up a step but made sure to toss one last grenade over her shoulder. "He's traveling for work for the next two weeks. To Sydney, Australia. Isn't that funny, Laney?"

Kayla smiled apologetically, but I only shook my head and plopped down on the seat Dean vacated.

"What was all that about?" he asked, eyeing me over the rim of his pint glass.

I flitted my hand in the air. "Nothing."

"What did she mean about sliding right back in with Ethan?"

"You know how she was. Always jealous," I said, skipping over the part about how Madison had a right to be jealous when we were in school. Even though Ethan and I didn't do anything while he was with her, it wasn't as if the way we'd flirted was completely appropriate. Or the few close calls of kisses when we'd sat at my kitchen table as he helped me with math homework.

Madison had never liked me. Liked me even less after she'd started going out with Ethan.

"But what's up her ass now?"

"I don't know, Dean," I said then downed her wine. "I'm the fallen prom queen. It probably delights her that I had to come crawling back home."

He blew out an agitated breath. "That's horseshit. You didn't come crawling back home." He smirked at me. "You flew on a plane."

"You should do stand-up."

"Maybe." He lifted a shoulder as his eyes snagged on something beyond me. "There he is!"

"Hey," Ethan said, setting his hand on the back of my chair.

I skipped the pleasantries. "Where've you been? You left me to circulate by myself."

He held his hand out to Dean. "You weren't alone."

I gave him a bland look, and his gaze roved over me, stumbling on my lips. "Mr. Kinney's here, so I was talking to him for a while. He wrote me a big check." He unfolded said check in front of my eyes.

"Five thousand!"

He nodded, smiling.

"Oh my god." I took it from him. "How'd that happen?"

"We've kept in touch over the years." Ethan lifted his hand to the bartender for a beer. "He basically got me into Princeton, and I had him read over my grad school thesis."

"But he gave you five grand?" Dean asked, tugging at the collar of his shirt before leaning against the bar. It didn't escape my notice how he tipped his chin toward a woman in the corner, giving her his best crooked smile.

"He won some money in the lottery a few years ago," Ethan

explained. "Put some of it away in stocks, and he's living the high life now." He took the check back from me, his index finger brushing over mine, and stuffed it back into his pocket. "Kinney's a good guy. He deserves it."

Dean stood up, his attention still on the corner of the bar. "All right, you guys good?" He didn't wait for their answer. "I'll be back in a bit."

Once he walked away, Ethan took his place, standing next to me, his arm along the back of my chair, his fingers brushing the ends of my hair. "How'd you do?"

"Nothing concrete yet. Besides the judgy eyes."

"Judgy eyes? From who?"

"Madison."

He shifted, covertly peering over his shoulder, probably for her. "I think you're imagining that."

I huffed. "She never liked me. You *know* she never liked me."

He hid his stupid half smile around a sip of beer. "No, but it doesn't matter. She doesn't matter."

"Talk to me when everyone you grew up with is looking at you with judgy eyes."

"I don't even know what judgy eyes look like," he said, bending closer to me.

"You know, like this." I narrowed my eyes at him. "Or this." I widened them, giving him my best Precious Moments stare.

He took a swig of his beer before letting his gaze run down the length of me, and I didn't know if he realized it or not, but he was talking straight to my breasts when he said, "I think I got one or two of those judgy eyes."

"From who?"

He zipped his eyes back up to mine, completely unembarrassed at being caught gawking. Although after our little romp together, he had no reason to be embarrassed. It had proven his point.

I wanted him.

And I wanted to do it again.

"I was talking to Caleb Reichenbach. He's apparently some big club promoter in Las Vegas now. The guy put on, like, fifty pounds of muscle and suddenly has judgy eyes."

"He was probably trying to intimidate you."

"Ha." Ethan pushed his glasses farther back on the bridge of his nose with his index finger. "Me, the coolest kid on the planet, intimidated?" He pointed to himself. "Nah."

"I remember a time when you weren't so cool. When you had to wear a neon jacket while you pushed carts around the parking lot of the grocery store."

He dropped his hand to my knee, squeezing, and the muscle memory sent a zing of pleasure straight between my thighs.

"I ruled those carts with an iron fist."

My laughter was disturbed by someone calling our names.

"Hey, Marrero, Laney."

We swiveled around, and Ethan jumped up at the sight of Gabe Madsen. They hugged each other.

"How're you doing, man?" Ethan patted Gabe on the back. "Why didn't you tell us you were coming home?"

"Last-minute thing," he said, dragging his hand over his long hair pulled back in a bun. "My grandmother's in the hospital, and I wasn't sure if I'd be able to come down…" He lifted his arms. "You know how it is. But I heard about this thing at school and thought I'd swing over to the old haunt, see who was here."

"I can't believe it." Ethan chuckled a carefree sound. "I'm so glad to see you."

"You too," Gabe said, then hugged me. "And how are you?"

There was no implied question or funny tone of voice. He was legitimately asking how I was doing.

"Great," I answered once we let go of each other.

Someone got up from a nearby stool, and Ethan snagged it, placing it down in front of Gabe. "Have a seat."

Gabe sat down next to me, and Ethan moved to stand right behind me as he reached around me for his beer. "So, what's up with your grandmother? Everything okay?"

He pulled a face. "She's got dementia and had an episode. My mom decided they need to put her in a personal care home, so I came down to help with the move and all that."

"Sorry to hear that," Ethan said, and Gabe elbowed him.

"What about you and your brother? Fill me in."

I was aware that Dean and his friends kept in touch through a group chat, much like I did with my girls, so it didn't take long to catch Gabe up on everything, and he knocked his shoulder into mine. "Still killing the game, eh?"

"Trying," I mumbled while Ethan curled his fingers around my neck, claiming otherwise.

"No, she's killin' it. Badass boss lady right here."

"Well, let me know what I can do," Gabe said, and Ethan nodded before launching into questions about Gabe's life in Boston.

After high school, he attended music school then accepted an associate professor position at Berklee and opened up his own school of rock. The whole time they caught up, Ethan found ways to touch me, his hand on my arm or brushing my hair over my shoulder. They were obvious familiar gestures that only someone who knew me well would make, and if Gabe noticed, he didn't say anything.

Dean eventually found his way back to us with Hank in tow, and I smiled at them all huddled together, laughing and joking around.

"We should jam while I'm here," Gabe said, and the others all heartily agreed, though their faces fell. The band was almost all back together. Patrick, the last member of their group, had died a few years ago from an opioid overdose.

Hank broke the quiet. "Remember when Patrick stole Ms. Rigle's word of the day calendar? She flipped out and put the class on lockdown. God, that kid had balls."

I studied the four men in front of me, grown from the four boys they used to be, best friends and bandmates, and missing a member of their tight-knit circle.

Dean and I had known Patrick since first grade, and he and Dean were pretty inseparable. Not to say the rest of the guys weren't close with him, but Patrick and Dean had known each other for so long that when Patrick died, Dean was absolutely crushed. They all were, including me.

Patrick was a great guy, creative and daring, a genuine sweetheart.

And to see these guys together, I couldn't help the sting in my eyes because Patrick wasn't there with them.

Dean raised his drink. "To Patrick."

The group followed suit. "To Patrick."

Finishing the last of my wine, I checked the time on my phone. It was barely ten o'clock, but I was exhausted from extroverting so much. Plus, I didn't want to crash the party these guys had formed any longer. "I think it's time for me to head home."

Gabe jerked his head back. "Already?"

"Yeah. Been a long day." Dean moved to get his keys and coat, but I stayed him. "Hang out for a while."

He frowned. "How'll you get home?"

I opened my rideshare app and put in the address, and when my driver's picture showed up at the bottom of the screen, I angled my phone so Dean could see. "Cynthia."

He pointed to the bar. "Why don't you stay here, and I can take you home later?"

"Because you need time to hang out with your boys, and I don't want to be out till all hours of the night."

Hank raised his fist. "Let's get wasted!"

Ethan palmed Hank's face, pushing him away as he tipped his chin toward the stairs. "I'll wait with you outside until your ride gets here."

I hugged Gabe one more time. "In case I don't see you again before you leave, I hope everything goes well with your grandmother and that your family finds peace with it."

He kissed my cheek. "Thanks, Laney. Good to see you."

Then I pointed at my brother and Hank. "No drinking and driving."

"I'm done for the night. I'll take 'em home if they get too rowdy," Ethan said with an easy smile as he followed me to the door. I ignored Madison glaring at me from the corner and waved to JT and his crew on the way out.

Leaning against the building outside, I held my phone up to track Cynthia's car.

Ethan gazed over my shoulder. "How long until she's here?"

"Four minutes."

He craned his neck up the street. "Black Volkswagen?"

"Yep."

With a quick glimpse at me, he said, "Wasn't so bad in there, right?"

"It was all right." At his surprised eyebrow, I folded my arms. "Is it terrible that I'm a little bit relieved Jennifer Hill is divorced twice, and Leslie Davis has three kids with three different people? I'm not the only one who's had the shit kicked out of them."

Ethan slung his arm around my neck and tugged me close

to kiss the top of my head. The wool of his jacket scratched against my skin, but I set my cheek on his shoulder anyway, wrapping my arms around his waist.

"I hope you don't think you need to hide from me."

Ethan Marrero was the one person I couldn't hide anything from. Even if I wanted to.

I tipped my head back to stare up at him. "I don't."

"Good." He dropped his lips to mine for one chaste kiss. "Go on a date with me."

I opened my mouth to answer, but before I could, he kissed me again, this time sliding his tongue along my lower lip. In the next moment, he had my back up against the building. It was cold out, but huddled together, exchanging hot breaths and even hotter swipes of our tongues, I was warm.

"You taste like wine," he said against my mouth.

"House Cabernet."

"Tastes good on you."

If he hadn't had me pinned against the brick wall, I would've swooned from that line, and he knew it. He smiled against my jaw as his hands roamed down my sides, tucking into my back pockets. "There's a show in Philly I want to go to next week. Come with me."

"Some indie band that no one has ever heard of but you?"

"Mm-hmm." He kissed my throat. "We can grab dinner before."

I turned away from him, but that only gave him better access to my neck.

"You've been working so hard for the fundraiser. Let me repay you."

I sucked in a clearing breath and stepped out of his grasp. "Ethan." I shook my head, unable to meet his eyes. "That's exactly why we can't."

He huffed, bending his knees, forcing himself into my line

of vision. "I can make you come with a vibrator, but I can't take you on a date?"

I pushed him away with a hand on his shoulder, annoyed with his tone. "I don't think you understand how it feels to lose everything because you couldn't keep business and feelings separate."

"I'm not him, Delaney." He threw his hands up at his sides, his voice rising uncharacteristically in agitation. "Number one, I'm not a dumbass, and number two, this isn't some huge worldwide business. This is a local fundraiser. You don't work for me. If you don't want to do it anymore, then don't."

"I don't want to quit. I've got big plans for that money from Mr. Kinney. Down payments for a couple of rentals."

His pinched face relaxed, his eyes pooling with tenderness. "You're doing a big favor for me, and I'd like to repay you."

I bit back a smile, my own irritation fading. "With sex?"

"With dinner and a concert," he amended in mock seriousness. "Repayment for helping out a friend."

I crossed my arms. "And everything else?"

"That," he started, crowding my space once more, "is me making up for being an idiot ten years ago."

As he moved to kiss me, Cynthia pulled up, and I pressed my hand to Ethan's chest, giving in. Because he wasn't the only one who was an idiot ten years ago.

"Okay."

"Okay?"

I stepped around him to my ride. "I don't know why you sound so amazed. I thought you knew I was a sure thing when it came to you."

"All that sweet talk, you'll make me have a heart attack before our first official date, Laney. I'll be real mad to miss it."

Between his boyish grin and his hand clutching his chest, a

loud laugh bubbled up from the back of my throat. "You're ridiculous."

"And you're wonderful."

I opened the car door. "Take care of my brother."

He saluted me and watched as I got in, waving as Cynthia drove off. By god was I a sure thing.

CHAPTER SEVENTEEN

4whoresmen of the apocalypse

I'm going out with Ethan.

BRONTE

As in on a date…or like boyfriend girlfriend?

SAM

My sweet summer child.

BRONTE

Shut up.

I'm going on a date with Ethan.

GEM

A literal dream come true.

GEM

Are you going to eat hot dogs?

I hope not.

SAM

How do you feel?

Nervous. Excited.

BRONTE

Where are you going?

To Philly to see some band he likes.

BRONTE

Fun!

GEM

Give us the play-by-play.

SAM

Or not. Hopefully you'll be too occupied.

GEM

True story. Ignore me.

SAM

We mostly do already.

GEM

SAMANTHA

GEM

You would kick me while I'm down and puking
my guts out?

SAM

I'm kidding. We love you. Who else would give
us shit about our carbon footprints if not
for you?

BRONTE

Can we get back to the good part? Laney and
Ethan.

Apropos of nothing, Ethan eats mostly
vegetarian.

GEM

I love him already.

BRONTE

I love him if you love him.

SAM

I will save my judgment until I meet him.

GEM

Where's the fun in that?

BRONTE

OMG THE DOORBELL JUST RANG WITH A DELIVERY

BRONTE

OMG LANEY

Four chicks and Three dicks

CHRIS

Well, well, well. Christmas came early.

CHRIS

And I must have been a very, very good boy.

JASON

?

BRONTE

OMG. Stop.

CHRIS

I got a present from Delaney.

You're welcome. Everyone else's should be arriving today too.

SAM

What is it? I'm at work.

GEM

HAHAHAHAHAHHAHAHAHAHA

JASON

What is happening right now?

GEM

Laney bought all the girls presents.

I mean...

They're not necessarily for single-player use only.

CHRIS

Yes. Ours is definitely a two-player game.

GEM

I'm opening mine right now. Are they all the same?

I tailored them to what I thought each of you would like.

SAM

OoOoOoh. Did the sex toys arrive?

JASON

I'm sorry, what?

SAM

Laney went to a sex toy party. I thought she was kidding when she said she'd buy each one of us something.

You know I take gift-giving very seriously. I put a lot of thought into it.

GEM

That's true. Thank you. I love mine.

JASON

I'm sorry, what?

SAM

Where did Bronte go? I would love to see her face.

GEM

I bet they're trying theirs out right now.

SAM

I want to see what I got. I'm still here for another two hours.

MIKE

I just finished with my client and

MIKE

Did I really read what I think I read?

SAM

Yep.

MIKE

Jesus

I assume that taking the Lord's name in vain in this instance means you're happy?

SAM

Good assumption to make.

JASON

I have a really important meeting in a few minutes. What the fuck, guys?

GEM

"a really important meeting"

JASON

Gemma.

GEM

Jason.

Everyone have fun!

GEM

Not me. I feel like garbage. I'm down eight pounds. I barely have enough energy to make it through the day, let alone have sex. This baby is kicking my ass worse than the first one.

JASON

Now, hold on a minute.

GEM

Jason.

JASON

Gemma.

GEM

No. You're putting Willow down, and I'm drinking a ginger ale and taking a melatonin gummy and going to bed early tonight.

MIKE

Sorry for ya, bro

MIKE

Delaney, you are a god among men.

Merely doing my civic duty.

GEM

Going to use yours with Ethan?

…

GEM

You sly dog.

JASON

Meeting's over. I'm coming home.

That was only like ten minutes.

GEM

"really important"

JASON

Gemma.

4whoresmen of the apocalypse

GEM

Laney, you've been holding out pertinent
information about you and Ethan. You hooked
up already?

The night of the party.

GEM

That was weeks ago!

GEM

And you didn't tell us?!

GEM

That goes against our friendship contract.

SAM

Meanwhile, I'm still here doing paperwork,
and Mike sent me a selfie with our present.

SAM

Something that looks like it comes with a
remote control…?

I thought about getting that one for the
Mitchells, but I know Gem likes to be the
boss. Ain't that right?

GEM

In and out of the bedroom. I only pretend he
has some say to make sure he sticks around.
You gotta trick 'em like that.

Welp. My job here is done.

GEM

Oh shit. Jason's home.

SAM

Go put your money where your mouth is.

BRONTE

So when is the big date?

She's alive! Five hours later!

BRONTE

I was busy.

Yes. I know. I thought my boy would enjoy a little pegging action.

BRONTE

No comment.

HA

The date's on Friday.

And I just realized I'm the one who is single and really does need to use my purchases. You guys all have the real things.

BRONTE

I'm sure Ethan wouldn't mind lending his services.

No. It's pretty much a sure thing.

CHAPTER EIGHTEEN

Laney

Dean clomped up the steps as read a text from Ethan saying he'd be here in a minute. He had messaged earlier to tell me traffic was horrendous, so he'd be picking me up half an hour earlier than planned. That meant I had to forgo my favorite jeans, which were still in the dryer, and throw on an old pair.

I stuffed my phone, ChapStick, and wallet into my purse and crossed it over my chest before bumping into my brother in the hall. He loosened the tie around his neck. "Where're you headed in such a rush?"

"I'm going to a concert." I checked the time, finally noticing how late it was for Dean to be coming home from work. He looked exhausted. "Staying in tonight?"

He shook his head and turned, shuffling backward to his room. "I'm going out with a friend."

I shot him a look. "Aren't you tired of it?"

"Of what?"

"You're doing too much. Between the firm and all these women. You're going to wear yourself out."

He leaned his shoulder against his doorjamb. "That's the point."

"Hey." I caught his attention before he stepped into his room. "Don't be dumb."

"You too," he said and pivoted around.

Outside, I was already waiting on the curb when Ethan pulled up. He rushed around to the passenger side of the car to hold the door for me.

I greeted him with a kiss on the cheek. "Hi."

Before I could get away, he wrapped his hand around my hip. "Why didn't you let me come to the door for you?"

But then his mouth was on mine, so I couldn't answer. He caressed my lips with his tongue, and he gently pressed me against his car as his hands found their way under my jacket, so high his thumbs dragged along the wire of my bra. I angled my head, drawing him closer, nipping and sucking at his lips, but at that point, it was hard to tell who was pushing and pulling, who was claiming whom.

With one last tiny kiss to the corner of my mouth, he cleared his throat and extracted his hands from where they were under my shirt. "Let me walk you to your door at the end of the night."

"Why?"

"Because this is our first *real* date, and I don't want to screw it up." He smiled like a young kid trying to impress his first girlfriend, and with his cowlick, graphic T-shirt, and zip-up hoodie, he may as well have been.

It was like we were starting from scratch.

"Okay," I said and dropped into the passenger seat. He shut the door and rounded the hood with his long strides. His fashion may not have progressed far past high school, but my eyes snagged on those hands that had certainly learned a few things since then, and when he sat down behind the wheel, he elbowed me gently.

"You all right?"

"Mm-hmm." I bit into the corner of my lip, and he nodded as if he knew I'd been thinking of what we'd done. Of what we still had yet to do.

He maneuvered the car onto the street and swiftly to the highway, where the traffic was bumper-to-bumper. He fiddled with the radio, tuning to some alternative station, but I smacked his hand away. He chuckled, letting me take over, even if that meant Adele. As I settled back into my seat with my hands in my lap, he linked our fingers together, and when I glanced over at him, his attention was on my thighs.

"They're ripped," he said, scratching over the distressed denim above my knee.

"I know." I hitched my brow at him, but he was still staring down. He poked his finger through the hole, lightly tickling my skin, and I didn't think he was giving me fashion advice. Especially when his mouth twisted into a half smile. "What?" I asked.

He focused on the road, slowly following behind the minivan in front of us. "Thinking about a memory. That's all."

"You can't say something like that and not tell me." When he still didn't answer, I shook his hand, twined with mine. "We don't have secrets, remember?"

I didn't know if that was still true or not, although it used to be. There had never been secrets between us. We told each other anything and everything. Except how we really felt about each other. But it was different now. It had to be.

No secrets. At all.

"It's stupid," he said after a while.

"Tell me."

"It was one time in your room," he started, and he leaned his elbow on the console between us, moving his hand out of my grasp to rest it on my thigh. "A couple weeks after home-coming," he said, and I understood his implied tone of voice.

Homecoming was when it had all gone sideways. He'd thought I was with JT, so he started going out with Madison.

"We talked a bit. I don't remember about what," he continued, absently stroking my knee with his thumb.

"The White Stripes, I'm sure," I suggested with a smile because he was forever trying to get me to listen to them.

"Probably." Then he shrugged. "You pulled me down to the bed, and we were sitting so close. I wanted to kiss you." He angled his gaze to me, his eyes the color of molten honey. "So bad."

I didn't know what this had to do with my jeans, but I loved hearing his side of our story, and I wasn't about to stop him.

"But then you got a message on your computer. It was JT. I didn't mean to look, but I saw that he asked you to come over to his house. He wanted you to wear the jeans with the rip in them."

I furrowed my brow, having absolutely no recollection of this.

"I had no right to be jealous." He briefly glanced at me before traffic finally started to let up. "Still, I was. I was the guy in your bedroom, but some other dude was trying to get you to wear jeans with a rip to his house because he said you looked hot in them. I went back downstairs so mad. I mean, I had assumed you two were together before then, but that text message made it obvious."

"Huh." I stared at his profile, reflecting on how JT and I had been together, occasionally flirting, but nothing had ever happened between us. A lot of people assumed things about me that weren't true, so it was probably easy for Ethan, as the new kid, to believe JT and I hooked up since we were often physical with each other, hugging and kissing each other's cheeks.

But I had never wanted JT. It had always been Ethan, my brother's best friend and drummer in the marching band. The math genius with those adorably big ears and messy hair. Apparently, no one in school would have believed the homecoming queen wanted him. Not even Ethan.

"So, when you came back downstairs to leave and you weren't in your ripped-up jeans, I was happy. Relieved. I didn't want you to dress for him." He played with the rip in my current jeans. "But now you're wearing them for me, and you do look super hot in them. And yeah, I'm taking a perverse pleasure in it."

I took perverse pleasure in it too. I was ready to let him in my ripped jeans and take whatever he wanted. Thinking of what he'd been already capable of, without ever getting me completely naked, sent ripples of heat over my skin, and I clamped my legs together, trapping his hand between my thighs. He tipped his head, grinning lasciviously, and I teasingly smashed my hand against his cheek, pushing him to look forward. "Just keep your eyes on the road, all right?"

He suppressed a laugh and drove. About forty minutes later, he took the Broad Street exit off I-95. "My uncle's got a little pub in South Philly. We could grab a bite, and you can meet some of my family."

Surprised and thrilled at the prospect of meeting more of his family, I tried not to get too far over my skis about it. It was still only a first date, after all.

He turned onto 11th Street. "It's no five-star place, but I thought you'd like it."

He parked in a tiny lot behind a brick building and took my hand as soon as I was out of the car, guiding me around to the front. There was a small patio with only one couple braving the cold wind, and I automatically lifted the collar of my jacket.

"Come on," Ethan said, towing me past the iron rod tables and chairs with the red umbrellas. "You'll warm up inside."

Above the door, a sign read Grady's in gold lettering, and Ethan held the door open for me. It wasn't what I was expected from all he'd said about the "little pub." It was gorgeous, with shiny wood floors and chestnut furniture. Walls portioned the restaurant off into different sections, some with big, oversized chairs around tables and others with picnic-style seating. Sconces and low-hanging chandeliers provided light and an old-world charm. Patrons were scattered all over the place, laughing and chatting. A waiter passed with delicious-looking food that smelled even better.

Ethan tugged me toward the bar, where a tall white man with salt-and-pepper hair waved and hauled Ethan into a hug. "Hey! Long time no see!"

Ethan returned the hug with one arm, not letting go of my hand with the other. "Hey, Uncle. How're ya?"

"Good, good. Glad to see you." He gestured to me. "And who've you brought today?"

"This is Delaney. Laney, this is my Uncle Tim."

"Nice to meet you." I shook Uncle Tim's outstretched hand before he pointed to the bar.

"Want to sit here or…?"

Ethan looked to me to decide. I smiled at them both. "Bar is fine."

Tim nodded and grabbed a couple of menus. "I'll be back in a minute," he said then disappeared toward the kitchen.

I removed my jacket and hung it and my purse on the hook under the bar. "So, he's your…?"

"My mom's brother. One of five, all born and raised here."

"Wow. Big family."

"Yeah. I have…" Ethan lifted his attention toward the

ceiling for a few seconds. "Twelve first cousins on that side. Every once in a while, we all try to get together. It's nuts."

I nodded, trying to remember Ethan's parents. I'd met them once, at our high school graduation. "What about your dad?"

"He's from upstate New York. My parents met in college."

"Are you—" My question was cut off when two women, not much older than us, waltzed out from the kitchen.

"Hey, cuz!" the one with fire-engine-red hair said.

Ethan hugged them both. "Hey." He pointed to me. "This is Laney. Laney, these are my cousins, Siobhan—" he gestured to the dark-haired one "—and Colleen—" then tipped his chin to the redhead.

Siobhan strutted around the bar. "You didn't tell us you were coming. We could've gone out."

Ethan sat back down. "We have tickets to a concert at eight."

"Oh, nice." Colleen tossed down a pair of coasters on the bar before grabbing two glasses from the shelf behind her. She filled the first with Guinness and plunked it down on Ethan's coaster, then asked me, "What would you like to drink?"

"I guess I'll have a Guinness too."

Siobhan leaned in toward me. "It's nice to finally meet you. Ethan never brings his friends around."

"Yeah, I was starting to think he didn't have any," Colleen added.

Ethan kept his voice monotone as he said, "Ha. Ha. Really original." Swiveling on his chair to capture my attention, he explained, "They like to catch up on the years of torment they missed out on since we were moving around so much."

Siobhan nodded, acknowledging the truth as she walked away. "Gotta get back to work. See you later."

Colleen placed my beer in front of me. "What can I get you guys to eat? The fish 'n chips are killer."

I tapped my hand on the bar. "Fish 'n chips, it is."

Ethan handed Colleen our menus even though neither of us had even opened them. "Roast beef sandwich for me. Extra horseradish."

"Got it."

She pivoted away, and I propped my elbow on the bar, my chin in her hand. "Tell me."

"Tell you what?" he asked around a sip of beer.

"About our time apart. I want to know everything I missed."

He ran both hands through his hair, messing up the way he had the front styled so it drooped to the side. His cowlick pointed in the other direction, making him look younger, and if it weren't for his five-o'clock shadow, I'd think we were back in high school.

"Everything?" he asked, setting his knees on the outside of mine.

When I nodded, he launched into his life for the past ten years. He talked about the countries he had studied abroad in, and the time he got lost in the middle of Oktoberfest in Munich, only to be found passed out on the side of the road by the police. He told me how even though he loved traveling, he loved being able to come home more. Said he'd never met any friends better than the ones he'd met at Holy Redeemer, and that made me smile.

I was falling for him. All over again.

"Here we go." Tim interrupted me telling Ethan about my girls to slide our food onto the bar. The plates were huge. "I put my special sauce on there," he said, referring to Ethan's sandwich.

Ethan rubbed his hands together. "Thanks."

Tim patted my shoulder. "Enjoy."

I smiled and bit into a fry as I spritzed my plate with malt vinegar, going back to telling Ethan about Gem, Bronte, and Sam. The fish was hot, crispy, and delicious, but I could barely finish it. Blowing out a big breath, I sat back in my chair. "I'm so full already."

"Uncle Tim must like you. Gave you a bigger plate than usual." Ethan gripped my upper thigh with a squeeze. "He's not the only one who likes you. But then again, you've always had a big fan club." He wove his other hand through my hair, wrapping a lock around his index finger. He tucked it behind my ear, sweeping the length of it aside to kiss the spot below my ear. I shivered when his breath ghosted my neck. "You smell edible."

"Are you sure that's not the roast beef sandwich?"

"Positive." He kissed me again. "We should get going."

I stood up and took one more sip of my Guinness. I'd barely drunk any of it but felt buzzed anyway, every cell and fiber in my body lit up like a Christmas tree.

After hugs to his uncle and cousins, Ethan slipped his arm around my waist, escorting me back outside to his car. The show was in Fishtown at The Fillmore, a converted warehouse with two concert spaces, a smaller room upstairs and an open space in the basement, which was where he directed me.

There were some seats along the outside of the room, for people to eat and drink, but the rest was standing room only.

"You want a drink from the bar?" he asked.

I shook my head. "But I'll have a sip of yours."

He ordered another beer and two bottles of water. I took one of the waters and chugged about half before we found a spot on the floor toward the right side of the stage. He slid his arm around my shoulders, offering me his beer. I accepted it and took a swig.

"You're normally a wine drinker, huh?"

I nodded and passed the lager back to him. "Although it seems you're turning me into a beer drinker."

He grinned into his beer right as the lights flickered. It was time for the show.

CHAPTER NINETEEN

Ethan

"You like the show?" I asked as the lights on the floor came back on, the crowd dispersing toward the doors on the left.

"Yeah."

"I thought you might." I curled my hand around Laney's as we walked toward the exit. I'd always had an eclectic taste in music, but she liked the softer pop stuff, which was why I guessed she'd enjoy this band. Like if Ben Folds Five played more R&B with a gravelly kind of Motown voice and Top-40 lyrics.

"Thanks for taking me," she said, and I kissed the back of her hand.

"My pleasure."

She snuggled into my side as we followed the throngs of people out of the venue and to the parking lot. The walk to the car wasn't long, but it was cold enough to see our breath. Damn early spring weather was all over the place.

"Did you want to hang out around here or head home?" I asked her, knowing there were some cool bars in the area, but as she got into my car with chattering teeth, I suspected her answer.

"Home, please."

I sat down behind the wheel and blasted the heat.

"You need butt warmers in here," she said, running her hands up and down her legs.

"Maybe in our next car."

Laney stilled momentarily but otherwise didn't say anything about my statement, whatever the opposite of a Freudian slip was. As far as I was concerned, I was ready to combine bank accounts and adopt a dog. Go to Target and buy one of those mats for the front door that said *Our Nest* or something equally as cheesy. Hell, I'd buy one for every holiday and season. Flamingos in the summer and one with a snowman for the winter. Go all out.

Though in the moment, all I did was point all the air vents in Laney's direction. "Better?"

She nodded, nibbling on her bottom lip, and I let her go, giving her space and time to think through whatever it was she needed to. As I got back on the highway, my mind wandered as well, over what it would take to keep Laney. Once we'd graduated high school, she was gone. She'd found her wings and hadn't looked back. I didn't know how much I had to do with her choices, but I assumed a little. What I did know for a fact was that she had felt stifled in West Chester, as if all eyes were on her.

The only current problem was I didn't know if she'd stay now that she was home. Or if the wind would take her off in another direction, away from me. I didn't want to lose her again and was determined to rewrite our history. I would tell her how I felt this time around, make sure we looked into each other's eyes when we came to our decision, whatever it might be, instead of running from each other.

Arriving back at Dean's, I shut off the ignition. "So?"

"So..."

"What did you think?"

"Of what?"

I circled my finger around, encompassing everything. "Of this. Of tonight. Of you and me."

She unlatched her seat belt and sat forward. "I don't know."

"You don't know?"

"I just..." She covered her face with her hands, muffling words that sounded like, "I don't know if I could get over you again."

"What?" I gently pulled on her wrists. "I can't understand you."

She fisted her hands, sighing. "Ethan, you broke my heart."

I let go of her to rake my hands through my hair then moved to reach for her again. "I'm sorry."

"It took me years to get over you. I avoided getting close to anyone for a long time."

I licked my lips, nodding. It had been the same for me too. "I was a stupid kid, but I was as heartbroken as you were. I didn't know how to fix it then. I didn't have the words or actions, but I do now, and I promise I won't hurt you."

In the dark of my car, Laney's eyes were like clear, glowing pools as they toggled between my own, and my heart contracted as if someone had their fist around it—as if she had her fist around it. Threading my hands into her hair, I crushed my mouth to hers. This might have been our first official date, but this conversation was a long time coming, and I used my lips as words, my tongue as punctuation. I didn't plan on stopping until I had her convinced.

"You are all I ever wanted." I pressed my forehead to hers. "You are everything to me, Lane." She smiled into another kiss, but I backed away from her. "Don't move. Let me be a gentleman this time."

She stayed seated while I rounded to her side of the car and opened the door for her. I linked our fingers together to walk her to the front door, but she paused, shaking her head slightly.

"What?"

"Dean went out with a *friend*." She motioned to the dark house. "And he's not home yet."

"Does this friend happen to be of the female variety?"

"Yes."

It was after eleven, and I shrugged. "Probably not coming home tonight."

"Too bad I'll have to be home alone in this big house by myself," she said, pouting.

I dropped my attention to her lips. "That is too bad. I wonder what we can do about that."

"Got any ideas?" She turned into me, skimming her fingers down my torso, and every single muscle in the vicinity clenched.

I smoothed my hands over her hips. "I've got a few."

Then she smiled that bright white smile and pulled her keys from her purse to open the door. I was immediately on her, hands and lips everywhere.

She threw her head back, laughing, as we bumped into the wall, the sofa, and the coffee table. I forced my mouth off her throat long enough for us to race upstairs, but in our haste, she tripped. I caught her with an arm around her waist to keep her from falling down then patted her ass a few times, rushing her up the last few steps.

In her bedroom, Laney flicked the lights on, her eyes blazing with excitement, and I had to once again pause. Or else I'd be coming in my pants like the kid I was trying to prove I wasn't. Attempting to gain control of myself and the situation, I reached for her, curling my palm around her neck, but she stopped with her hands up. "Don't make me regret this."

"Never," I promised. The first of many promises I planned on making to this woman.

When I dipped my head to kiss her, she ducked away and shoved me onto the bed. I chuckled and gave in, offering up control for a little while. Crossing my arms beneath my head, I noticed her gaze drop to where my T-shirt lifted, revealing a thin band of skin, and her eyes darkened. A litany of bumbling, awkward memories filled my mind. After all this time, I was finally getting a redo. Another chance to be honest. Another chance to be together.

She slipped off her shoes, removed her jacket, then surveyed me as if she wasn't sure where to start. I offered her a suggestion. "Take my belt off."

She didn't hesitate to strut toward the bed, her long, straight hair like strands of wheat, her plump lips wet and the bottom corner tucked into her top teeth, failing to hold back a smile. She followed my instruction and unbuckled my belt, sliding it from the loops before tossing it to the floor. My shoes and socks were next, then she climbed on the bed, straddling me to peel off my zip-up and T-shirt. With a hand against my chest, she pushed me to lie back down, and I clamped my hand over hers.

"I can feel your heart beating," she said, and I wasn't surprised. It was attempting to burst out of my chest. I was about to have sex with the girl I'd been dreaming of for the last ten years; of course I was full of nervous energy. I wanted to make it good for her, show her how badly I wanted her. How much I craved her.

But she seemed intent on making me wait, and the longer I had to wait, the shorter my fuse got.

She shimmied down my body, leaving openmouthed kisses on my chest, licked over my nipple, and scratched her teeth down my stomach. I grabbed for her as my breath hissed out of me. She slanted an eyebrow at me, obviously knowing *exactly* what she was doing, and continued down the line of dark hair to my jeans. If this was payback for the other night with her battery-powered friend, I'd take it. Although I wasn't sure how long I'd last.

After tugging the zipper of my jeans down, Laney reached inside my pants, pressing the heel of her hand down the length of my cock, straining toward her, and I reflexively canted my hips off the bed. She wrapped her fingers around me, and I had to close my eyes to the sight of her long, pale fingers against my darkened skin. Then she lowered to close her mouth around me, causing my eyes to fly open as I wrapped her hair around my hand. She put those magnificent lips to work, hollowing her cheeks as she sucked, her tongue swirling at the tip, and the sound that left my body was *unholy*.

She released me with a pop, laughing at my expense, and I narrowed my eyes at her, tugging on her until she was in my lap. When she tried to kiss me, I shook my head and flipped so she was on her back. Then I stripped my jeans and boxers off, drawing her attention down to my shaft, shining from her treatment of it.

"My turn," I said, wasting no time in unbuttoning her shirt. It looked good on her, but it hid my favorite assets, and I tossed it on the floor. Then I went after her jeans, peeling them down her long legs until she was left in only her bra and underwear. I glided my hands up and down her thighs, from knee to hip and back, and she let out what sounded like a sigh of contentment. I smiled. "Don't get too comfortable. We've got a long way to go."

I fused my lips to her chest, biting into the flesh barely contained by her bra. Unclasping it, I pulled it off and cupped my hand around her breast, licking her nipple, and she locked her legs around my waist. I moved to her other breast, kissing and sucking it until her breath was ragged and her back arched into me. Only then did I lift my head for a moment, taking in my handiwork, the light teeth marks and the red scratches from my stubble. She was still muscular, evidence of her past as an athlete, but she had softened around her hips and belly, become supple and plush in the best places.

"You're gorgeous," I said then tapped her hip in a sign to help me take her panties off, and she stared up at me with those eyes that told me she needed to be more than that to me. And, of course, she was. I bent over her, kissing the spot beneath her ear. "You're also honest and generous, and I am privileged to be here with you."

She breathed my name against my ear, and I broke the light hold she had around my neck, saying, "Let me show you."

I set my glasses on her nightstand and sank down to the floor at the foot of the bed, towing her toward me by her ankles to hook her legs over my shoulders. I hovered my mouth above her pussy long enough to make her whine. With a smile, I dropped my head for my first taste of her, strong and sharp, a little bit salty and metallic, and so goddamn delicious my dick surged even thicker.

I hadn't gone down on her the first time around, and I planned on making it up to her. As many times as possible. I started light, with only the tip of my tongue, occasionally teasing her with kisses to her thighs, and she trembled. "I'm ticklish."

I hummed my appreciation against her, and this time, she not only trembled but squirmed her hips. I pinned her down with an arm across her lower stomach. I alternated kissing and sucking, reveling in each and every moan, and the quake of her thighs. She was close, and I backed away from her, licking her flavor off my lips as I dragged my hand over her slit, pushing in one then two fingers, crooking them until I found the spot that had her almost levitating off the bed.

"So this is what I've been missing out on all this time," she panted, and I chuckled against her leg before dipping my mouth back down to her center, using my tongue and fingers on her. Her sounds soared higher and higher as she grasped my forearm, her fingernails digging into my skin. I sucked harder in response, and I could feel her clenching around my fingers, but I didn't stop, intent on wringing out every ounce of pleasure I could from her.

When she sagged against the mattress, her skin slick with a sheen of sweat, I stood up, sucking her wetness off my fingers before stepping away to grab a condom from my wallet. I'd hoped this was where we'd end up and didn't want to chance it so I tucked the foil packet away before I left my house. But she stopped me from ripping it open.

"Ethan."

I pivoted back to her, and she combed her hand through her hair, pushing it from her flushed face.

"I want you to know that after everything happened with..." She cleared her throat and sat up. "I was tested to make sure because I didn't know..."

I sat down on the bed, wrapping an arm around her, my heart sinking at her obvious discomfort and embarrassment about her past, though a boulder settled in my stomach with anger for that fucking prick. I kissed her temple, intent on soothing her worries. "I've always used condoms and—"

"This isn't about me thinking you're careless." She shook her head, her focus on her wall. "I trust you, and that's why I'm telling you. I'm on birth control, and Bobby and I didn't use condoms because I thought..." She slowly dragged her eyes to me. "I thought he loved me. I loved him, so we..." She dropped her attention to my collarbone as she straddled my lap. "I wish I could take a lot of things back."

With her naked, wet skin on me, I stayed excruciatingly still and held on to her waist, forcing her eyes back up to mine, needing to hear whatever it was she wanted to say. "What is it, Laney?"

She licked her lips, easing even closer to me, the tip of my cock perilously close to reaching heaven. "I want you. I trust you."

I nodded, unable to speak but *same.*

"I trust you more than I ever trusted him. I don't want to compare you to him, and I'm sorry I ever did." She rested her hand over my heart, barely whispering the last part. "I need you to…"

My skin prickled as I mentally filled in the blank. She wanted to erase that Australian bastard from memory, and I was more than happy to assist. "I'm going to make you feel so good you won't be able to remember your own name, let alone his."

She smiled, and I lifted her up a few inches then positioned myself at her entrance so she could slide down me, soft and hot and wet and tight perfect bliss. I exhaled the breath I'd been holding for the last ten years. Because Laney was finally home with me.

But then she started to move, finding the speed and rhythm she needed, and my mind reeled off the track. I dropped my chin toward my chest, squeezing my eyes shut to the sensory overload.

A few moments later, she stilled, her hands on my shoulders, and it took a second for me to come to, finding her wide grin. "What are you saying?"

I blinked. "What?"

"You're mumbling something. Sounded like numbers."

"Oh." My chest tightened, along with my throat. Like a sudden allergic reaction had ravaged my body. At this point, maybe that would have been better than the truth. "I, uh, didn't realize I was saying it out loud."

"Saying what out loud?"

"Prime numbers."

Laney looped her arms around my neck, her naked breasts against my chest, her laughter echoing not only in my ears but through my ribs too. I tried to hide my face in her hair, but she forced me to look at her. That was when I blurted out, "I'm trying not to come in fifteen seconds here, but all I want to do is fuck the shit out of you." I squeezed her waist. "You know how often I've thought of this? Of you? God, Lane, fuck..."

Her smile faded to something more feral, and she rolled her hips as if to challenge me. I'd just given her a goal—to make me come in fifteen seconds—but whether it required reciting prime numbers or not, I'd give her a night she wouldn't forget.

With one palm supporting her lower back and the other on her breast, I spread my knees farther apart, offering her more room to work with and take what she needed. I dragged my teeth over her shoulder, her jaw, her ear, any part of her I could taste. With her fingers in my hair, she ground her hips against mine, rolling them faster and faster as I plucked at her nipple and sucked on the skin of her neck.

"Yes, Ethan," she murmured, and I captured her mouth then wrapped my arms around her hips and ass, lifting her up as I stood.

She yelped in surprise. "What are you—"

I pushed her up against the closest wall, not letting her get the rest of her question out, and held her left thigh up in my arm to thrust hard into her. "When you say my name like that," I said, plunging into her again and again, "it drives me crazy."

She dug her fingers into my biceps, letting her head fall back, and I licked her throat, salty with sweat. She groaned out my name again, and I tucked my face into the crook of her neck, grunting until I couldn't stand any longer, my blood pumping hard and fast, my orgasm building in my lower back. I needed to slow down.

I guided her back to the bed, grabbing a pillow to put under her hips as I laid her on the mattress and held her legs up against my chest.

From this angle, I could admire her face, see how her lips formed a silent O when I pushed inside her, hitting a spot that elicited tiny gasps. I dragged my hand between the valley of her breasts, down her stomach, to where I was buried inside her. I petted the little bud of her clit with my thumb. "I want you to come again." She thrashed around, muttering incomprehensible words, and I had to grit my teeth to keep from losing it. "Come on, Laney. I want to feel you." I stroked her, driving harder and faster into her until she finally cried out, and I bent over, pushing her thighs up toward her chest, nipping at her earlobe. "That's my girl."

Then I let myself go, giving in to the wave of heat rising over me, a spark of light flashing behind my eyelids as I released into her. For a minute, we lay together, me on top of her, only breathing.

"No regrets?" I asked once I found my voice again.

"No regrets. At all," she said with a tired smile, and I kissed her shoulder, telling her I'd be right back before hopping off the bed.

I cleaned myself up in the bathroom then returned with a warm, wet cloth. Laney stretched her arms above her head, plainly relishing how I gently swiped the washcloth against the pink and swollen flesh between her legs. When I finished, I kissed her stomach, tossing the cloth into her laundry basket in her closet. Laney was the untidy twin, with no rhyme or reason to how she ordered her clothes and random items strewn on the floor.

Before I could tug her down next to me, she rose to use the bathroom, her naked hourglass figure striding gloriously away, the dimples of her lower back calling to me. I vowed to make friends with them later, although when she sauntered back into the room a few minutes later, all thoughts left my brain. With her hair down and mussed, her nipples pert and darkened in color, the thin patch of hair between her legs, she was a goddess.

"Don't look at me like that," she said, crawling back into bed to lie on top of me.

I welcomed her weight. "Or what?"

"Or we might not sleep."

"I wasn't planning on it," I said, and she snuggled her cheek against my chest. I traced my fingers down the divots of her spine and wrote my name above those dimples on her back.

"I could stay like this forever."

I agreed with a happy hum. "I wouldn't mind."

After a few minutes, she rolled to her side, locking her eyes with mine. "Remember when we went to the beach and—"

"Don't finish that sentence." I placed a kiss on her collarbone.

She huffed out a laugh. "Why not? I want to talk about it."

"You want to talk about how I was a fumbling idiot who had no idea what he was doing? No thanks, I'll pass." When she laughed again, I slid my hand over her hip to her thigh, squeezing it to prove a point. We didn't need to rehash the night we both lost our virginity to each other.

Like every graduating senior class on the East Coast before us, we all went to the beach for a week. The Hargroves had said they would only allow Dean and Laney to go if they rented a house together, looked out for each other. So, they'd each rounded up a few friends, and we'd all driven down to a big but broken-down house in Ocean City, Maryland. It had been during that trip when Laney and I'd finally had it out, after a few too many warm beers. On the back porch after everyone else had gone to sleep, we had argued about whose fault it was.

Why didn't you tell me you liked me?

Well, why didn't you tell me you liked me?

All these years later, I couldn't remember much of what we'd said, only that all of a sudden, we were kissing and groping each other. And then the next night, we'd made plans to go down to the beach after everyone was asleep again. I'd brought a blanket and a condom, and I'd made a fool of myself. I'd had no idea what I was doing and practically blacked out in ecstasy from even being naked with her.

I had never worked up the nerve to tell her how I felt about her, and I'd certainly needed a lot more practice at pleasuring her. But then I'd had to leave to attend a summer program at school. I hadn't thought of telling Laney about the program before because it didn't matter...at least it hadn't *before* our senior week trip. When she found out I was leaving in July, she'd been pissed.

I would never forget how Laney had physically pushed me away, her eyes glistening with unshed tears, shouting at me in a whisper that she couldn't believe I hadn't told her. That I'd kept it from her. I had tried to hug her, touch her, comfort her, but she'd only shaken her head and walked away. And that was that.

I had regretted it every day since.

"I'm not going to hurt you again," I told Laney now. "And I sure as hell know what I'm doing." To make sure she understood, I planted my hands on either side of her, nestling my already hardening length between her legs, giving my hips an experimental roll against hers. She parted her lips but didn't invite me to do more.

Instead, she held her hands against my chest. "I want to talk about how you made me feel."

With a petulant moan that earned a soft giggle, I moved off her and turned on my side. "Okay. Tell me."

She stuck her left palm under her cheek and kept her right hand between us, so I echoed her position, linking our fingers together.

"I was never afraid to be with you," she said. "I was never afraid to be honest or open." Though, she tipped her chin down a few centimeters as if the next part was hard for her. "But I never felt good enough. I know it sounds silly to say when I was a popular girl or whatever, but sometimes I felt like that's all people cared about with me."

I let go of her hand to trail the pad of my thumb along her jaw, lifting her chin so she'd meet my eyes. I wanted her to finish her thought.

"You made me feel like I was more," she admitted quietly, and I held her so she couldn't move or float her gaze away.

"Because you are more."

"I know, but after everything..."

After everything with that fucking Bobby Magnate, she felt used and discarded, like she didn't matter. I didn't need her to verbalize it for me to know. All Laney had ever wanted was for someone to see *her*, not the perfect veneer she put on every day to please those around her.

Delaney Hargrove was not only a pretty face. She was not a placeholder or prop or trophy wife or any other absurd label that inspired my homicidal thoughts about anyone who'd ever made her think that about herself. I kissed her once then towed her to me, positioning her head on my chest. "After everything, you're still the girl who isn't afraid to get up after she's fallen. You're still the girl who can find the bright side of any situation and make a really bad day better with your laugh. You're still the girl who's had my heart since the first day of school when she ran into Dean with a pencil stuck in her mess of hair."

"You remember that?"

"How can I forget?" I tangled my fingers into her hair, and I could feel her growing smile against my breastbone.

"You know how to melt a girl's heart," she said, and I kissed the top of her head.

"Yours is the only one I want."

CHAPTER TWENTY

Laney

I swam through a thick fog in my brain, waking up to the sound of my name, stifled like I was in a cocoon. But then I lifted my head and realized I *was* in a cocoon, one made of Ethan's arms. I usually slept on my stomach, spread out to every corner of the bed, so the couple of rounds I went with Ethan last night must have truly exhausted me that I didn't mind sleeping cuddled up all night.

"Laney?" Dean's voice cut through my exhaustion, and I sat up, checking the time on my phone. It was just after eight in the morning, and my brother was getting closer. "Delaney?"

I snapped my head to Ethan, still sound asleep, and hit him awake.

He blinked up at me, confused. "Huh? What?"

"Dean," I hissed, flapping my arms in panic.

Ethan's eyes shot open in alarm, and he fumbled for his glasses, looking around as if to get his bearings. But he didn't have long to collect his thoughts because my bedroom door was wide open, and Dean's footsteps plodded at the other end of the hall. In my younger days, I was known to be a pretty fast runner, but I'd never be able to make it to the door in time to close it before my brother saw something he wasn't supposed to.

As Dean reached the doorway, I shrieked and used the bedsheet to cover my body while Ethan threw it over his head. If I weren't so hysterical, I'd probably laugh because there was absolutely no way to hide his long body. Especially since his feet poked out over the end of the mattress.

"Whoa!" Dean shielded his eyes. "What the hell, Laney?" He whirled around, his back to me. "You could've warned me or something."

"You could have not barged in here like an animal," I said, jumping out of the bed and taking the sheet with me, which exposed Ethan's naked-as-a-baby form.

Like a cartoon, his eyes got real big before he covered himself with his hands and army-rolled off the bed. He hit the floor with a loud thump and a, "Shit."

Out of the corner of my eye, I noticed Ethan grab his head as my brother spun back around.

"What's going on?" Dean's eyes drifted to the floor, where Ethan was mostly hidden by the angle of the bed.

I tried to play it cool, or as cool as I could after being caught in bed with my brother's best friend. "Nothing. Why? What's up?"

He folded his arms, glaring at me. "This is my house, Laney."

I didn't appreciate his patronizing tone. He wasn't my parent, and I hadn't done anything wrong.

"This is my house too," I said, sounding more like a child caught with my hand in the cookie jar than a grown adult, and I hated that.

He pointed to the now-empty bed. "Yeah, but you can't bring some random dude here whenever you want."

I fumed, readjusting the sheet around me, in order to better go after Dean. I got up in his face, poking him in the chest. "You go out all the time and have sex with random chicks you pick up from bars or wherever-the-hell, but I bring someone home one time, and you flip out like you're some saint? You don't get to judge me. And Ethan isn't some random guy. I—"

Three things happened simultaneously as my words registered with all three of us in my room. Dean's jaw hit the floor as his eyes moved over m shoulder, Ethan leaped up from his hiding place with a pillow covering his groin, and I slapped my forehead, cursing myself and my wandering mouth.

The jig was up. And it was officially the weirdest moment of my life.

Dean pointed to Ethan as if he couldn't believe that was who was in front of him. "Marrero?"

Ethan nodded. "Yep."

"You and Ethan?" Dean asked me, flicking his finger between us.

"Yes."

Dean's brow crimped like he was working out an advanced calculus problem. "Seriously?" When neither Ethan nor I answered, he threw his hands up, storming away. "What the actual fuck?"

I didn't move for a few seconds, a deer caught in headlights, but Ethan shrugged, a nonchalant smile curling his lips. "Could've been worse."

I fell back on the bed, too embarrassed and overwhelmed to do anything else. No, it wasn't the *worst* thing to happen to me, but it ranked pretty high on the list of most embarrassing moments. Only second to that time I was walking out of English class at college with the girls, and I was going on and on about how hot the professor was. Turned out he was right behind us.

I was about to close my eyes and abandon the start of the

day, but then Ethan dropped the pillow, and I was once again treated to the sight that was Ethan Marrero.

The guy was a golden god, and he didn't even know it. He was lean yet cut in all the best places, with broad shoulders and a tapered waist. He bent down, the muscles in his back bunching when he grabbed his clothes from the floor, and stepped into his underwear then jeans, covering up his solid thighs sprinkled with dark hair.

That was when he caught me staring. Leaving his fly open, he strutted over to me and wrapped his hands around my arms, pulling me to stand up in front of him. He gently held my face between his palms and smoothed his thumbs over my cheeks before kissing me sweetly. As if he still needed to persuade me.

He didn't. I'd lost the war, waved the white flag, and enthusiastically yielded to him. He dragged the tip of his nose along my temple then buried it in my hair. His chest rose and fell on a deep breath. "You smell good in the morning."

I pressed up on my toes to align our bodies and kissed his neck, fanning my words out against his skin. "You *feel* good in the morning."

"My plan for my morning with you was very different. It involved way more of you naked and way less of your brother."

As quickly as my desire bubbled to the surface was as quickly as it fizzled out at the mention of Dean.

"Do you think he's really mad about us?" I asked, frowning.

Ethan untangled his hands from my hair. "It'll be all right," he said. "We'll work it out, but first, you have to get dressed."

He kissed me once more then dropped the sheet from my shoulders, exposing my body to him. His leering smile told me he'd rather be doing other things besides putting clothes on, yet he snatched his T-shirt from the floor and lifted his chin, in a silent order to raise my arms. When I did, he pulled the shirt over my head, but not before his fingers traced over the sides of my breasts and rib cage. Following the edge of the shirt, he caressed my hips and down to my backside, squeezing hard enough to pry a squeak out of me.

"Pants?" he asked with a tap to my thigh.

"Bottom drawer." I motioned toward the dresser, and he dug through until he found a pair of gray sweats. He held them out for me to step into, and once I was fully dressed, he finally kissed my neck. The process of him dressing me was almost—almost—as good as him undressing me.

He finished buttoning up his pants then covered up his top half with his hoodie, zipping it up. After his socks and shoes were on, he gathered up his wallet, cell phone, and keys, then grabbed my hand. I must have looked nervous because he kissed my palm. "Don't worry."

But I was worried. I worried this would affect his friendship with Dean, not to mention my relationship with my brother. I still wasn't sure what this thing was between me and Ethan, and I didn't know what to tell Dean besides the fact that we'd had mind-altering sex last night. Though I didn't think I should lead with that.

Ethan followed me into the kitchen, where Dean waited on the brewing coffeepot.

"Hey," I said.

He didn't answer, but his fingers did ball up into fists on the countertop.

"Can we talk, man?" Ethan asked, coming to stand in front of me.

I peeked around his shoulder in time to see Dean pivot away from the counter. His eyes narrowed on Ethan, even though his voice remained casual. "Sure, about what? How you fucked my sister?"

"Dean! You—"

"Hey. Whoa, whoa." Ethan interrupted us. "It's not like that. I understand you're angry, but this wasn't some flippant decision. This wasn't a one-night stand."

"Then what is it?"

Ethan stuck his hands on his hips, most likely trying to find words, and I took the opportunity to answer for him. "It's a long time coming."

Dean scratched at his jaw. "What do you mean? How long?"

"Since high school," I admitted, stepping up to Ethan's side. "We have history since high school."

"I knew it! You were always sneaking off, talking to each other real quiet and secretive." Dean thrust his fist in the air. "I knew it."

He seemed almost victorious, and I glanced over at Ethan, gobsmacked.

"You're not mad?" Ethan asked.

Dean dropped his hand back down to his side. "Yes, I'm mad. I'm mad you guys had something going on way back then and you didn't tell me. I'm mad something is going on now, and you're still doing it behind my back."

"I didn't think you'd be too happy if you found out," Ethan said.

I nodded in agreement. "And I didn't want to come in between you two."

"Well, you sure as hell did." Dean ping-ponged his attention between us. "And I'm not too happy about it. What if it doesn't work out between you? Where does that leave me?" He angled his body like he wanted to cut Ethan out of the conversation with me. "How do you think I felt when everything went south for you in California?" His voice wobbled at the end as he tugged on his earlobe. It wasn't often he let his emotions get the best of him, and he stared down at the floor to hide it.

A few moments passed until he picked his head up. "I think I'm a pretty easygoing guy, but I wanted to kill that son of a bitch for what he did to you. And I don't even really know him. What's going to happen when something like that happens again?"

"What are you insinuating?" Ethan took a half step forward, enough of a movement to reveal he was pissed at Dean's assumption, and I wrapped my hand around Ethan's forearm. Even though they both were angry, I didn't think it would come to blows, but...just in case.

"I'm not insinuating anything. I'm only saying it's a pretty asshole thing to do. To go behind my back." Dean shoved his hand out, palm up, to accent his point to Ethan. "You're my friend." He gestured to me. "And you're my sister." Then he pointed above him. "And you had sex in my house."

Ethan reached for my hand, even as he talked to Dean. "I understand why you're upset. I'm sorry I wasn't up front with you from the beginning, but—"

"But," I interrupted, attempting to quell the argument, "we don't want to get ahead of ourselves. Why make a big deal out of nothing, you know?"

This time, Ethan cut me off with a stern look. "But this *is* a big deal." His attention turned to Dean. "Laney and I are a big deal."

And I couldn't help the grin that stretched across my face at his proclamation. It wasn't a proposal or an I love you, but it was enough for my hopeful heart to sprout wings and try to fly from my rib cage.

Dean eyed us both critically for a few seconds then shrugged and spun back to his coffee. "Fine."

"Fine?" I repeated.

"Yeah. Fine. I'm not happy about how I found out." He glanced over his shoulder at me. "But fine. If you're going to date anybody, it should be someone I like." Then he narrowed his eyes at Ethan. "Don't make me hate you."

Ethan lifted one shoulder. "You could never."

Dean carefully poured cream into his coffee. "I can if you make me. Don't hurt my sister."

"I won't," Ethan promised then I dragged him out of the kitchen, down the hall, and shoved him against the wall in the living room, kissing my appreciation into his lips.

"I said I'm fine with it, but I'm not fine with you guys doing it wherever!" Dean yelled, and I tossed my head back to the ceiling, grumbling.

Ethan stifled his laughter. "I should leave anyway." When I pouted, he kissed it away, holding my hands between us. "Lane, I meant what I told your brother. I'm in this."

"Me too," I said, taking the leap with him. Despite not being sure of what my future looked like, I wanted it to be with Ethan, to figure it out with him. "I'm all in."

CHAPTER TWENTY-ONE

Ethan

The beginning of April brought about sunshine, the first inklings of warm weather, and the first holiday of *Laney and Ethan: Together Again.*

Laney had to go to Easter brunch with her parents and Dean, but she'd planned to meet me at my parents' house later. Although, if she didn't arrive soon, Trace would be facedown in a candy coma. He was already bouncing off the walls with chocolate smeared around the edges of his mouth from the missing bunny foot, and he'd been asking about the egg hunt every five minutes.

"Honey, I promise we're going to do it," my mom said. "In a little while."

"Gigiiiiiiiiii," Trace whined, hanging on to her leg. "I'm boring."

Leah set her glass of iced tea on the counter. "Bored. You're bored."

"Yeah." Trace reached for the handle on one of the cabinets, no doubt to empty all of its contents.

Leah stopped him. "Come on, let's watch *Zootopia.*"

Trace took his mom's hand. "Okay, but at the song part?"

"Yes, at the song part."

Trace danced out of the kitchen, toward the bottom floor. Justin and Dad were down there already, and I could hear Trace shouting at them, "Baseball off! We're watching *Zootopia!*"

I caught my mother's gaze and we both laughed, though I quickly realized that we were alone and this was my chance to talk to her about the thing that had been knocking around in my head for a while. I gnawed on the inside of my cheek.

"What's up, Eth?" Mom opened the refrigerator. "You have something on your mind?"

I grabbed the platter of cookies when she handed it to me. "How'd you know?"

She shrugged and brought out another tray, this one of carrot cake. "I'm your mother. What's up?"

"Well…"

With her hands on the kitchen island, she waited patiently for me to continue. She was much shorter than I was, though with thick-framed glasses and dark-brown hair, some people could probably be convinced we were biologically related.

"Ever since Justin was diagnosed, I've been thinking about, maybe, contacting my birth parents."

Mom nodded as if that made total sense then peeled the plastic wrap off the desserts. "I'm surprised it's taken you this long."

I pushed off the counter and moved to stand next to her, snagging a sugar cookie. "Seeing what happened when Justin tried to contact his…it, I don't know, freaked me out."

She rubbed a hand up and down my back. "Understandably, but that was a totally different situation. If you're ready, you can try to contact your birth mother."

I munched on my cookie. "What exactly do you know about her?"

Mom rolled her head up to the ceiling, in much the same

way I did. "Um, not much. All of our contact was through the agency. She'd wanted pictures and updates when you were younger, but the older you got, the harder it was to keep up. Plus, I think maybe she had found peace in her decision." My mom met my eyes with a small smile. "Or, at least, I hope she did."

As I thought more on that insight, Mom stuck her index finger in the air and jogged out of the kitchen, her slight footsteps padding on the carpeted staircase. Two minutes later, she returned with a closed manila envelope. She slid it in front of me on the island and then covered my hand with her own, squeezing it. "When you're ready."

I smiled at her, looping one arm around her, and she wrenched me down to kiss my cheek. "I love you, honey, but you need to shave." She patted my chin. "Especially with your girlfriend coming over."

"Speaking of..." I leaned back, checking for the hundredth time if she'd arrived yet. "Don't embarrass me."

"*Moi?*" My mother's jaw hit the floor, her hand on her heart. "I'd never." When I eyed her, she dropped the pretense and lifted her hands in innocence then bit into a cookie, zipping her lips with the rest of it after.

I nodded, although I didn't believe her, and stepped into the small foyer when I heard a car door close outside. A few seconds later, the doorbell rang, and I swung the front door open, grinning at Laney.

She quirked her lips to the side. "Hey, speedy, how'd you answer the door so fast?"

I propped one arm on the door, all cool-like. "I've kind of been watching the door for you to come. No big deal or anything."

"Oh no?" She laughed, and I hauled her into me, kissing her smile away. I pressed my hands against her lower back, and she bowed into me, letting out a soft moan. This woman and her softness, from her lips to her skin to her sounds, I was addicted. So absorbed that I'd forgotten to close the door and voices were filtering in from somewhere behind us.

"Daddy, is someone at the door?"

"Do you feel a draft? Why is the door still open?"

"Ethan! Who is it?"

"I think he said his girlfriend was coming over."

"Ethan has a girlfriend?"

"Oh, is it Laney? She's been so great with the fundraiser."

Laney breathed out a giggle against my lips, and I let my forehead drop to hers. No use in pretending we couldn't hear my family. She leaned away from me but kept her index fingers around my belt loops, her attention like a lazy river down the length of my body. I did the same to her.

"You're wearing your ChapStick," I noted with a swipe of my tongue across my bottom lip.

She nodded, staring at me from under thick eyelashes.

"And your hair is curly."

She nodded again.

"And you look super sexy." I flicked at the collar of her striped dress that was basically a knee-length button down shirt, belted at her waist and, for some unknown reason, crazy hot. Maybe because it reminded me a little of a school uniform. Between her miles-long legs and the open button hinting at her cleavage, I'd rather be anywhere than at my parents' house about to partake in an Easter egg hunt.

"It's almost like you're trying to seduce me, Delaney Hargrove."

Her perfect teeth nibbled on her bottom lip. "Is it working?"

I crushed my mouth to hers, sucking at that lip. Then I teasingly snapped at it. "Not at all."

She batted at me, letting out a big burst of laughter, which she immediately tried to cover with her hand. As if that would help.

I linked my fingers with hers and guided her into the kitchen, where my mom stood, lips pursed, and I knew she was about to say something totally inappropriate.

"Mom, this is Laney. Laney, my mom, Rita."

"Laney!" My mother clasped her hand then dragged her in for a hug. "Nice to see you again."

"Mom," I warned quietly, but she only wrapped her arm around Laney's shoulders, escorting her down the short flight of steps to the basement of their bi-level home. "Everyone, this is Laney. Ethan's been in love with her since high school."

"Jesus Christ, Mom," I muttered, smacking my forehead as I turned in a tight circle while Laney's laugh reverberated around me.

"I'm kidding," Mom told Laney, only slightly more serious. "But he used to come home all the time saying, 'Laney said this...' or 'Laney told me to...' or 'I've got tutoring with Laney...'" She smiled as if she weren't stabbing me right in the back.

Laney glanced over her shoulder, face bright and eyes full of amusement, and I toggled my hand back and forth. "That's only half true."

She snickered then faced my father, who ran his palm over the middle of his head, where it was balding—my dad could pass for Jason Alexander, only a little taller—then he hugged Laney too. "I'm told you're doing a great job with the fundraiser."

"I'm trying," Laney said and bent down to Trace, who ran at her for a hug. "Nice to see you again. Whatcha been up to lately? Any good dance parties?"

"Oh yeah! We can do one later. Do you want to have a

dance party wif me?" Trace held up his fist to his chin in question. "But what are you doing here?"

"I came to hang out with you."

"You're gonna look for Easter eggs wif us?"

Laney glanced back at me for reassurance before answering. "Yeah. That's exactly why I'm here."

"Woo-hoo! I so excited." He wiggled around in a circle, and Laney stood back up, reaching for Leah.

"Nice to meet you in person."

Leah laughed and patted her back. "You too."

Then Justin reached out his hand to Laney. "I'm Ethan's brother. I don't think we've ever met."

"No, but I've heard so much about you."

"If Ethan told you, then none of it's true," Justin said, draping his arm around Leah's shoulders.

"All good things. I promise."

With everyone sufficiently charmed by Laney, Mom gestured back upstairs. "Should we have dessert before we do the hunt?"

"Yeah!" Trace bellowed and froze with one arm in the air for a moment, like a slo-mo cartoon, then hightailed it to the kitchen. "Cookies!"

My parents followed Leah and Justin up, while I hung back for a few seconds.

"I didn't really talk about you that much in school," I told Laney.

"It's cute how you think I'd believe you." She kissed my cheek, whisper-shouting, "Come on! Cookies!"

I tamped down my grin and patted her hip as I motioned for her to go ahead of me. In the kitchen, I filled up two glasses of iced tea and passed one to Laney before standing next to her, my hand on her waist. Justin pointedly raised his brow at the action, but I ignored him. I'd had girlfriends before, none of them serious, and certainly none whom I'd have over while babysitting my nephew or whom I would invite to a family gathering like this.

Probably because I'd been waiting and hoping on a wing and a prayer.

And now I was soaring through clear blue skies.

"Laney, would you like a piece of carrot cake?" Mom asked, dropping slices onto decorative paper plates.

"Yes, please." She accepted it with a smile and grabbed a plastic fork, digging in. "Thank you for letting me intrude on your holiday."

"You're welcome any time," Dad told her, reheating his coffee for probably the fourth time today. Whenever Trace was around, he tended to forget about his food and drink.

"So, you guys were friends in high school, right?" Leah asked, wagging her fork back and forth between Laney and me.

"Yeah, he was good friends with my brother. And me, I guess," she said, slanting her gaze to me for a second, a little secretive smile solely for me.

"It's so sweet you guys found each other again," Leah said. "Like it's meant to be."

I dragged my hand up Laney's back. I couldn't answer Leah without talking with Laney first, but from the heated look she sent me when I squeezed her shoulder possessively, I assumed I wasn't the only one in this for the long haul. Because it was meant to be.

"Is it time yet?" Trace asked, barely hanging on to his stool at the kitchen island, cream cheese frosting smeared on his top lip.

"After everyone finishes eating, buddy," Justin told him. "You have to be patient a little longer."

"Yeah, Mommy isn't done with her cake yet," Leah added.

Trace growled, transforming into a dinosaur.

"Uh-oh. He's back, Traceasuarus!" I held my hands up. "Don't eat me!"

Trace hopped off the stool and attacked me. Laney scooted out of the way as I grabbed Trace at the waist to hoist him upside down so he erupted in a fit of giggles. "Do that again!"

Following orders, I reversed course, set Trace back on the floor, then picked him right back up again.

"You're gonna make him puke," Justin said, but I only tickled Trace's stomach, making him laugh harder. Over my nephew's kicking feet, I met Laney's eyes. They were rounded and faraway, a dreamy smile—one I'd never seen before—graced her lips, and I wondered what she was thinking.

I didn't have to wait long because a minute later, my parents handed everyone a wicker basket and opened the back door, herding us outside. "You know the rules," Mom said. "Whatever you find, you keep."

"Ready, set, go!" Dad put his fingers in his mouth and blew a whistle. Trace was off like a shot, Justin and Leah laughing and jogging after him, while I held my hand out for Laney's.

"Am I really allowed to find eggs?" she asked.

"Of course."

Gleefully, she tugged me toward a row of tulips beginning to bloom by the fence. She picked up an egg. "What did your mom mean when she said whatever we find, we keep?"

"Because it's not always good stuff." I took the pink plastic egg from her and opened it to find a scratch-off lottery ticket, already scratched. I showed it to her, and she frowned. "Since we lived all over the place, we didn't always celebrate holidays and stuff a lot, so when Trace came along, it was their chance to redo it. Make everything bigger. And they thought it was funny to put some gag gifts in Easter eggs. Or, in this case, a losing scratch-off."

She snorted a laugh. "Amazing."

I put the ticket back in the egg, capped it, and tossed it in her basket before we searched for more. "What were you thinking about?" I picked up a green egg, this one filled with jelly beans. "In the kitchen."

"With you and Trace?" she clarified, sneaking a white jelly bean before I closed the egg back up. When I nodded, she spotted another egg by the bird feeder. It had a few pennies in it. "I was thinking about you and me and the future."

"And…?" I snagged an egg with packets of soy sauce.

"And…" She turned away from me, watching Trace, Leah, and Justin for a minute.

I found another egg, this one with a small chocolate bunny, which I offered to Laney. She ate it in silence until Justin straightened from where he'd been helping Trace at the other end of the yard. He jerked his head toward our parents, yelling, "You know you can't leave liquor bottles around for our four-year-old to find, right?"

Dad pointed to Mom, who smacked him, and Laney leaned into me, laughing. Justin shook his head at our parents and put the egg into his basket. Leah waved at them. "Next time, make it gin for me."

Mom gave her a thumbs-up, then swept her attention to where I held Laney next to me. "What'd you guys find? Anything good yet?"

"No treasure yet," Laney called.

"There is a crisp George Washington out there for one of you," Dad said, his hands in his pockets.

"George Washington was the first president!" Trace shouted helpfully.

"He's also on the dollar bill," Dad said, and Trace took off in another direction.

"A dollar! Oh my gosh!"

I pointed out a pink egg hidden under the grill, and Laney

grabbed it. No dollar bill, but it did have a very long CVS receipt. "So, what were you thinking about?"

"Bobby didn't want to settle down," she said but thrust her hand out as if to take her words back. "I'm not comparing. It's a fact. He said he felt like I was forcing him to do something he wasn't ready for." She puffed up her cheeks as she let out a breath, her eyes skirting behind my shoulder.

"And you are ready to settle down," I guessed, and she darted her gaze to me, nodding.

"I've always known I wanted to get married and have a family." She motioned to the whole of the backyard, to my parents laughing about something on the back patio, to Trace hollering about a dollar bill, to Justin leaning into Leah and kissing her temple. "Like this."

I had known the Hargroves to be nice people but not particularly approachable...or loud. Not like my own family. "Like this?"

She tucked a lock of her curly hair behind her ear. "Yeah. Like this."

Finding the courage I didn't have ten years ago, I stepped up close to her. "With me?"

She raised up on her toes and answered against my mouth. "With you."

CHAPTER TWENTY-TWO

Laney

It might have sounded crazy, and if it were anyone else, confessing how they'd fallen for someone new only a few weeks after a traumatic breakup, I might have agreed. But this was me and Ethan—Ethan!—and we'd already lived a whole lifetime together. Now that we'd both matured and experienced the ups and downs of life, I was sure of myself. Sure of what I felt for the man in front of me now, sure of the memories which shaped the woman I became, and sure that we could have a wonderful life together.

Ethan slipped his arm around my middle, tugging me right up against him, smiling possibly the biggest smile I'd ever seen out of him, which was really saying something because the guy was constantly smiling. "I love you, Laney." He curled his hand around my jaw, his thumb sweeping a few times across my cheek. "I love you like flowers love the sun." He kissed my forehead. "Like birds love the sky." Then he pressed a kiss to the center of my mouth. "My happiness doesn't exist without yours."

I huffed, surprised to find a single tear on my cheek. "Please don't make me cry in front of your parents. I want them to like me."

"They love you," he whispered and kissed the tear away. "Because I love you."

When he let go of me, I dropped my chin to sniff back the rest of my emotion so I didn't turn into a puddle when I said, "I have loved you for a very long time." Then I laughed at a memory and smiled up at his affectionate eyes. "Probably ever since that time I was changing for volleyball practice after school. I was walking out of the trainer's room with a couple of tampons in my hand, and you were coming out of the band room. I wasn't looking where I was going, and I ran into you. I was so embarrassed, but you only shrugged and bent down to pick up the tampons I'd dropped."

"I remember," he said, biting back a smile. "I said, who's afraid of a little uterine lining."

"I was shocked that you'd know what that was. That any high school boy would know."

He tipped his head in the direction of his mother. "Living in other countries showed her how abysmal the sex education is here. Wanted Justin and me to know better. So you can thank her."

I found his hand and twined our fingers together. "For raising the son I love." I pressed the back of his hand against my cheek. "I love you, Ethan."

He bent like he was going to kiss me again, but Justin called out, "Another one! My god, Mom!"

Ethan and I both turned to his mom, who lifted her hands. "What? Everyone likes those tiny bottles of wine."

"Oh yeah," Ethan said, gesturing for his brother to give it to him. "We'll take that."

Justin capped the purple egg and threw it to Ethan, who fumbled the catch. I was the one to grab it. Ethan clucked his tongue. "That's my girl, reflexes like a cat." I opened the egg, revealing a miniature Sutter Home Moscato, and he slung his arm around my shoulders. "Ooh, come on, there's another egg."

After the egg hunt ended—there weren't any more bottles of alcohol, but there were paper clips and a few loose gummy bears Ethan told me not to eat because he didn't trust that they weren't fifteen years old—everyone settled back inside to chat for a while. Trace promptly fell asleep, coming down from his sugar high, while Rita and Tom told some stories about their travels abroad. Snuggled into Ethan's side, I sipped on a coffee until I had to excuse myself to use the bathroom.

When I left the powder room, I found Ethan leaning against the wall with his arms crossed over his chest. I tilted my head in question as to why he was standing there, and he slipped his arms around my waist in answer, pushing me backward and closing the door behind him.

I laughed, my lower back bowing against the sink. "What are you doing?"

"Sneaking a feel." His voice rose at the end so it sounded more like a question. Like he was asking permission.

I curled my arms around his neck, inviting him to take whatever feel he wanted, and he coasted his hands down my hips to squeeze my thighs before guiding me up to sit on the counter.

"Your family is right out there," I warned when his mouth eased down my throat.

"I know. I know. I'll be quick. I just can't stand seeing you in this dress. Such a tease. One little breeze outside, and the bottom woulda gone right up," he said, the hint of humor in his words even as he nipped at my collarbone, like he wanted to teach me a lesson.

He opened enough buttons to expose my right breast, and he tugged down my bra cup, sucking my nipple into his mouth.

When I moaned, he covered my mouth. "You want us to get caught?"

I bit his finger and he stood up straight, removing his palm from my mouth. "Ouch. Jesus, Lane."

"You started this," I whispered. "If you don't want them to hear us, then take me home."

He put my bra back in place, grumbling, "Take away all my fun."

I rolled my eyes as I buttoned my dress back up, shoving him toward the door. "The quicker we get out of here, the quicker I can make it up to you."

He grabbed my hand and tugged me into the hall. "I like the sound of that." Down in the living room, he waved his arm. "Laney and I are going to head out."

All except Trace, who was still asleep, stood up to say their goodbyes. Rita packed up all our eggs into a bag, making sure they didn't "forget" to take our finds.

"Yes, what would we ever do without that CVS receipt," Ethan joked as he gave Justin a one-armed hug.

"Hey," Tom said, "there are reward points on there."

Justin nodded solemnly. "Yes, for all the shopping they'll do there."

Rita kissed both Ethan and me on the cheek and walked us to the front door, saying, "Come back soon, Laney. I got a lot of those little bottles of wine."

"Can't wait."

Ethan told me to follow him to his place, which wasn't too far a drive, and once we were in his apartment, it wasn't too far of a walk to his bedroom. And it was only a minute before he had my dress off and his glasses somewhere behind him. I hadn't even gotten a chance to look around, see what knick-knacks he had on his dresser, how he arranged his clothes in his closet, or if he had any dirty laundry on the floor.

There was no time. Not with my back on the mattress and his fingers exploring my skin. When he skimmed his hand over my underwear, I arched my neck, and he kissed where my pulse beat against my flesh before dragging his teeth along the line of my chin.

Permitted to be as loud as I wanted now, I let out a moan when he teased at my opening, circling my clit with a featherlight touch until I was breathing Ethan's name over and over. Then he plunged his finger into me and kissed me like he was trying to convert me to a new religion.

"I love you," I told him as the first crest of my orgasm peaked, and he sank lower toward the foot of the bed, urging me on with his lips and fingers, prolonging the tidal wave of pleasure until it crashed over me. My legs spasmed and my mouth went dry from breathing so hard, and I yanked at his hair, wanting him on top of me.

He bit my inner thigh. "You grabbing at my hair like that only makes me want to stay down here longer."

"But I want you inside me," I whined, and he laughed against me.

"It's our time down here," he said then dragged the flat of his tongue up my slit.

"Did you…" I panted, pushing my hips up. "Did you just quote *The Goonies* to me with your head between my legs?" His answer was mumbled, and I slapped a hand against my forehead as he crooked his finger inside me, another peak rapidly rising. "You're the nerdiest person I've ever known."

Whatever words he replied with were lost over my keening, and he sat up, grinning, his lips shiny. "Seems like you kind of like it."

Yet even then, he didn't let up. I was wrung out and so slick with desire, I couldn't take it anymore. I shook my head, silently pleading with him, but he merely leveled himself over top of me, his fingers still working their magic. "I want to feel you come again. One more time," he rasped, "because once I'm inside you, it'll be like the beach all over again. Two-pump chump."

"You're ridiculous." My laugh was cut short by a moan.

"No, you are." He licked at the hollow of my throat. "It's ridiculous that you love me. That you expect me to be able to last that long when you and your fucking perfect mouth say I love you like it's the most normal thing in the world."

He was taking me higher and higher.

"Any man would be lucky to have you," he murmured against my ear, "but you picked me."

I grabbed hold of him, curving my hands around his jaw to keep him steady, even as my body fought against every cell to thrash and ride out my ecstasy. "*You* picked *me*. You loved me then, before I even knew who I was, and when I thought I was unlovable after coming back here, you showed me how wrong I was. *I* am the lucky one to be loved by you."

Without saying a word, he settled over me, pushing his cock all the way inside me with a single thrust, his gaze never leaving mine. I brushed my fingers over his cheeks and his furrowed brow, his concentration so obvious I couldn't help the laugh that escaped my lips. Then he smiled too, his apparent warning coming true.

"I told you," he murmured, his eyes sparkling with humor and adoration, and I wanted to live there forever. "You feel too good."

But then he ducked his head to the crook of my neck, breathing heavily next to my ear, and I locked my feet around his waist, trying to get as close to him as possible, meeting his every thrust. I clawed at his back, directing him with words like *faster, harder,* and he complied until I sank my teeth into his shoulder, a flash of heat engulfing me. A second later,

Ethan grunted with one final thrust before collapsing on top of me.

I combed my hands through his hair, his neck clammy and hot, until both of our breathing slowed back to normal. Then he raised his face to mine for a kiss. "You're staying over, right?"

"Even if I wanted to leave, I couldn't. You melted my bones."

He rolled to his side. "Perfect. Exactly how I like you."

CHAPTER TWENTY-THREE

Laney

At Ethan's alarm, I blinked awake, my brain slowly recognizing the pins and needles in my hand and arm, and I curled my fingers into a fist, attempting to release the tingles in my sleepy state. I lifted my arm from where it'd been above my head, but it was dead weight and fell back down to my side, smacking Ethan's leg.

"Hey," he mumbled, reaching to silence his cell phone, his voice gruff with sleep. "G'morning."

"I can't feel my hand," I said, twisting into his side, admiring his naked chest in the morning sunlight streaming through his window.

Without opening his eyes, he found my hand and lifted it to his mouth, kissing my palm then nibbling at my index finger. I pulled away from the ticklish grazing, and he finally turned to me, his eyes full of mischief.

"It's too early in the morning for you to be looking at me like that," I said.

He mumbled a disagreement, pulling me back to him with his arm around my waist, but I snagged my own cell phone to check my messages. There were two from Bronte on the **Four**

chicks and Three dicks thread, including a picture of Chris in bunny ears, and another from Bobby.

I smacked my phone down on the mattress a little harder than I meant to, and Ethan lifted his head, his hair sticking up adorably on one side. "What is it?"

"Nothing."

"Liar. What was it?" When I didn't answer, he backed away, eyeing me seriously. "What's wrong?"

I had nothing to hide and offered him my phone. "Bobby's been texting me, calling me."

Ethan reached over to grab his glasses before reading Bobby's latest text, asking to talk. His lips skewed to the side as lines creased his forehead.

"I haven't responded," I told him, assuming he needed reassurance, but he stayed silent, his thumb scrolling up so he could read through the other messages.

"Why not?"

I shrugged my answer.

"He wants to get back with you."

"I don't know," I said, and he shook his head.

"That wasn't a question. He wants to get back with you."

"Well, I don't want to get back with him."

"Then why haven't you called or texted him back to tell him that?"

It was too early in the morning to dissect the relationship I'd had with Bobby, and I rolled my eyes to the ceiling. "Because I don't want to. He doesn't deserve any more of my time or energy."

A frustrated sound left Ethan a split second before his glasses were off and his hand was around my breast. With his mouth on me, I shrieked out my shock, knocking my cell phone from his hand. "What're you doing?"

"*You* don't have any more time or energy, but I've got plenty," he said as I got a look at the photo on my screen. Ethan had taken a picture of him sucking on my nipple, his eyes glaring at the screen, his fingers digging possessively into my skin.

"What's this for?"

"Send it to him," he said, sitting up. "Tell him you're done."

I started to laugh but stopped. "You're serious."

He stared at me. Deadly serious. "You said he keeps calling and texting you, so tell him to stop. Tell him you moved on. Tell him whatever the fuck you want, but you don't need to put up with him contacting you."

I pulled the sheet up to my neck, feeling overly exposed at the moment. "I have moved on."

He pushed his hand through his hair. "Then why don't you block him?"

"Do you want me to block him?"

He crawled closer to me, and the jealous glint that previously darkened his eyes was replaced by concern as they rounded. "I would never tell you what to do."

"But you want me to."

He held my face between his hands. "Because I don't want you to be upset, and I can see that you are."

"I'm not."

He flattened his mouth.

"Not really," I corrected.

"I know you can't say no to people—apparently not even to assbags like him—but this one time, I think you need to."

I pouted. I could say no to people. I did it all the time. *Would you like a refill? No, thank you. Can you meet at two? No.* "I can say no," I mumbled, and he smiled into a kiss. "I can!"

"Prove it. He keeps reaching out, and you don't want him to, so I think you've got to either talk to him and put it to bed or block him."

I nodded, but after everything went down, even after

Bobby had made me feel completely worthless and exchangeable, I still had trouble convincing myself I could do it.

I was raised to be polite at all times, to be sugar and spice and everything nice. I made friends with everyone, was a shining example to my community, and would never dream of making anyone uncomfortable or distressed.

Even if it made *me* uncomfortable or distressed.

"Lane," Ethan said, knocking his knuckles into my thigh, seizing my attention from my mental spiral. I turned to him, and he dropped his head toward his shoulder, smiling. "I love you."

I raised my arms to hug him, the sheet dropping down to my waist, and he threw himself at me, tackling me back to the pillows. When I screeched out a laugh, he chuckled, nipping at my throat. "Love that laugh too."

He smooched loud kisses on my shoulders, across my chest, and up my neck until I was a giggling mess. "Stop! Stop!" I smacked at his shoulder, trying to wiggle out from under him. "You're making me claustrophobic."

He lifted his head a few inches, hitting me with a suspicious glare. "You're not claustrophobic."

"You're not letting me up." I dug my index finger into his left pec until he howled.

"Hey!" Then he went after me again. "You're never getting away now." He tickled my sides as I thrashed under him.

"Come on," I whined, locking my hands around his wrists in an attempt to push him away. "Don't you have to work?"

He grumbled and stopped fighting me, only to drop his dead weight on top of me.

I let out a strangled laugh. "You weigh an awful lot for a twig."

With his face muffled in my hair, I didn't catch his words. "What?"

"I said," he started, leaning up on his elbows and pressing his growing erection against my thigh. "You're going to give me a complex."

I snorted. "You're going to give *me* a complex." When a line formed between his eyebrows, I pointedly dropped my gaze down my body. While I was comfortable in how I looked and loved the lush parts of myself, my hips and breasts, I could probably snap him in half. He was basically a stick figure with glasses. "I'm, like, twice the size of you."

He nodded, humming into a kiss, parting my legs with his knees. He dipped his head to my breast, swirling his tongue around my nipple as he pushed inside me. Turned out I didn't need much more than some of his sweet talk and kisses to be ready for him. "I love every bit of you."

He dragged his hand down my side to lift my leg around his waist, breathing out his words against my throat. Words about how gorgeous I was, how good I felt, how soft and sweet I was, how he wanted to stay like this forever. He lifted himself up enough that I could sneak my fingers between us, circling my fingers where we met.

"Get there," he grunted, staring down at me. "Come on, Lane."

And when I reached my climax, he wasn't far behind, rolling me to the side to nuzzle against my neck.

"You're going to make me late to work," he mumbled, and I flicked at his arm around my waist.

"*I* am going to make you late? You're the one who wouldn't get off me."

I felt him grin against me. "Well, that is your fault. You make it difficult to get out of bed."

I was about to answer, but my stomach beat me to the punch, and Ethan flattened his hand against it. "I guess we really have to get up." He massaged my hip then rolled away from me with a tap to the back of my thigh. "Come on. I've got to feed my lady."

While I traipsed across the hall to use the bathroom, I heard Ethan make his way to the kitchen. "I'm going to start the coffee," he told me. "After a shower, I'll make breakfast, okay?"

I only laughed, pressing my hand to my forehead that he would ask if it was okay. As if I'd ever say no to him wanting to take care of me.

Even though Bobby was a literal world-renowned chef, he almost never made food for me. He was always too tired and said the last thing he wanted to do when he came home from work was to cook.

Now Ethan wanted to make me breakfast before he went to work. It was nearly impossible to imagine how I had myself convinced that I was happy with Bobby, when what I had with Ethan, what I felt for him, was so much bigger and better than anything else in my life.

And a few minutes later, I was still smiling about it when Ethan strolled into the bathroom, naked and singing "Always Be My Baby." I laughed as he took my hand, circling me under his arm, even with his toothbrush in my mouth. After he let me go, he looked me up and down, noting I was back in my bra and underwear. "You're dressed."

"Not really," I said, finishing up with my teeth to pass him the toothbrush.

He took it and squirted some more toothpaste on it. "I thought you'd shower with me."

I pointed my thumb over my shoulder to his sage-green shower curtain. "I don't have any of my stuff."

He heaved out a petulant sigh. "Fine." When he hunched over the sink to brush his teeth, I stepped back, but he caught my wrist. "Send that picture to me."

I frowned in thought. "The picture?"

"The one of me eating your boob."

I rolled my eyes, refusing to laugh. "No."

"No? Why not?"

"Because." When he raised his brows, waiting for me to go on, I gestured to his crotch. "Are you going to send me a dick pic?"

"Yeah. If you want. I mean…" He shrugged, his hand holding his junk. "Dicks aren't as pretty as boobs. But go get your phone. Take one right now."

"Oh my god," I moaned, spinning away from him. He followed me to the bedroom, where I slipped into my clothes from the day before.

"What's wrong?"

"I just…" I shrugged, buttoning my dress back up. "Ever since everything happened with Bobby, it's opened my eyes to how much of myself I was putting out into the universe, and I…" I lifted my eyes to his and bit into my lip in amusement at how he was so intent on me and yet still so naked. "I don't want to do that anymore."

He narrowed his gaze a fraction of an inch, his lips pinching for a moment before he wiped the emotion away, replaced by his usual easygoing smile. "So, we're not going Instagram official?"

I'd wiped a lot of my social media from the last three years of my life. So much evidence of exactly how often I'd invited perfect strangers into my life, or at least into some made-up version of myself. It had taken turning my world upside down to realize how thick of a veneer I wore. I had to strip completely down to understand that I'd been trying to keep up with a lifestyle I didn't truly enjoy. And I didn't want to go backward, not with something as important as the man I loved.

"Not any time soon."

He ran his hand through his hair, his lips wrenching to the side like he was chewing on the inside of them, but before I could ask what he was thinking, he nodded and turned back toward the bathroom. "Give me a few minutes to shower and get dressed. I'll make toast and eggs," he said, glancing over his shoulder at the door. "I've got a grocery list on the fridge. Add what you like to eat in the mornings to it."

Then he stuck his toothbrush into his mouth, ducking out of sight, and I sat on his bed, considering the last few minutes. Something was bothering him, and I had to assume it was because of Bobby.

Ever since Ethan waltzed back into my life, he was so sure of himself, so sure of *us*. I knew he didn't appreciate Bobby texting and calling me all the time, and maybe—even more than his irritation at Bobby still communicating with me— that I had been hesitant to make any decision about it. But everything seemed almost too good to be true, and I couldn't help to wonder if the other shoe would drop. I still needed time to get used to everything.

It was a lot to take in, after all. I'd left my entire life in California to start all over again. Sure, I had Ethan to lean on, yet I didn't have a job and was still mooching off Dean for housing. I wasn't exactly in a place where I felt proud of my accomplishments. And I wasn't going to shout it out to Internet strangers.

Although I could send Ethan the picture. That was easy enough. I texted it to him along with a couple of emojis, then made my way to his kitchen, writing a few things on his grocery list: Greek yogurt, cherries, spinach, frozen pineapple, super tampons.

CHAPTER TWENTY-FOUR

Ethan

"So, how's everything going with Laney?" Justin asked in between sips from a water bottle, his eyes on Leah and Trace while they played in their backyard.

"Good." I backtracked with a stiff shake of my head. "Great, actually."

"Yeah?" He faced me, a hint of a smile at the corner of his mouth. "You really like her?"

"I love her," I said without equivocation. "I'd marry her tomorrow if she'd say yes."

"Oh, whoa." He laughed. "It's like that?"

I nodded, glancing over at Trace when he shrieked at how high Leah pushed him on the swing.

"Moving a bit fast, no?" Justin asked.

"Not really. I think if I hadn't been an idiot when we were kids, we'd probably be married already. I wouldn't have been able to wait." I imagined I would've gotten down on one knee as soon as I had the money to buy a ring. Maybe even before that. She was it for me.

He blew out a low whistle in amusement. "So, all this time, you've been in love with her?"

"Basically." I met my brother's curious stare. Sure, we'd

talked about personal matters before, but I never had much to contribute to the conversations. Not until now. "Yeah."

He patted my knee twice. "Good for you, man. I'm happy for you."

I nodded my thanks. "I, uh, wanted to talk to you about something else, though."

He struggled to screw the cap of the water bottle back on for a few seconds before he succeeded. Then he set it down next to him and crossed his ankle over his knee, giving me his full attention. "About what?"

"Mom gave me the contact information for my adoption agency, and I got in touch with them. My birth mom is willing to talk to me."

He leaned his elbow on the arm of the bench. "Wow."

I swallowed down my fears. "I have her email address."

Scratching at his eyebrow, he asked, "Did you email her yet?"

When I shook my head, my brother lifted his arm along the back of the bench. We didn't need to exchange many more words. He already understood what I was feeling, the trepidation and anxiety and clamped his hand on my shoulder, squeezing it lightly.

"I don't know what to say," I said.

"Hi is a good start," he joked, and I shot him a glare as I pulled my cell phone out of my pocket, handing it to him with my email draft open. He took it, reading it over to himself.

"Is it good?" I asked after a while.

He handed my cell phone back. "Yeah. It's the basics. You want to get to know her, and you're hoping to stay in contact."

"You don't think I need to tell her anything about myself? Where I live? I had a really long one written up but deleted it. It felt like I was on a first date." I laughed at myself. "Hi, my name is Ethan, and I live in West Chester, and my favorite color is blue, and I like to cook and play in a band."

Justin shook his head. "You're not auditioning for anything. You have nothing to prove, all right?" Then he dropped my arm around my shoulders. "No matter what happens, you have your family, and we love you."

I shifted to hug him, patting him on the back. "Thanks, man."

"Love you," he replied quietly, ruffling my hair like I was a kid again, and my chest burned with love for my big brother.

"Love you too."

When we pulled apart, Trace ran toward us full bore, screeching with his arms out. "I'm a pterodactyl! Look at me, Uncle Efan."

I caught him, hauling him into my lap. "Whadya eat today, guy? You're going a million miles an hour."

Leah sauntered over, pointing at Justin. "Made chocolate chip pancakes for breakfast, let him have leftover Easter candy for a snack, and a waffle with syrup for lunch."

"What?" My brother raised his hands. "It's the weekend, and weekends are for eating whatever, right, Trace?"

My nephew nodded, spinning around to face me. "Where's Laney?"

"Funny you should ask," I said as Justin snorted. "Let's call her up."

I held my phone so we were both on the screen when the FaceTime call went through.

"Hey!" Laney said, waving, her smile as big as ever. "What's going on?"

"What are you doing?" Trace asked, moving his face so close to my phone that only his forehead and left eye were on the screen.

"What am I doing? I'm out running errands for your daddy's party."

"Party!" Trace bounced on my lap. "We're having a party?"

"Yeah, baby." Leah ran her fingers through his curls. "Remember when I told you we're going to have a big party in a few weeks to help people like Daddy."

"Oh, um…" Trace poked his finger against his chin. "Yeah. So are you coming over, Laney? Uncle Efan is eating dinner wif us. Can you eat wif us too?"

I glanced at Laney's raised brows on my phone then smiled down at Trace. "You want Laney to come over? I think you need to ask your mom."

Leah shrugged, saying in a loud voice, "Come on over, Laney. Justin's grilling."

I raised my palm to Trace for a high five and moved the phone so only my face filled the screen when I asked, "Are you going to come over?"

"Should I bring anything?"

"Just your pretty little self."

"All right. Text me the address."

"Okay, love you," I said, hanging up to text her, and Justin repeated my words in a high voice, taunting me.

"Okay, love you."

I punched him in the arm.

"Does Laney like this love-sick thing you have going on?"

I nodded.

"Pussy-whipped, huh?"

"Language," Leah hissed, backhanding Justin as I grinned.

"Oh yeah, for sure. And I would live there if I could."

"All right, all right," Leah said, tapping Trace on the shoulder to nudge him off my lap. "Let's go inside and wash your hands. You can help Mommy cut up strawberries." She gave me and Justin a warning look to watch our mouths.

Justin merely smiled at her. "Love you, babe."

"I think you two are really cute together," Leah said to me then narrowed her dark eyes at my brother. "And if you ever want to see *mine* again, Justin, you better keep that language contained around our son. Because if I get a call from preschool that he's running around saying he's pussy-whipped, you'll be beating it in the shower alone."

I tsked my brother, who licked his lips at his wife. "You know I love it when you get stern with me."

Leah cocked her hand on her hip, eyeing him for a moment before Trace yelled from inside, "Mommy! Where are the strawberries?"

When we were left alone again, I pushed Justin's shoulder. "You fucker."

He laughed. "Should I start writing my best man speech now or what?"

"Let's see if you even get invited. Leah might murder you first."

He rubbed his hand over his chest, inhaling audibly, his gaze over at the window, where we could see Leah's head bent over at the sink. "Yeah. That woman owns me." He sucked air through his teeth then turned to me, a more somber expression on his face. "Don't wait too long, okay?"

It was moments like this when the uncertainty of Justin's disease reared its head. It was not necessarily the end of the line, but it also didn't guarantee anything, including time.

"I won't," I said and then pressed send on my email to my birth mother before the two of us sat in silence for a while.

About a half hour later, Laney showed up with some store-bought dessert and hugs for everyone. After handing the platter of cupcakes to Justin, she tucked into my side, slipping her hand into my back pocket. She grinned up at me. "How's your day been?"

"Good. How's yours?"

"I signed the contract for the location, went to the party supply store to order some things, and sent out all the invitations."

Leah snapped her fingers. "I keep forgetting to give you the name of my friend's sister, for the catering." Grabbing her phone from where it charged in the corner of the counter, she tapped on the screen. "Let me do that now before I forget again."

Trace came careening into the kitchen. "I went potty and didn't get any on the floor!" Justin held his fist out, and Trace jumped up to bump it with his own before noticing Laney. "You're here! You're here!"

"I am, I am," she said, letting go of me to sink down to his level. Trace promptly wrung his little arms around her neck, and she laughed, hugging him back. "Nice to see you too."

"You want to play wif me?"

"Yes, of course. That's why I'm here."

She stood back and took his proffered hand, tossing a smile to me as Trace led her outside. "Look, it's like a playground out here. See? See? You want to go on the slide wif me?"

"Race you," she said and took off with a giggling Trace running after her.

"All right," Justin said, smacking a pack of burgers into my chest. "Put your googly eyes away for now and open this for me."

Outside, Justin got the grill going, and I popped the top of a beer for each of us while Leah and Laney each had a bit of wine, talking and laughing. Laney pushed Trace on a swing, one hand holding her drink, the other waving about as she told some story, and I couldn't take my eyes off her. That was until my cell phone buzzed in my pocket, and I grabbed it, finding a new email. "Oh my god."

Justin turned, a broad spatula in his hand. "What?"

"She got back to me already." I met my brother's gaze. "My birth mom."

"What'd she say?"

I silently read over the short response three times before reading out loud, "Hello, Ethan. I've always wondered if or when you would try to reach out, and I admit I'm not as calm about it as I thought I would be. I would love to stay in touch and look forward to getting to know you. Marcela."

I let out a breath I felt like I'd been holding my entire life.

"Holy shit," I murmured then downed almost all my beer. "Marcela, that's her."

Justin patted my back. "You all right?"

"Yeah, but it feels like…" I blinked a few times and shook my arms out as if I could get rid of the nervous energy.

"One step at a time," he said. "Take it one step at a time."

I nodded, trying to rein in my imagination. I had been so afraid to reach out to end up with the same results as my brother, but now that I had and she'd responded, my brain was off and running about what I wanted to say and ask, what she might have to tell me.

"Why don't you go get the girls? These are done." Justin began piling up the cheeseburgers on a platter, and I started away, waving to Laney, Leah, and Trace.

"Food's ready," I said, closing in on the play set, and Laney slowed Trace down so he could hop off the swing. He ran off toward Justin, and Leah followed, leaving me alone with Laney.

She wrapped her arms around my waist. "Do you feel okay? You look a little pale."

I ran my hand through my hair then dropped my arm around her shoulders, holding up my now-empty beer bottle. "Maybe a little dehydrated," I lied, not wanting to tell her the truth of my digital exchange. As Justin had said, I needed to take it a step at a time, and I wasn't quite ready to let anyone else in on my situation, still wary of what the outcome might be. "Could use some water."

She narrowed her eyes the tiniest bit, as if examining me, and I bent my head to kiss her temple. With the fundraiser right around the corner, and this new, yet amazing relationship, I needed to keep that my focus. I couldn't worry about what may or may not happen in the future with Marcela.

"Your birthday is next weekend," Laney said after a few moments. "You want to do anything special?"

I hugged her closer as we walked back to the patio. "*Do anything special? We could try out the other vibrator I saw you had.*"

She smacked at my stomach, laughing. "I meant for you. What do you want to do? It's your birthday."

I nodded. "Yeah, and that's what I want to do."

"Okay." She pursed her pink bee-stung lips at me. "Then what I bought from Seraphina's party might be of interest to you."

I pushed my glasses back with my knuckle, brows rising. "As it happens, I am *very* interested." When we reached the table, I whispered, "We could try it tonight. Early birthday present?"

My little tease didn't answer, only dragged her hand down my back, patting my ass before taking a seat, launching into some animated story with Trace.

Cruel woman.

CHAPTER TWENTY-FIVE

Laney

Unlike Ethan, I didn't "hang out" with my parents. Closing in on retirement, my dad, Dr. Aaron Hargrove spent most of his days at a hunting cabin or golfing with pals, while my mother, Katherine Hargrove, V.P. of ComTech Resources, was still going strong, keeping a tightly packed schedule that I often thought even Bronte would be jealous of. Which was exactly why I found myself in a pedicure chair on Wednesday afternoon, meeting my mom at one of her biweekly nail appointments. "Have you looked over the sponsorship packages yet?"

She nodded distractedly, her eyes on the TV screen above us as a couple hunted for a vacation home in Bali. "Yes, I have a check from your father for the bronze package."

I forced my mouth into an appreciative smile. Dean and I had never lacked for anything, lucky enough to come from a family with wealth, both of our parents very successful in their respective careers. So, I had no reason to complain. Except that the Hargrove pull-yourself-up-by-your-bootstraps method of thinking didn't, couldn't, and shouldn't always apply to every-thing, including when I was heading up a fundraiser. My father had more than enough money to part with. He could afford more than the $500 sponsorship package.

"What about ComTech?" I asked, referring to the human resources firm she worked for.

She turned to face me, a barely there frown creasing the left corner of her mouth. "I didn't think it would be appropriate for me to ask." She nodded as if I should know that. "It's a conflict of interest."

I hid my eye roll but couldn't contain my huff. "What's the difference between asking for a donation to a really good cause and a parent of a Girl Scout selling cookies?"

"Nothing," she answered resolutely. "There is no solicitation. It's company policy." Then she gave me an impatient smile. "It's nice you're doing this for your friend, Delaney, but shouldn't you be focused on getting a job?"

"I am focused on that. I can do two things at once."

Mom pinned me with an expectant gaze.

"I contacted a headhunter," I said in response.

"Wonderful."

"And secondly, Mom, Ethan isn't my friend. We've started dating."

She twisted in her chair, giving me her full attention. "You're dating?"

I nodded, fiddling with my cell phone in my lap as I watched the nail technician buff my toenails.

"This is Dean's friend Ethan, right?"

"Well, he was my friend too."

"In high school," Mom said in a funny voice that had me lifting my gaze.

"Yeah."

A grin broke out across her face. "I always thought he had a thing for you."

"You what?" I almost shrieked.

Our mother-daughter relationship was good, but it wasn't

the open kind where we'd gossip or talk about the latest boy to break my heart.

She shrugged. "He was at our house all the time, and he always seemed to be…" She twirled her hand in the air, aluminum foil on her fingers to remove her gel nail polish. "He was close to you a lot. If you were standing by the kitchen counter, so was he. If you were sitting on the long couch in the living room, so was he. And you—" She snorted a laugh that sounded exactly like mine. "You were so popular, I could never understand why you weren't going out with different boys all the time, until I came home from work one night and the two of you were at the kitchen table, doing something, I don't know what."

"Probably calculus homework," I guessed, and my mother eyed me. She was the one who demanded I get a tutor, after all. Lest I be the first in the family to get a C in any class.

"You were sitting so close together, you were practically in his lap."

"Mom," I chided, my cheeks heating with secondhand embarrassment for my teenage self.

"It's true." She shook her head in mock scolding. "You know your father and I weren't sure about the two of you together at the beach. When Dean told us he was inviting Ethan, we really considered making you and your friends go a different week, but you know your dad." She puffed out a short burst of air. "He didn't want to pay for two different rentals."

"What did you think was going to happen?" I asked, full of indignation. It wasn't as if we'd gone on a weeklong bender. It was a bunch of recent high school graduates drinking warm beer and gorging ourselves on pizza.

My mother pursed her lips, letting her silence answer, and that's when I realized me and Ethan had done exactly what my parents were afraid of—we had sex during that trip—and I played with my hair, trying to hide the growing blush I felt creeping up from my neck. My mother threw her head back and laughed. "Guess maybe we should have sprung for that second house for you and your girlfriends, huh?"

"I plead the Fifth," I said, which only caused her to laugh louder.

"Well," she said when she quieted down, "I'm happy for you." She patted my arm. "Does that mean you're looking to be here on a more permanent basis?"

Even though Ethan and I had officially been together a few weeks, we hadn't talked about it. But now that my mother had brought it up... "Yeah, I think so."

She smiled, patted my hand once more, then faced forward, smiling at the nail technician when she started painting her toenails the usual maroon color. "Well, let me know how it goes with the headhunter, or if I need to take a look at your résumé."

I inhaled deeply. "I got it covered, Mom."

She raised her hands in innocence. "Just checking."

An hour later, I was headed back inside Dean's house when my phone buzzed with a text from Gem. I squinted at the picture for a moment before I recognized what it was.

OMG.

I didn't pay attention to the two men in the living room as I threw myself into the closest chair, my fingers flying over her phone screen.

IS THAT MITCHELL BABY #2?

Another picture came through, a black-and-white photo of what looked like two tiny hands balled into fists.

BRONTE

Looks like they want to fight.

SAM

I can't tell what I'm looking at. I need a
diagram.

I laughed, and my brother said, "What could you possibly be looking at that's so fascinating?"

"Porn," Ethan guessed, and I momentarily paused my typing to shoot my boyfriend a glare. He gave me one of his lazy grins in return.

GEM

Is this clear enough for you?

She sent another photo. This one with a circle around what looked to be nothing.

Sam sent back a side-eye emoji.

SAM

No, it's not any clearer. You could tell me I'm
looking at an elephant baby, and I'd believe
you.

I cackled, and seconds later, a FaceTime alert came through. Gem flattened her mouth to a faux annoyed slant as all of us appeared on-screen. "I'm gestating a human not an elephant, Samantha."

Sam lifted one hand. "It looks like blobs to me. What's the point of the tech circling anything?"

"It's the gender," Gem said, and Bronte was the first to shout out.

"It's a girl!"

"Three against one," I crowed.

Sam pumped her fist up and down. "You finally have your army."

The soon-to-be mother of two girls laughed. "That's right."

"Who're you talking to?" Dean asked, lifting the remote to turn the volume of the television up. "It's like surround sound."

I curled my lip, snarling at him. "My best friend is having a baby. So sorry our happiness is bothering you."

Ethan gestured me over to him, saying, "He's in a bad mood. He's got some new coworker riding his ass to be top gun."

"Who's that?" Sam asked from her phone.

Gem swiftly followed up. "The high school heartbreaker?"

Dean grumbled as I sat on the couch between him and Ethan, spinning my cell phone so the girls could see Ethan. Bronte, Sam, and Gem all waved and talked over one another.

He grinned. "Nice to meet you, ladies. Laney's told me a lot about you."

"That's funny. Because she's told us almost nothing about you," Gem teased, and I lifted my middle finger to the screen. "I'm kidding." Gem fluttered her hand in the air like she was swatting at a fly. "I was the one visiting her in San Francisco when she found out about the Australian's assholery."

"Oh." Ethan nodded. "You were the one who puked on him."

She dipped her head in a magnanimous bow. "The one and only."

"You know, I feel like we need to rework our murder scheme," Sam said, and that got Dean's attention. With his arms crossed, he raised one brow at me.

"Not real," Laney said. "Not yet, anyway."

Dean shook his head. "I don't want to know."

"It's all theoretical," Bronte said cheerfully, and I turned my phone so my brother could see my friends.

"I don't know if we've ever met." Bronte waved. "I'm Bronte."

"The nice one," I said.

"Sam." The woman in question pointed to herself.

I nodded. "The brainy one."

"And I'm Gem, the resident antagonist."

I didn't have anything to add to that, and all four of us laughed.

Ethan threw his arm around my shoulders. "Which one are you?"

"Laney's the glue," Gem said.

"That's why I'm stuck to you, huh?"

"Jesus Christ." Dean groaned like he had a stomachache and tossed his hands out. "I'm going to get changed."

I watched as my brother stomped upstairs, loosening his tie. He hadn't even changed out of his work clothes, and yet he'd opened up a beer, evidenced by the bottle on the coffee table.

"He texted me to come over," Ethan murmured in my ear.

"Maybe he's upset I interrupted your guy time." I pulled my lips to the side, wondering if I should take my call somewhere else, but Ethan only held on to the hand in my lap.

"Don't worry about it," he said. "Dean'll be fine." Then he looked back to the screen. "So, I guess congratulations are in order?"

Ethan charmed the girls for the next few minutes, and I was even more in love with the man than before I'd walked in the door. I could tell my friends approved of him too. Bronte was almost in tears by the time he'd finished explaining why he wanted to start the nonprofit, and Gem and Sam were likewise impressed with his travels and easygoing storytelling.

Right before we hung up, Bronte slipped in a reminder. "I know it's a long way off, but I'm going to be confirming our rental for New Year's. It's a cabin outside of Tacoma, seven bedrooms, three bathrooms, sauna and hot tub, game room, wraparound porch, and not that we'll want to use it, but it also has an outdoor pool."

"Sounds good to me," Sam said.

Gem sucked air through her teeth as she grimaced. "We'll have a second kid with us by then. Is that still okay with everyone?"

Bronte rolled her eyes like *of course*, and I brought my phone close to my face. "Can't wait to see you all, especially the newest little blob and smoosh her face."

"Okay, well, it's time for me to have my third popsicle for the day," Gem said and signed off.

Bronte and Sam followed suit, leaving Ethan and me gazing at my blank screen.

"You think they like me?" Ethan asked, removing his glasses to swipe the hem of his shirt over the lenses.

"They *love* you."

"Yeah?" When I nodded, he grinned and popped his glasses back on. "What's up with Gem's popsicles?"

"She gets really sick when she's pregnant. Can't keep much down until the last trimester." I cuddled in closer to Ethan's side, and he skimmed the tips of his fingers down along my shoulder and arm as I hummed thoughtfully. "Maybe we should do a couples Zoom so the guys can meet you."

"Their boyfriends need to vet me too?"

"Two of them are married, but yeah, kinda." I tipped my head back to him. "If you're going to come with me to the cabin, it's probably best if you're not meeting them for the first time."

"Cabin?" he asked as Dean clomped back down the stairs.

"That's what Bronte was talking about. It's a new thing we're trying to do. Annual New Year's vacation, all together. Bronte's planning the whole thing. You want to come?"

"Yes." He kissed my temple. "Definitely."

Dressed in jeans and a T-shirt, Dean grabbed his car keys from the side table. "All right, let's go." He gestured for Ethan to follow him out of the front door. "I texted Hank to meet us."

Ethan got up from the couch. "Where are we going?"

"Birthday drinks," Dean said, and when Ethan looked between me and Dean in confusion, my brother sighed, scrubbing his hand over his face. "I figured you'd be going out with Laney tomorrow, so Hank and I want to take you out tonight. Plus, it's most likely the last time we'll see him for a while with the baby due next week."

Ethan snapped his fingers in recognition. "Right. Right." He leaned over, kissing me on the mouth. "Talk to you later."

I smiled. "Have fun."

Dean tipped his chin at me, mumbling something about still not being used to us making out.

"You've been so grouchy lately," Ethan said, smacking Dean in the arm. "When was the last time you got laid?"

I laughed as the door closed on them.

CHAPTER TWENTY-SIX

Ethan

After a few emails back and forth with basic information about where we lived and what we did for work, and the reason for I reached out in the first place—Justin's diagnosis—Marcela and I exchanged phone numbers with a promise to speak on my birthday. I wasn't nervous per se, but I did have to change my T-shirt twice because I sweat through the other ones.

When my cell phone finally did ring at exactly 4:30, the agreed-upon time, I scrambled to reach for it, like I hadn't been staring at it. "Hi! Hello?"

A few seconds passed until she spoke softly. "Hi, Ethan."

"Hi," I said before standing up then sitting right back down on my couch. "Ho-how are you?"

"I'm fine. How are you?"

I dragged my hand through my hair a few times. "I'm good. Really good."

"Good," she said quietly. "I can't believe we're talking, that I can hear your voice."

"I know." I blinked over to the framed family photo I had by my TV. "It's wild."

She made a sound of agreement then went quiet, but I wasn't sure what to say either, so silence descended.

"Are you, um, doing anything special today?" Marcela asked after a while.

"I'm going out to dinner with my girlfriend."

"Oh." Her voice brightened. "You have a girlfriend?"

"Yeah." I relaxed against the back of the couch. "Delaney."

"Delaney," she repeated. "Have you been together long?"

"Not really, but it's...complicated."

"It always is." She laughed. "What's complicated about it?"

"We, sort of, had a thing when we were in high school, which was weird and complicated because..."

"Because that's high school," she finished for me, and I smiled.

"Exactly. She was living in California for the past few years, but she came home at the end of January, and since then, it's been..." I smiled. "It's been perfect."

"You sound happy."

"I am. What about you? Are you happy?"

She sighed, and I wished I could see Marcela in person to know if that was a good or bad sigh. "I am happy now, yes. Especially talking to you. Knowing you are happy makes me feel better than I have in a very long time."

I nodded to myself. "Do you have... I mean, are you...with someone too?"

"No, I'm not," she said. "I've never gotten married, but I haven't given up hope of finding someone."

I chewed on the inside of my cheek for a moment. "So, you're not with the...my biological father?"

She didn't hesitate to answer. "No. I haven't seen him in a very long time. Since before you were born, actually."

I connected some of the dots in my mind about the information the adoption agency had given me. "He didn't want to be involved then, obviously."

"No." She huffed. "He was not at all interested in helping

me, which is part of the reason why I made the decision to give you up." Then she exhaled a shaky breath. "Hearing you now, I don't regret what I did, but I have carried around a lot of guilt. I often wondered if you resented me or felt unwanted or carried some trauma from adoption."

"No, Marcela, no." I raised my hand to my empty living room. "Please don't worry or feel guilty. I have a wonderful life, my parents—" I stopped, not wanting to offend my birth mother, but she seemed unruffled.

"From what you've told me, your parents gave you everything and more than I could have hoped for."

Another few seconds of quiet passed, and as if she could tell I was nervous to ask, she said, "I suppose you'd like to know why I decided on adoption."

"If…" I cleared his throat. "If you want to tell me."

She spoke after a long moment. "My parents immigrated from Mexico, and I was raised being told that this was the land of opportunity, that if I tried hard enough, I could achieve the American Dream. I was the first one in my family to go to college, on a full ride to Georgetown, but then I met a boy." She let out what sounded like an exhausted breath. "How all trouble starts, I guess, with a cute boy."

I smiled, relieved that she was okay with telling me this story and that she didn't sound too distressed over it.

"He was handsome, tall with green eyes…looked a little like Jason Priestly."

"Jason Priestley?"

"He was on *90210*." At my silence, she went on. "Anyway, he was on the rowing team and came from an…entitled background."

I snorted, imagining the type of guy my biological father was.

"We met in a philosophy class freshman year and were on

and off for a while. When we returned to campus for our second year, we went to some party, and I guess we both had a little too much to drink because neither one of us thought about birth control. A few weeks later, I found out I was pregnant, and when I told him, he asked how I knew it was even his. We weren't officially together, so how did he know I hadn't been with anyone else." She sniffed. "But that was just an excuse. He knew I hadn't been with anyone else. I thought I loved him."

"I'm sorry," I said.

After an audible inhale, she continued, "My parents were strict Catholics. I didn't know how to tell them that their only daughter with a scholarship to school messed it all up."

I rubbed my fingers across my forehead. "Yeah, I understand that Catholic guilt."

"Oh yeah?"

"I went to Catholic school."

Marcela laughed quietly on the other end, and I grinned at our commonality.

"So, there weren't many options for me," she said. "But I knew if I told my parents, they would want me to leave school, they'd take on extra jobs to help me raise the baby, and I couldn't do that. I couldn't give up all of my hard work, all of *their* hard work. Brad was not going to help me, so adoption was my only choice."

"I understand," I said, because I did, although I hated the man who gave me half my chromosomes. To take no responsibility whatsoever and leave it all up to Marcela was an awful thing to do. Then to break the silence, I said, "His name was Brad? You had to know he'd turn out to be terrible."

A big burst of laughter erupted from Marcela. "Too right."

"Thank you for explaining it to me," I said after she quieted.

"I want you to know that I thought—think—about you all the time, every day, but especially on your birthday. For the first three years, I'd get a few pictures. I was able to see you blow out your candles, and I was so grateful to your mom for allowing me a small snippet, but I couldn't bear to see them anymore. I knew you had a good life, and I realized that if I was going to be the person I was meant to be, achieve all the dreams I was supposed to, I couldn't hang on to you any longer. I had to let go, so I did. But not one day has ever gone by that I didn't think of you and holding you for a few minutes in the hospital."

I took my glasses off to wipe my eyes.

"I'm so glad you reached out, Ethan. I..." She sniffled and cleared her throat before continuing, "If you would allow it, I would like to talk more, text and call."

"I would really love that," I said, putting my glasses back on.

"I want to hear more about your family and how your brother is doing, and more about Delaney. I want to know everything."

I grinned. "I want to know everything about you too. I told you about the fundraiser and—"

"Oh yes, please text me the link to the website. I'd like to give a donation."

"Thank you. I will. But I was going to say, I'll be really busy next week, so maybe we can find a time to talk after. Maybe even Zoom?"

"Yeah, that sounds really good."

I stood up, pacing the length of the living room, unsure what to say.

"Well, I guess I should let you go since you're going out tonight," Marcela said. "I hope you have fun."

"Thank you."

"And text me, okay?"

"I will," I promised. "As soon as we hang up."

"Okay." When silence descended yet again, she laughed. "I think we'll get better at this the more we try it."

I chuckled. "I think so too."

"Have a nice night, Ethan. Take care."

"You too." As soon as I hung up, I texted her the link to the website, as promised, along with the message.

> It was great talking to you.

MARCELA

> I can't wait to do it again.

Tossing my phone down, I headed toward the bathroom to shower and change, all the while thinking about how well our chat went. Hopefully, after we talked more, we would be able to meet in person. I already had an amazing family; to get a bonus parent would be the cherry on top. And now that I knew what Marcela was like, I felt comfortable telling Laney about her. I couldn't wait to, and I was still smiling when I answered my door, but it dropped when Laney stepped inside.

She cocked her head to the side, closing the door behind her. "What's wrong?"

I licked my lips and blinked. Then I blinked again, proving I was still in semi-control of at least some parts of my body. I couldn't speak for a certain organ below my belt.

I touched the loose material of her dress, fluttering it slightly, and she quirked a brow. "What are you doing?"

"Shh." I shook my head. "Don't speak, or else we won't be going anywhere."

"What are you—"

"I told you," I said, grabbing her by the waist to pull her close, my hands balling the soft cotton in both of my fists, at her lower back. "We will not leave this apartment if you open that mouth of yours." I nipped at her lips, and she gasped, arching into me. There was no way she didn't feel how hard I was.

"What's gotten into you?" she murmured, looping her arms around my neck.

I huffed, tightening my hold around her, lifting her slightly to take her weight against me, her full and perfect tits pushed against my chest, accentuating the cleavage already spilling out from the low neckline of her dress. "You literally look like you walked out of one of my fantasies."

She tipped her head back, laughing, and I kissed her throat. "I'm serious, Laney. I can't stand it. My dick can't take it."

She wiggled out of my grasp to drop her gaze below my waist, like she needed proof.

"Your hair is curly," I said, wrapping a strand of it around my index finger before tucking it behind her ear and dropping my fingers to her chin. "You have on your berry ChapStick." I rubbed the pad of my thumb along her lips, then skimmed my fingers down her throat to her collarbone and lower to the tops of her breasts. "And this dress. It's..."

I shook my head and stepped back, my eyes roving over her. "It's so innocent with the tiny flowers, but..."

"It's just a sundress."

I grabbed her again, sucking at the skin below her ear. "It's not a sundress." I brushed my hand up her thigh, under the flimsy skirt she excused as a sundress. "It's a goddamn wet dream."

She backed away from me, fixing her denim jacket. "I made reservations."

"But it's my birthday."

"And I was really looking forward to the scallops."

"I can't go out like this," I said, drawing her close again, pressing my hard cock against her hip.

She sighed, snaking her hand between us to tug on the belt loops of my jeans. "I guess we could spare a few minutes."

Then she dropped to her knees, right there in the entryway of my apartment, and smiled up at me. "Happy birthday, Ethan."

I reached my hand out for the wall, so I didn't fall over dead.

Delaney Hargrove on her knees as she undid my belt, there was never a more perfect sight.

"Jesus Christ," I muttered, my mouth dry, as she pushed my jeans and underwear down. My dick bobbed out toward her, long and hard and already glistening at the tip. She didn't hesitate to take me in her hand, licking the flat of her tongue over the sensitive spot just under the head, and my breath hissed out of me.

She'd had her mouth on me before. I'd witnessed her take me between those plump lips of hers, but never like this. Never with wide blue eyes staring up at me. Never with her wearing that delicate-looking dress I wanted to rip off. Never with her chest heaving like she was enjoying this as much as I was.

"You're everything," I told her, sinking my fingers into her hair, gripping the back of her head. "You're so sweet and beautiful and—" I sucked a sharp breath in when her teeth lightly scraped along my length. The tiny hairs all over my body stood on end in pleasure and pain. "Ah, shit, Lane."

The corners of her eyes tipped up as she hummed an amused sound, and I narrowed my eyes, tightening my grip in her hair. "You think you're so cute, huh? Stop teasing me and suck."

She wrapped her hands around the backs of my thighs, taking me all the way to the back of her throat, and I didn't dare to even blink. Her eyes watered as she gagged, and I don't know why I liked that so much. Maybe because this perfectly polished woman was getting sloppy for *me*. Everyone else got the shiny version of her. But I was blessed to have her on her knees, her fingernails digging into my skin, her cheeks red, saliva leaking out of the corner of her lips, her throat contracting as I fucked her perfect mouth.

"That's it," I told her quietly, holding the back of her head even as my shoulders inched up toward my ears, my orgasm barreling down on me. I thrust into her mouth. "I'm the only one you get on your knees for."

She nodded, her mouth full, and I dragged my thumb across her jaw and down her throat. "I love watching you do this." I thrust again and again, barely holding on, and I felt my spine start curving with my need to release. "I love you so much, and I know you don't like to swallow, so you have exactly three seconds before I come."

Instead of backing away, she hallowed her cheeks, sucking me so hard I shuddered, spilling into the back of her throat. Her fingers circled my balls, gently pulling on them, prolonging the rolling wave of my orgasm, and I slapped my hand on the wall again.

I hung my head, my grip on Laney's hair easing, and I blew out a breath, hoping she might find some pieces of my brain on the floor next to her.

"All right?" she asked, wiping her fingers over her mouth.

"All right?" I huffed and hauled her up off the floor, pinning her against the wall, one hand on her hip, the other at her throat. "No, I'm not all right." Her lips were swollen and red, her eyes still slightly glassy. "You just tried to kill me."

She laughed.

"Not funny, Lane. I could have died."

"From getting your dick sucked?"

I nipped at her lips. "I love when you talk dirty, and, yes, you almost killed me from sucking my dick so hard. How would you explain that to the police?"

"I wouldn't," she said, batting those baby blues at me. "I'd call the girls to help me bury your body. Though…" She clucked her tongue. "I would miss you."

I inched my fingers on her throat higher, nudging her chin up to kiss her. My hips reflexively pressed into hers, and I realized my pants were still down by my ankles. I knew we had a reservation. I knew Laney wanted the scallops. But my cock was already getting other ideas. I groaned into her mouth, allowing myself one last swipe of my tongue along hers. Then I hiked my jeans up. "We better go."

"Don't sound so sad about it." She laughed. "It's your birthday."

CHAPTER TWENTY-SEVEN

Laney

Once we finally arrived at the restaurant, Ethan and I gorged ourselves on seafood and took our time sipping a crisp Riesling, followed by a slice of chocolate cake, though I ate most of it.

"You should have the last bite," I said, holding up my fork to him. "It's your birthday."

The corner of his mouth tipped in a half smile. "I know how you like your sweets. You eat it."

"If you insist." I lifted a shoulder and ate the last bite, licking the fudge icing off the back of the fork with the tip of my tongue, and he moved his leg so it leaned against mine under the table.

"Lane," he rumbled, "when did you become such a tease?"

I widened my eyes, pressing my hand to my chest in innocence, and he lifted his brow, shaking his head ever so slightly like I'd pay for it when we got back to his place.

I hadn't expected his reaction when he'd opened the door tonight. The dress had become a bit snug over the years as I'd gained weight, but it was too cute to waste in the back of my closet, especially when the weather was so nice. And, yeah, I did want to tease him a little when I was on my knees, but *he* was the one teasing *me*. With his hand in my hair, drawing me into him, directing me to take him deeper, but still smiling down at me so playfully. A soft top if there ever was one.

"You ready to head out?" he asked, even though he didn't require an answer since he was signaling for the check.

"You in a hurry?"

He threw me a bland look and didn't even peek at the bill when it came, simply offered up his credit card.

"I'm supposed to pay," I said, flicking at his hand, and he grabbed my fingers, twisting them up to his mouth. He kissed my wrist.

"Whatever gets us out of here faster."

A minute later, he was towing me outside with his hand on my back. He all but shoved me into his car and jogged around to his side. "If I had to look at your tits any longer in that dress, I'd be held liable for public indecency."

I backhanded him as he started the ignition, and he glared at me in fake outrage. "There is only so much a man can take. And," he said, driving out of the parking lot, "there are only so many math facts to mentally recite."

"Then I guess I shouldn't show you this, huh?" I asked, presenting him with the small, nondescript black box that I'd stowed away in my purse.

He spared it a glance as he changed lanes. "What's that?"

"Your present."

"My present? Pretty sure I got that already."

"Oh, okay." I shrugged. "Well, if you don't want to play with it, I guess I'll send it back," I said, earning his full attention after stopping at a red light.

"Play with it?" he asked deliberately, and I tamped down my smile. "You had a sex toy in your purse the whole time?" He inhaled so loud and long, rubbing at his forehead, I couldn't help but giggle. He sent me an anguished scowl then drove on when the light turned green. "You want to hear about the two French mathematicians who are the fathers of probability and statistics?"

I snickered. "If it'll help."

He leaned his elbow on the console. "Not even your appetizer before we left helped." Then he wrapped his hand around my thigh, squeezing it roughly. "So, okay, in the seventeenth century, these two guys, Blaise Pascal and Pierre de Fermat, were thinking about gambling."

I leaned my head back against the rest and listened to Ethan drone on about games of chance and probability and something called Pascal's Triangle until we arrived back at his apartment, where he stripped me of my jacket and wrapped me up in his arms, kissing me like I was his dessert. I certainly felt like it from the way he licked into my mouth, moaning quietly like I was the sweetest thing he'd ever tasted. When he reached for the straps of my dress, I backed away from him, a little unsteadily. "Wait, hold on." I stepped out of my shoes. "I need to use the bathroom and want to brush my teeth. I probably taste like seafood."

He flicked at the skirt of my dress. "Not at all."

I wrapped my hair up into a bun at the top of my head and secured it with an elastic from my wrist. "But it'd make me feel better."

"Okay." He let out the sigh of all sighs. A king disturbed by the wish of a peasant. "Fine."

I smiled as he pivoted around to pick up the black box, weighing it slightly in his hand before opening it. I raced to the bathroom, not wanting to keep him any longer, and sat on the toilet. A few moments later, he strolled in behind me, and I gasped, covering myself. "Ethan!"

Grabbing his toothbrush, he barely acknowledged me. "What?"

"I'm going to the bathroom," I overenunciated it as if he couldn't hear the sound of me peeing inches away. "I'd like a little mystery between us, please."

That made him turn to me, foam at the edges of his mouth as he brushed, his brows narrowed, apparently in disagreement. I flapped my hand, trying to chase him out. "I need to wipe."

He smiled around his toothbrush, his words garbled.

"I didn't catch any of that."

He spat into the sink. "I said, are you really going to force me out of my own bathroom?"

I squeezed my jaw together, widening my eyes at him, and he shook his head in amusement. "Fine." He stuck his toothbrush in his mouth and closed the bathroom door after himself, calling out, "Happy?"

Instead of answering, I finished up, washed my hands, and opened the door to find him leaning against the wall outside it. "Better?"

"Yes, thank you," I said, all snooty, and he brushed past me, dragging his fingers along my stomach, then spat one more time in the sink and rinsed off his toothbrush. "You haven't even moved in yet," he said, knocking it on the side of the sink, "and you're already setting down rules."

I wrenched my head back. "I...what?"

"It's quite forward of you, don't you think?" He squirted more toothpaste onto the brush and held it out to me.

I stuttered, not understanding where this was coming from, and he lifted my right hand, placing the toothbrush in it like I was his personal mannequin.

"You come in here, acting like you own the place, when you haven't even moved in yet." He crossed his arms over his chest, and the cogs of my brain started clicking back into position.

"*Yet?*"

"Yeah." He lifted one shoulder. "I'll let you have this one, but no more until all your clothes are moved in, okay? I want to see your entire legion of hair products in there," he said, tossing his head toward the bathroom closet then his chin to the drawer in the vanity. "Tampons there." Releasing his arms, he grabbed my left hand from where I had been tugging at the neckline of my dress. "I want all your clothes in my closet and your shoes next to mine, or no more kicking me out of the bathroom. Got it?"

I nodded in silence, too stunned to speak, so he kissed the corner of my mouth, nudging my nose with his, as if to wake me up from her trance. "Hurry up, brush your teeth. I want you naked in two minutes."

I proceeded to brush my teeth in record time and slipped out of my dress, hanging it on an open hook on the wall, then released my hair from its bun, fluffing it out since my soon-to-be live-in-boyfriend loved it down so much. Sauntering into his bedroom, I smiled at the picture of Ethan stripped down to his boxer briefs, turning over the C-shaped sex toy in one hand while he held the directions in the other. As if sensing me standing there, he lifted his head. "Hey, gorgeous. Ready to play?"

I pointed to the paper in his hands. "You had to read the directions?"

"I am nothing if not thorough." Then he flung the paper somewhere behind him and stalked toward me, removing his glasses in the process. "I don't know if you remember this, but when I turned eighteen, I went out to Applebee's with the guys."

He wrapped one arm around my waist, pulling me flush against him, and I shook my head. So far, this memory sounded completely foreign.

"You came down before we left and caught me in the

kitchen while they were all outside. You told me how your first grade teacher would tug on the kids' ears for their birthday for good luck."

"Oh." I gave in to a laugh even as his fingers sank below the thin material of my underwear, dragging along the tops of my cheeks. Mrs. Tesatore gave every kid seven tugs on their birthday.

"Then you tugged on my ear eighteen times. I had to hide how hard you made me just from you tugging on my ear."

I might have laughed if I wasn't busy melting against him when he nipped my earlobe before sucking on the skin below it. "Does that mean you want me to tug on your ear twenty-eight times?"

"No, I was thinking we aim for twenty-eight orgasms."

This time, I did laugh. "That's not physically possible."

He backed away, grinning, as he held up our new vibrator between us. "Let's call it a statistics and probability experiment."

We didn't get close to twenty-eight, but Ethan earned points for his tenacity.

———

The next morning, I woke up to the sounds of running water and the smell of coffee. As I sat up, the sheet slipped off my naked chest, and I took account of the tender places all over my body, including the few red marks on my breasts. I flopped back to my pillow, throwing my arm over my head, still too exhausted to get up.

"Ethan?" I called, my voice so scratchy it barely came out. I cleared my throat and tried again. "Ethan!"

The running water stopped, and a few seconds later, he

popped his head around the bedroom doorway. "You're up already."

"*You're* up already?"

"I was going to make veggie omelets. That okay with you?"

With him in only his glasses and a pair of athletic shorts, I let my gaze drift down his golden bronzed torso.

"Hey," he said, forcing my eyes up to his. "Stop looking at me like that. I need to refuel."

I playfully rolled my eyes. "Fine."

"We've got all weekend. No rush," he told me then ducked away, presumably to fix up our breakfast, and I smiled to myself that sweet and nerdy but excessively good in bed Ethan Marrero was mine. I instinctively reached for my phone, then remembered he had, at some point, plugged it in to charge. Rolling over to his side of the bed, I grabbed it from the charger, my attention catching on his phone, next to mine, with the kids from *Goonies* on his lock screen.

I picked it up to get a better look and noticed the few alerts, including a text message from someone named Marcela. Normally, I would have thought nothing of it, except that it said **Let me know how the fundraiser goes. XO**

XO?

Frowning, I keyed in his passcode. Because there were no secrets between us, I knew it was 3141, the first four numbers of pi, like he knew mine was my birthday, 0124. I didn't hesitate to open the text thread between Ethan and this Marcela person.

It was great talking to you.

MARCELA

I can't wait to do it again.

MARCELA

Let me know how the fundraiser goes.

MARCELA

XO

Swiping my hair back from my face, I took a calming breath and assumed there had to be a logical explanation. There was no way Ethan would be cheating on me.

Yet the crushing weight of feeling *not enough* had me opening his contacts. Marcela's area code was unfamiliar, but they'd had a phone call for a half hour yesterday afternoon. Before I had come over to see him, Ethan, my boyfriend, the man I loved, and who asked—demanded, really—that I move in, spoke to a woman named Marcela for half an hour and exchanged text messages, including one from her that was signed with hugs and kisses.

Blinking away the tears threatening my eyes, I tried to shake some reason into my head, unsure of what to believe. But I refused to open his social media apps to investigate. No, I wouldn't give in to my worst instincts. Instead, I slipped into my underwear, pulled on a pair of his sweats and an old Princeton T-shirt and calmly walked into the kitchen with Ethan's phone in my hand.

CHAPTER TWENTY-EIGHT

Ethan

I had just thrown the spinach and cheese in to finish off the omelets when I heard Laney shuffling up behind me. I circled around, spatula in hand, ready to pull her in for a kiss. But I didn't.

Not with her red-rimmed eyes and frown marring her plump lips.

I set down the spatula and hooked my index finger on the bottom of my shirt that she wore, towing her closer a few inches. Though she barely budged. "What happened? What's wrong?"

She cleared her throat and held up my cell phone. At first, I couldn't even focus on it, didn't care about it. I only wanted to know why she was upset. But when she didn't say anything, I drifted my focus to the little screen, jerking angling my head back a few inches to see it.

"Who is Marcela?"

I took the phone from her hand and set it on the counter. "Is that why you're upset?"

"Yes." She huffed out a watery laugh, her eyes glassy, and I opened my arms to comfort her, but she stopped me. "Are you..." She swallowed thickly. "Are you cheating on me?"

I wouldn't take no for an answer. I needed to touch her, and I took hold of her wrists to clasp her hands to my chest. "No. I am absolutely not cheating on you. I'm so sorry you ever experienced that, but I am one hundred percent in love with you."

She still didn't make a move toward me, as if she didn't believe me. A tear fell from her eye, and I smudged it away with my thumb, promising myself that if I ever came across Bobby Magnate, I'd punch that shithead in the face. "Laney, do you really think I'd cheat on you?" I curled my hands around her face. "I've never hidden anything from you. I've never lied to you. You think I'd start now?"

Her eyes shifted to where my cell phone lay on the counter. "I don't know what to think."

I nodded, exhaling slowly. I had a lot of patience and was pretty laid-back, but the fact that she didn't believe me was testing my usual unflappability. "I've got to be honest, it stings that you don't trust me."

She backed away, out of my grasp, and folded her arms over her chest. Giving her the space she needed, I grabbed two plates and put an omelet on each one then set them on the kitchen table. I snagged two forks and two napkins before sitting down, gesturing to the chair opposite me. "Please sit?"

With her jaw set, she dropped her chin to her chest, her bare feet wiggling as if she needed to think about it.

"Please, Laney. Let's talk about this. Let me explain."

"So there is something to explain," she said after a while, her voice flat and cold.

"Yeah, so can you sit and eat? It's kind of a long story."

She guffawed. It was an annoyed puff of sound, nothing like the laugh I loved so much. Although she sat, she didn't pick up her fork, so I didn't either.

"First off, I want to say that I know you're still carrying

around baggage from your last relationship," I said. "I get it. I understand it, but I don't know how to help you."

She rolled her eyes. "You don't need to help me. This isn't like a broken leg. I don't need rehab. I need the truth. I need honesty."

"I've always been honest with you, Lane. Always."

She pursed her lips in apparent dissent then pointed to my cell phone.

I sat back in my chair and set my hands on the table, raising my fingers. "I can see why you made an assumption, and I'm sorry I didn't tell you about Marcela before, but..." I combed one hand through my hair a few times as I tried to find my words. "I haven't told anyone yet except Justin."

"Told Justin what?" she snapped, and I rubbed my fingers across my forehead.

"Told him that I got into contact with my birth mother."

Her breath left her with an audible exhale, and she deflated, propping her elbows on the table.

I took her silence as a sign to keep going. "I don't know if I ever told you this, but when Justin turned eighteen, he decided he wanted to find his birth parents, and it was a wild-goose chase that he went on for years, only to come up empty-handed. It was really upsetting to me, to see my big brother go through all that for nothing. I didn't want to go through that either, so I decided that I wouldn't ever try to look for or contact mine. Until he was diagnosed."

Across from me, Laney scratched at a chip on the corner of the table.

"It made me realize that it might be a good thing to do. I'm older and..." I shrugged, chewing on the inside of my cheek for a moment. "I can handle it now, so I talked to my mom about it."

"I thought you said you only talked to your brother about it," she said, lifting her gaze from the table to meet mine.

"Well, I had to ask my mom's opinion about it, and she gave me the starting point to contact the adoption agency. My adoption was semi-open, so she'd sent pictures to the agency to forward on for a few years."

Laney brought one foot up on her chair, leaning her chin on her knee. "So, Marcela is your birth mother?"

I nodded. "At first, we were only emailing each other, and then yesterday, we talked for a bit on the phone." I tried for a smile. "I heard her voice for the first time."

Laney sucked her bottom lip between her teeth, her eyes going teary again.

"I didn't tell you about it before because I was afraid," I said.

"Afraid of what?"

"Afraid of the outcome. Of everything falling through, like it did for Justin. Of what I might find or who they might be. I didn't want to get my hopes up, you know?"

She dropped her forehead to her knee, so I couldn't see her but still heard her sniffling. A few seconds later, she said, "I don't know because you didn't tell me."

I sat on the edge of my seat, troubled that she was upset but also a little offended that she wasn't excited or happy about me finding Marcela. It was a pretty big deal.

"I'm sorry, Laney," I said, and she finally raised her face to me.

"I'm sorry you felt like you couldn't talk to me." She wiped her cheeks with the back of her hand. "This is really important, and I would like to be there for you for whatever you need."

"You are there for me."

"After the fact." She shook her head slightly, her blue eyes —now bloodshot—focused on the ceiling as she blinked rapidly. After a moment, she dropped her full attention on me once more, her face and eyes dry. "I bet this has been really hard for you but also, maybe, really nerve-racking." When I nodded, she narrowed her eyes. "And you've been hiding it from me. This is a big part of your life, and it feels like you purposely kept me out of it."

"I kept everyone out of it," I said in defense of myself, though I immediately realized it wasn't much of a defense.

"I'm not everyone."

"No, you're not." I wrapped my fingers around her hand on the table. "You mean everything to me."

"But not enough to tell me."

"Laney," I said on a sigh. "I'm sorry I hurt you. I'm sorry I kept this from you, but I think you're making it into a bigger deal than it is."

"That's what you think," she said, taking her hand back to set it in her lap. "But I'm telling you how I feel. Not even five minutes ago, you said that you gave me no reason to distrust you, saying you've never lied to me, yet you did."

I lifted my glasses to rub the heels of my hands in my eyes. This was not how I'd pictured this conversation going. "I was going to tell you about Marcela, today even. I told her all about you."

She shrugged. "Okay."

"Don't do that," I said, motioning to her placid features in place. That perfect veneer she so often wore.

"I know I have trust issues." She placed her hand against her chest. "I can't help that. And I know you're not Bobby, which is the reason we're having this conversation instead of me running out your door, but I can't help feeling left out."

"I'm sorry," I repeated, frustrated that I had to keep saying it. "I won't do it again."

Silence sat between us like a physical obstacle on the table, and I finally picked up my fork. "We should eat. This is probably almost cold."

"I'm not really hungry," she said and stood up.

"Seriously?" The question came out with more anger than I intended, and she threw me a look over her shoulder as she walked away.

"Seriously. I'm going to change and go home."

My fork clattered on my plate as I pushed away from the table to follow her. "You're really that mad at me over this?"

In my bedroom, she turned her back to me, lifting my shirt over her head. "I'm not mad. I just don't feel like sitting around here today."

"So, you're that *upset* with me, then?"

She didn't answer, only tugged her dress over her head, the skirt covering up her butt and thighs when she wiggled out of my sweats, almost as if she didn't want me to see any part of her. She put her hair up in a hurried knot, a few loose curls dangling at the nape of her neck, before she spun around in search of her shoes. I found them on the floor by the closet and handed them to her.

"That summer," she started, slipping her feet into them, and I didn't need it pointed out which summer she referred to. "You never told me you were going to school early. You let me think we had *all* summer. I started getting a funny notion in my head about us being together for the long-term." She lifted her arms at her sides. "I imagined us visiting each other at school. I thought we could've made a real go of it." She dropped her hands back down, and they landed with a smack against her legs. "I got my hopes up, and then all of a sudden, you had to leave. You told me last minute, as if you thought it was no big deal."

"I know. I was dumb. But you can't keep punishing me for that." I tossed my thumb over my shoulder to our past. "For that! For trying to keep what we had a little longer. You still can't be mad about that."

"I'm not. I'm only trying to explain that, back then, you didn't think it was a big enough deal to tell me. And it's the same thing now. I understand you have a lot going on in your life. Believe me, I know what it feels like to want to keep it to yourself, but I'm trying to tell you how I feel. Which is out of the loop. You were trying to protect yourself then like you are now, and it makes sense." The corner of her mouth dropped as her voice cracked. "Only, it makes me feel like shit. You want me to implicitly trust you, although you don't implicitly trust me. At least, not enough to include me."

I stood, slack-jawed at her explanation. I never intended to make her feel like that, and never even considered how keeping the situation with Marcela to myself might hurt her. But when she put it like that, I felt guilty.

"Or, ya know..." She forced a smile. "Maybe I'm making a mountain out of a molehill because I can't shake my baggage with Bobby, and that's not your fault. Either way, I don't feel like sorting it out in front of you, so I'm going to head home. Okay?"

Not that I would ever force her to stay, but I answered anyway. "Okay."

She brushed past me with a murmured, "I'll talk to you later."

Then she walked out to the living room, the quiet snick of my door like a bomb going off in the silence she left in her wake.

CHAPTER TWENTY-NINE

Ethan

Technically, Laney talked to me, but with our argument being mere days before the fundraiser, we didn't have time to get together and hash it out. I'd given her space to cool down and waited for her to call, which she did, although it wasn't much more than *I'm sorry* and *me too* before she moved right on to her never-ending to-do list.

Laney had single-handedly put this whole event together, and I couldn't have been prouder. I'd agreed to meet her early to help finish the setup. However, by the time I'd arrived at the hotel, I was stunned. I blinked around the room, astounded that *this* was a big ballroom and not an actual carnival. Red and white fabric hung from the ceiling like a circus tent, and booths were set up around the perimeter of the room with games and food, as well as some information tables from medical centers and hospitals. The silent auction was in front of the stage, where a DJ was setting up. Outside of the small dance floor were high-tops mixed in with larger tables, big enough to sit ten people.

In the middle of all of it was Laney, directing someone to set up balloons.

I headed right for her. "Lane," I said in a hushed tone,

touching her elbow so she spun around to me. "This is amazing. You are amazing."

With black heels, dark blazer, and her hair straightened into a sleek ponytail, she looked all business, and I was so into it. She grinned. "You like?"

"Do I like? I love." I bent to kiss her cheek. "I love you. Thank you."

She shrugged as if it was nothing, but I knew better. She'd spent months putting this together, all out of the goodness of her own heart. She wasn't getting paid for this.

"I feel like I owe you. Big-time." I moved my hand up her arm to curl around her neck. "What can I do to show you how much I appreciate this?"

Her eyes drifted behind me, and she nodded to someone, waving hello, before meeting my gaze. "Nothing. This is going to be a great night, and we're going to raise a lot of money. This is what you wanted, right? To help your brother, Trace, other families like yours."

I nodded, rendered momentarily speechless at the generosity of this woman. I could only stare at her, take in her light eyes, my favorite color blue, and her lips, my favorite flavor. "Do you want to come over tonight? After all this is over. I need to talk to you."

"Yes. Of course." She smiled. "I have something to tell you too."

"Yeah?"

Her explanation was cut off by a guy jogging toward us. "Hey, excuse me. Laney, we've got an issue with the sno-cone maker."

She squeezed my bicep. "You've got some time to check everything out. If you want something changed or moved, let me know, 'kay?"

"Sure," I said, although I wouldn't touch a thing. This was her show.

With a finger wave, she followed the man over to the sno-cone maker problem, leaving me to my own devices. After a slow lap around the room, where I met and thanked each person for offering their services and help, I took a picture and posted it on Instagram. I tagged Laney because she deserved to be recognized. I wrote a caption about her being an incredible woman and added a little red heart even though we weren't social-media official.

Yet.

After a few minutes, my parents, along with Justin, Leah, and Trace, arrived, and they had the same reaction as I did.

"I was here yesterday and saw a lot of this," Leah said, "but now that it's all put together…wow. Just wow."

I grinned. "I know, right?"

"Pretty spectacular," Justin added.

"You have a gem on your hands, Ethan," Mom said, referencing Laney, where she stood a few yards away by the pretzel stand, laughing about something with an older woman behind the counter.

"Look, look, look!" Trace pointed to the face painting booth. A young woman set out a sandwich board sign with pictures of kids with animals and twisty fairylike designs on their faces. "A tiger! Can I get a tiger?"

Justin patted his shoulder. "Sure, buddy, but I think you need to wait a few minutes."

Laney appeared suddenly, greeting my family with hugs. "I thought I heard someone say they wanted to have their face painted. Hmm?" She tapped her finger on her chin. "Who was it? Ethan?"

Trace held up his arm as he jumped at her. "Me! It was me!"

"Oh, you. Okay. Well, come on." She held out her hand to him. "There's no waiting for my favorite kid. Let's go turn you into a tiger."

Again, I couldn't have forced my attention off her even if a hurricane ripped through here. She led my nephew over to the booth while the woman opened up her paints, and by the time Trace had been transformed into a tiger, guests had started arriving. And that was the last time I'd been able to talk to Laney.

The music turned up, food was sold, and kids ran wild with ring-toss prizes. I caught up with Dean and the guys from poker night as well as the Anchormen, including Hank, his wife, and their very *new* baby.

"We wouldn't miss this," Hank said, slapping my arm.

Angela agreed, gently rocking the car seat, where little Grayson slept. "He's pretty easy to travel with now."

"How are you feeling, though?" I asked her. "You only got out of the hospital a couple days ago. I can't believe you're here."

"I'm feeling okay, thanks for asking." She shrugged. "But we needed to get out of the house."

"It feels like all we're doing is tracking how often he eats and poops. Our whole day is waiting until his next bottle," Hank said, staring at his baby with a goofy head over heels in love smile. I had to admit, I was a bit jealous. I wanted that same feeling too. "My life is all about his poop now," he added.

"As opposed to yours?" I joked, and they both laughed. "I gotta keep making the rounds. I'll catch up with you guys later."

I strolled over to the silent auction, checking out the popularity of each item. That's where Seraphina Bianco caught up with me, elbowing my side, saying, "You going to bid on that one?" She pointed toward a dark basket, with black stuffing and foil wrapped around it. "That was donated by my friend. Laney really enjoyed the party we had."

"The party?" I repeated, confused for only a moment. When I finally understood, I grabbed a pen, clicking it wholeheartedly to write down a bid for the covert "Couples Date Night" package.

Seraphina laughed. "I really like Laney."

"Me too," I said. "Thanks for your donations." I gestured to her generous auction gift, but she'd also signed on with the highest sponsorship level.

"My pleasure." She smiled and patted my back on her way around him. "I'm going to grab a funnel cake."

I turned, only to find Mr. and Mrs. Hargrove. I shook their hands. "Thank you so much for coming."

"We had to come see what Laney's been up to all this time," Mr. Hargrove said, with a touch of pride in his voice.

I spread my arms. "Pretty great, right?"

Mrs. Hargrove nodded. "That's Delaney." Then she leaned in closer to me, lowering her voice. "She's told me you two are dating now. I have to say, I always liked you, and I'm glad to have her back home. Hopefully she stays now that you two are together."

My smile faltered for only a second before I recovered because I didn't even think that was an option, her moving away again. Then again, she did say she had something to tell him. The mere idea of her leaving again made me queasy, but I tried not to think negative thoughts. This was a party. It was supposed to be fun.

"Well, come on, Aaron. Let's place some bids." Mrs. Hargrove tapped her husband's arm. "I have my eye on that landscaping package. You brought your checkbook, right?"

Mr. Hargrove huffed but followed her anyway.

Spotting Laney, I lifted my hand, and she waved me over.

"It's time for speeches," she told me, holding up her clipboard so I could see her schedule. "I'm going to grab the mic from the DJ. Do you have your notes?"

I patted my pocket with the printed list of all the sponsors and people I needed to thank, as well as a few sentences about why I started the nonprofit.

"When you're finished, you can pass the mic back to me, and I'll finish up."

"Got it," I said and followed my boss babe up to the stage, where she signaled the DJ to pause the music and handed the microphone over to me.

I introduced myself and talked a little off-the-cuff about my brother's diagnosis and how I wanted to learn as much as I could about Huntington's and raise awareness about it. Then, as per instructions, I thanked everyone on my list, "especially the beautiful and brilliant woman to my right, Delaney Hargrove," which received a bunch of hoots and hollers. After, I passed off the mic to her, and she reminded everyone the auction was closing in twenty minutes and to stop by the health and medical booths to find out more information on Huntington's and how to help people suffering from it, as well as to sign up for the newsletter from RAHD. She grinned at me when she said that because she never did convince me to change the name.

"Once again, we're so happy to see so many people here and thank you for the support. And PS, Marilyn over at the soft pretzel booth will make you an everything pretzel if you know the secret code." She lifted her hand to her mouth and whispered into the microphone, "It's confetti." Then she raised her voice back to normal volume. "But don't tell her I told you. Have a wonderful night, everyone!"

I exchanged a few words of gratitude with the DJ, who hit

the music as I looped my arm around Laney's waist, escorting her off the stage.

"How do you think it's going?" she asked me.

"I think it's perfect."

"Yeah, I think—" Next to me, Laney froze.

"What?"

She didn't answer, only stared ahead, in the direction of the exit doors, and I followed her gaze.

"Is that—"

"Bobby."

My jaw hit the floor. Bobby Magnate was here, at *my* fundraiser, smiling and waving at Laney as if he didn't cheat on her, turning her whole life upside down. "What the hell is he doing here?"

She dropped her hold on me and started off toward Bobby. But there was no way I wasn't going too.

I was hot on her heels as she exited out of the carnival and into the hall which led to the lobby of the hotel.

"What are you doing here?" Laney asked.

"I came to see you," Magnate said, his voice thick with an Australian accent. "You wouldn't answer my calls or texts."

I rolled my eyes. I knew it. I knew the situation would escalate. Though I didn't expect him to show up here.

Bobby reached for Laney's hands, but I cut him off, and he angled his head to the side. "Oi, hey mate." He put on a friendly smile. "I came to speak to Laney alone, yeah? Mind giving us a minute?"

"I do mind, actually," I said, stepping in front of her.

Bobby, who was about the same height as me, but had more than a couple pounds on me like Laney had said, smirked. "And who are you?"

"Ethan," Laney said, her hands on my waist, gently pushing me to move aside. "It's fine. I got it."

And yet I was an immovable stone. I glared at this asshole Aussie. "I'm Laney's boyfriend. Who are *you*?"

He shifted his gaze to Laney, his brow narrowing. "Joey, really?"

Laney let out a tired sigh. "Bobby, please, this really isn't a good time."

"*Joey?*" I repeated, toggling my gaze between cocky-as-shit Bobby and a weary-looking Laney.

"Pet name," Magnate explained with a fucking grin that had my hands curling into fists at my sides.

"I'm gonna ask you, nicely, to please not call her pet names. And while I'm at it, you need to stop calling and texting her. She clearly does not want—"

Laney grabbed my shoulder, forcibly moving me. "Ethan, don't. I told you, I will take care of this."

"Yeah," Bobby repeated. "*Joey* will take care of this." He laughed, turning his eyes to Laney. "Babe, since when do you like people speaking for you?" He stuck his hands in his pockets, like this was all a funny coincidence that we were here, and rocked back on his heels.

"You're an uninvited guest," I ground out, stepping closer to Bobby. "You need to leave."

Bobby squinted like he was thinking about it then shrugged. "No, I'm good." Once again, he reached for Laney, this time making contact, wrapping his hand around Laney's wrist. "But if you could let Laney and me have some time alone, that would be good."

"No, it's not good." I tugged Laney away. "No one wants you here, including Laney."

"You're not going to let her speak for herself?" Bobby shook his head, as if I didn't know anything about the woman we were currently fighting over. "She hates that."

"You know what else she hates? You."

Bobby snarled, getting right up in my face. "You have no idea—"

"No." I shoved him back, ignoring Laney's pleas to go back inside. "*You* have no idea. You cheated on her. You threw her away."

"You have no idea what you're talking about," Bobby snapped. "I love her."

I growled, my jaw tight. "You don't deserve her."

"Just get the fuck out of my way." Bobby pushed at my right shoulder, which only gave me more room to cock my elbow back and finally follow through with the promise I had made myself. If I ever saw Bobby Magnate in real life, I'd punch that son of a bitch.

CHAPTER THIRTY

Laney

I gasped in shock as Ethan's fist met Bobby's cheek, knocking him back a few inches, but Bobby recovered quickly and lunged at Ethan, who was cupping his right hand in his left like he was in pain.

"Stop!" I tried to put myself in between them, but it was a losing battle. I had to do something quick before anyone noticed them brawling, so I did the first thing I thought of and dialed my brother. He picked up with a laugh. "Why are you call—"

"Get your ass out to the hall right now! Bobby's here." Then I hung up, attempting to pull Ethan from Bobby, but they had their hands wrapped around each other, wrestling on the floor.

"You need to stop," I said, uselessly tugging at Bobby's shirt when he maneuvered Ethan to his back.

"You don't know when to give up, do you?" Ethan goaded, even though his glasses were long gone, and Bobby had him by the scruff of his shirt.

"Shut your fucking mouth," Bobby seethed.

"Fuck you," Ethan said, kicking his leg, trying to wiggle out of Bobby's grasp. Right as Bobby raised his fist, Dean burst through the doors.

"What the—" He threw himself at the fighting pair, knocking Bobby sideways, giving Ethan enough time to scramble to his feet, holding his hands up, as if he wanted to go another eight rounds. Dean held his arms out, separating them. "Ethan, go back inside. You don't need this trouble right now. Not tonight."

"Yeah, run along." Bobby flicked his hand like he was brushing away dirt, and Ethan stepped toward him, but Dean thrust his arm out.

"Be smart, man." Dean grabbed a fistful of Ethan's shirt and shook him, and after a moment, Ethan blinked at him. "Go back inside," Dean said slowly and definitively.

I could see Ethan's jaw working, but he eventually gave in with a nod to Dean, bent down to grab his glasses, and then faced me. He raised his eyebrows expectantly.

Dazed over the clash that had just taken place, I didn't move.

"Really?" he asked in almost a whisper.

I didn't speak, and he offered his hand, probably assuming I would go back inside with him, but I couldn't. I had to take care of this. He shook his head, his gaze darting between me and Bobby. "I told you," he said quietly, his teeth clenched together. "I told you."

I swallowed my guilt at not putting an end to this situation earlier, but I had nothing to be sorry for. I wouldn't apologize for something that wasn't my fault, especially Ethan's anger or the fight between him and Bobby. "I know."

A few more moments passed, as if he was waiting for me to change my mind, but I stayed in my place, and he grumbled a curse before stalking off, back into the ballroom.

Then Dean swung his attention to Bobby, his own eyes full of ire. He marched over to my ex. "We've never had the displeasure of meeting. I'm Dean."

"Laney's brother," Bobby filled in. "I've heard a lot about you."

"Yeah. Same, but nothing good."

Bobby combed his fingers through his hair and fixed his shirt as if his appearing more presentable would erase the last five minutes. "Well, I've come to make it right."

Dean tossed me a look, and I lifted my hands. I was as shocked by all of this as he was. I'd never expected Bobby to show up, and never in a million years had I thought Ethan would ever punch someone. Although I had to admit—in the very back part of my brain, filled with smut and hidden desires —it was kind of hot, his being all protective and jealous.

Though, this was the real world, and Ethan could have ruined his own fundraiser. If anyone caught wind of the fight, this would be the first and last RAHD event.

"What do you want me to do?" Dean asked me.

"Go check on Ethan, please."

He gave me one single nod then headed back inside, while I breathed deeply through my nose, holding it for a while, closing my eyes to picture a serene river in nature, then slowly let it out. But once I opened my eyes again, the calming visualization faded, and my blood boiled.

"How did you even know where I was?" I asked, coming to stand right in front of Bobby.

He grinned as if he hadn't created a nightmare by showing up. "Instagram. You weren't exactly hiding this event, which, great job, by the way, babe." He clicked his tongue, winking at me. "You know how to throw a good party."

I ignored his flirtations. "Why are you here?"

"I came to talk to you, like I said. You haven't responded to me at all. What else was I supposed to do?"

I swiped the back of my hand across my forehead, wicking away the sheen of sweat that had gathered there. The whole incident had probably only lasted a few minutes, but I felt as if I'd been out here for hours. I only hoped it wouldn't take that long to sort this all out.

"You were supposed to take me ignoring you as a sign that I was ignoring you for a reason. Why would you think I'd want anything to do with you?"

"Babe," he said, wrapping his hand gently around my arm. "Come on, let's sit down."

I let myself be pulled toward the lobby, hoping that if I gave him a few minutes, that was all it would take. Bobby found two chairs, upholstered in an ugly flower pattern, and he dragged them to face each other, our knees almost touching. He scrubbed his hands over his face a few times then leaned his elbows on his knees, holding my hands between both of his. "Laney, I am sorry. There aren't enough words to tell you how sorry I am for what I did."

I blew out a breath and sat back, slipping my fingers out of his grasp, but he wasn't to be deterred. He sat up tall, drawing attention to the physical attributes I'd admired him for, the set of his shoulders, the muscle of his chest, the physique of a swimmer. But as quickly as I remembered why I'd found him attractive was as quickly as I shook my head. "I accept your apology, but that doesn't mean I'm interested in getting back together."

"Come on, joey, we were so good together."

I crossed my arms over her middle. "I used to think that nickname was cute. Now it makes me sick to my stomach."

"No, babe, why?"

"*Why?*" I surprised myself when my laugh came out all watery. I couldn't help the tears that formed when I forced myself to recall how hurt and angry I was. "Because you made me feel insignificant, like I meant nothing to you. I—"

"That's not true," he said. "You mean everything to me."

"Clearly not enough to say no to Suzette."

Bobby's brow crimped like he was annoyed. "I told you it was a one-time thing. It meant absolutely nothing to me."

I lifted one shoulder. "That makes me feel worse. You threw away everything we had for something that meant nothing to you. I'd at least understand it better if you had feelings for her. But..." I waved my hand between us. "You can't say I mean everything to you and then choose to have sex with someone who supposedly meant nothing to you."

He hung his head with a sigh, rubbing his hand along the back of his neck. After a few seconds of silence, when I wiped my fingers under my eyes, he lifted his gaze to me again. "Please tell me what I can do to prove it to you. Prove that I love you."

"You can't." Even if he could build a time machine to go back and undo what he did, my answer would still be the same. Now that I knew what true love and comfort and security and fun felt like. Ethan was everything to me.

"But I love you," he said, his voice pitching higher, like he was really desperate. "Nothing has been the same since you left." He touched his hand to his chest. "I haven't been the same."

I huffed a bemused laugh. "I think you're getting confused between love and need."

"No, I—"

I stopped his argument, slicing my hand through the air. "You needed me, Bobby. You needed me to make you feel good, to pick you up when your day was stressful. You needed me on your arm and liked when I wore that long black dress with the slit up the side. You liked when your friends complimented me, complimented *you* for having *me*," I said, shaking my head at the memories. "Made you feel like *the* man, right? Having the woman with the big tits with you. The girl with pretty pictures online who knew all the perfect angles and exactly what to say."

"That's not—"

I moved forward, barely sitting on my seat anymore. "That's exactly right, Bobby, and you know it. You used me like you would an assistant. I took care of your everyday life, plus improved your social media outreach tenfold, all while taking a pay cut. But I did it because I loved you." I tipped my head to the side. "Or, at least, I thought I did. I gave up a job I loved for you. I gave up my own dreams to help you succeed. And for what?" I opened my hands like I'd finished a magic trick. "Nothing. Absolutely nothing except for heartbreak and a few kicks to my self-esteem."

Bobby's face paled, and he sat back, gnawing on his upper lip. "I'm so sorry, Laney. Truly, I never meant to hurt you. I wasn't thinking."

"I know you weren't. I was the brains of the operation."

He gave in to a laugh at that. He was always one for an easy joke. "You really were." He rubbed at his scruffy chin, watching me, and I refused to break eye contact. I had to make him understand that I was not going to change my mind, even when he said, "Come back and work with me. You can have whatever title you want and the paycheck to go with it."

For a moment, less than a moment, I considered it, but... "No. I have a life here. I am not going to work for you."

"You have a life here, eh?" He tipped his chin toward the direction we'd come from. "With your boyfriend?" he added with a slight curl to his lips.

"You sound jealous."

He nodded. "I won't deny it." He spread his legs wider, an alpha move I had become well accustomed to. "Moved on fast. Like, maybe it's a rebound."

I shrugged. "Or maybe you were the rebound."

Bobby angled his head, his hazel eyes narrowed. "What?"

"Ethan and I have a long history. Longer than you can imagine."

"That's his name. Ethan?"

I nodded.

"And you love him?"

I nodded again.

"And you won't even consider coming back to work for the Magnate Corporation?"

"I considered it," I said honestly. "For a second. But, no, Bobby. I have moved on from you and your company."

His chest rose on a breath. "So, I guess…"

"That's it." I stood up so there was no argument otherwise.

From his seated position, Bobby took me in, his gaze roaming over me for a moment, then he stood too. "Walk out with me?"

I agreed, silently gesturing him toward the door. For as much as this was not the time nor place, at least I was getting closure on this chapter of my life. It was time to move on without worrying about what was behind me.

Stepping out into the warm spring night, Bobby opened his arms for a hug, and I thought about ignoring him but eventually gave in. For the last time, I hugged Bobby Magnate, patting his back a few times while he smoothed his hands down my spine. That was when I broke away.

He eyed me, evidently finding determination in my gaze. I was not going to acquiesce to his usual charm. "I'm sorry," he said, taking a step back. "I imagine I will be for a long time." When I didn't respond, he held up his hand. "Goodbye, Laney."

"Bye, Bobby."

He tossed me a smile then turned his back on me, shuffling to the parking lot. After a few yards, he pivoted around, curving his hand by his mouth. "Tell your boyfriend I had him. That was a cheap shot he got in."

I snorted a laugh then raised my arm as I spun away from him. "Bye, Bobby!"

Walking back into the hotel, I ducked into a bathroom to check my appearance. My eye makeup was slightly smudged, and I spent a few moments fixing it before retying my ponytail and running my wrists under cold water. I needed a shower and a stiff drink, but seeing as how I had a job to finish, I'd get neither any time soon.

Inside the carnival, the celebration had pretty much died down. I'd missed the winners of the silent auction, which the DJ had taken care of, and now there were only a few groups of stragglers. Spying my brother, I made my way over to where he stood at a high-top table.

He dropped the few pieces of caramel corn he had in his fingers to hold my shoulders. "Hey, what happened? Are you okay?"

"Yeah, I'm fine." I swatted at the air around my face. "He left."

"Are you sure?" He darted his gaze around the room suspiciously.

"I'm sure. I walked him out."

He finally let go of me. "And what happened?"

I shrugged, not really in the mood to rehash it all yet. "What you'd expect. He's sorry, wanted me to come back, blah, blah."

"You're not going back, are you?"

"No, of course not."

His shoulders curved in as he leaned back on the table. "Good."

I craned my neck around the room. "Where's Ethan?"

"He headed out a little while ago. I told him I'd wait for you."

I deflated. "He left?"

"Yeah." Dean chomped on a handful of popcorn. "The party's basically over. It was a big hit. Everybody was hugging him, shaking his hand. Some people were asking about you, but..." He let out a gravelly noise. "I told them you were handling an emergency."

I turned in a circle, checking out who was left, mostly volunteers and workers. A handful of attendees clustered around Seraphina as she held court in the corner, and a couple with a child, who was throwing a fit over what looked like a stuffed animal.

"Okay, well, I guess all that's left for me is to shut everything down." I hated that I had missed the rest of the event, but there was no way I could've avoided the *emergency*. The only thing I could do now was make sure everything was cleaned up and head over to Ethan's. "Make yourself useful," I told Dean with an elbow to his side. "Go gently kick out Seraphina and her friends. I'll take care of the screamer," I said, pointing to the opposite sides of the room.

Dean agreed and tossed his popcorn before holding his arms out in a grand gesture, shouting to the women. "Ladies, what's going on over here?"

I let out a small laugh then made my way to the toddler having a tantrum to offer him a balloon. The quicker this all got cleaned up, the quicker I got to see the man I'd put it all together for.

CHAPTER THIRTY-ONE

Ethan

I opened up my front door with a little more force than I meant to, and it banged into the wall. I toed off my shoes and tossed my wallet and car keys down before throwing, myself on the couch, stretching out along the cushions. The night had started off so well and ended up a shitshow. Although, I'd played it off pretty well for a guy who had never been involved in acting. From the way I'd walked back into the fundraiser, smiling and laughing after punching Bobby fucking Magnate in the face, no one knew the difference.

Except I did. I knew what it was like to face down the man who broke Laney's heart. To hear her plead with me to leave it alone. Yet, I didn't. I couldn't and wouldn't stand by and leave her to deal with *it* on her own. I had hoped Laney would follow me back inside the party, leaving that asshole to stew outside in his own arrogance, but she didn't. In fact, she never came back at all.

And that really pissed me off. Laney and I had been in a good spot, save for the little hiccup about Marcela, but I didn't think she would hold that against me. At least not until Bobby and his line of bullshit showed up tonight.

I couldn't help but be jealous that she allowed Bobby to stay in communication with her. I couldn't imagine a scenario where she would want her ex in her life, but him showing up out of the blue tonight was proof of how giving an inch turned into a mile. At this point, I didn't know what to think. I didn't know how to feel about her staying to talk to him or what she could possibly have said to him.

As far as I was concerned, Laney was it for me. I only hoped that our second chance wasn't completely spoiled because of some miscommunications and an asshole Australian.

With a deep breath, I sat up, deciding on showering away my stress. Afterward, I'd call Laney and make sure everything was status quo and get back to my original plan of having her over tonight. We would have *a lot* to talk about.

I scrubbed my body under cool water, checking out the red marks over my knuckles that were still a little sore, though the pain was well worth it. After a few minutes, I shut off the water, grabbed a towel, noticing three missed calls on my cell phone that sat on the counter. They were all from Leah, and she hadn't left any messages. A pit formed in my stomach as I picked up my phone to call her, but before I could, it vibrated in my hand with another incoming call from my sister-in-law.

"Hey, Leah. What's going on?"

"Justin," she said, and I could hear Trace shrieking in the background. "He fell down the steps, and I called the ambulance." Her voice was in near tears. "Trace is freaking out. I can't get him to calm down."

"Okay, okay," I said, racing to my room. "Where is Justin right now?"

"The EMTs took him a few minutes ago," she said, crying now. "Ethan, I need your help."

I tripped onto the bed in my haste to get pants on one-handed while I spoke to Leah. "Listen, you stay there with Trace. He needs you right now. I will go to the hospital and call my parents on the way."

"Tracey, baby, shh," she said, her voice far away, and I tossed a T-shirt over my head.

"Leah, did you hear me? Can you hear me?"

"Yes," she said and cleared her throat. "I'm going to try to get him to bed, but I don't know how long that will take. I just want to make sure Justin is okay. I need to know he's okay, Ethan."

"I know. I know you do, but you can't be in two places at once," I said, stepping into sneakers. "I'll tell Mom and Dad to go to your house, then you can come to the hospital, okay?"

"Okay," she whispered over the line as Trace cried. "I didn't know what else to do. I couldn't get Justin up, and Trace was so upset, crying for his daddy, I called 9-1-1."

"You did good, Leah. Everything will be okay," I reassured her, although at the moment, I didn't feel all that confident. "Everything will be okay. You sit tight for now."

She sniffed a few times. "Okay."

"I'm heading out the door right now. I'll talk to you soon."

I hopped into my car and hit the gas, tires squealing as I pulled away from the curb, calling my mother's cell phone. I skipped the pleasantries when she picked up and said, "Mom, Justin fell, and Leah called the ambulance to get him. I'm going to the hospital to be with him until Leah can get there. Can you and Dad go to their house? Trace is really upset."

"Oh my god." Mom called for my Dad. "Tom! Get your shoes on! Justin's hurt, we gotta go!" Then she said to me, "We're leaving right now. You call me as soon as you know what's going on."

"I will."

"I love you, honey," she whispered like she was about to cry, but I hung up to concentrate on driving. I made it to the hospital not long after, practically drag-racing there, and ran into the emergency room, where the nurse at the check-in station showed me to Justin's room.

It was empty.

"Where is he?" I asked, spinning in a panicked circle like my brother was able to up and disappear, which wasn't possible, so it couldn't have been anything good.

"I suspect the radiologist has him for X-rays."

I swallowed down the jagged pebbles in my throat and clasped my hands behind my head, breathing like I'd finished a sprint.

"Are you okay?" the nurse asked me, adjusting the curtain at the doorway.

"Yeah, yeah, I'm good," I panted.

With a nod, the nurse pulled the curtain, leaving me to call my mother and let her know I'd arrived before texting Leah to tell her my parents would be there any minute. Then I waited.

I checked my phone for any missed calls and paced the length of the tiny room. Between my anger about what had transpired with Laney and Bobby and my stress about Justin, I couldn't sit still.

And I waited some more.

I called my mom. Trace was finally calm and in his room with Leah. I texted Laney, but when she didn't respond after a few minutes, I rolled my eyes and tucked my phone away in my back pocket. It was almost dead, and I needed to conserve the battery as opposed to looking at it every five minutes for a call or message from her.

It was after eleven before Justin was finally wheeled back into the room on a gurney. He looked exhausted but managed a smile, and my pent-up emotion hit me like a brick wall. My eyes stung with tears as I reached out for his brother's hand when Justin extended his.

"What's up, bro? You look wrecked."

I choked on a laugh as I wiped at his eyes. "You're the dick who fell down a flight of stairs."

He shifted to get more comfortable in the bed as the doctor entered with a couple of X-rays. She slid them into place on a light box, showing us where Justin had broken his left ankle. "Your CT scans look good, but we'd like to keep you overnight for some observations and tests to be sure," she said, giving Ethan a quick look then lifted her hand, continuing, "I know you said this wasn't a balance or ambulatory issue, but we want—"

"I slipped," Justin interrupted, and the doctor's face broke out in an empathetic smile, but with the way Justin turned to me, it was as if he *needed* me to know this was a fluke, a complete accident. "I had socks on. You know how damn slippery those wooden steps are."

I patted his shoulder. "I know."

"I've been meaning to put something on them for a while. Especially with Trace."

"I know," I said again, trying for levity. "Maybe now, you'll finally cover them, huh?"

His eyes drifted down to his hands in his lap, seemingly defeated, and I kept my hand on his shoulder. I didn't know how Justin was feeling—maybe embarrassment for falling, guilt over never getting around to covering those goddamn steps, fear of his disease progressing, or all of the above—but I was determined to make sure he wasn't alone. In any of it.

The doctor stuck her hands in her coat pockets. "We need to be careful with your diagnosis, take some extra precautions, that's all."

Justin nodded, his head still down.

"We'll try to get you out of here as fast as possible and coordinate with your doctors at Penn. They'll probably want to see you up there."

She tapped two fingers to the metal bar at the end of the bed before leaving, and I took her place. "Hey." When Justin raised his attention, I smiled and clasped my hand on Justin's non-broken ankle. "I love you, brother."

"You too," he answered quietly. "Have you talked to Leah? How's Trace?"

"She was putting him to bed and—"

The curtain to the room flung open, revealing Leah, out of breath and wide-eyed.

"And she could tell you herself," I finished, moving out of the way. After some hugs and kisses, Leah sat on the bed next to Justin as we filled her in.

"I wish I'd known you were staying overnight. I could've brought some toiletries for us."

"Us?" Justin repeated, shaking his head.

"Yeah. I'm staying with you."

"No." He let out a self-deprecating laugh. "No, honey, you don't need to stay here."

She raised one eyebrow then deliberately plopped down in the chair I had vacated, setting her purse down on the floor with a plunk. Justin rolled his eyes to the ceiling like he was asking for heaven's help, but she only said, "Your parents are staying with Trace, who is fast asleep. I'm staying here, whether you like it or not."

"I don't even know when I'll get moved to a room," Justin argued. "*If* I'll get moved to a room."

Leah reached for the television remote connected to his bed. "Well, it's a good thing I'm here to keep you company, then, isn't it?"

I covered my growing grin with a swipe of my hand. "All right, well, seems like you guys are all good. I'm going to head out." I bent to kiss Leah's cheek then clasped my brother's hand. "Text me tomorrow."

When he agreed, I headed back out of the emergency room, waving my thanks to the nurses station, and gulped in lungfuls of the fresh air once I stepped outside.

Ever since Justin's diagnosis, I—and probably my whole family—had been on edge. As if we were waiting for something bad to happen. And in the grand scheme of things, a broken ankle was nothing. It could've happened to anyone, but in the moment, it felt like the worst thing happened. Especially sitting in the empty room with the bland walls and antiseptic smell. My mind had run away from me.

Though with the night behind me, I reminded myself that Huntington's was not an immediate death sentence. It was a long, uneven road that would no doubt be difficult at times, but I had been blessed to have my older brother around for twenty-eight years. Hopefully we would have another twenty-eight years together.

Back at home, I plugged in his dead phone then stripped off my clothes and took my second shower in the last few hours before sinking face-first into my bed, ready to sleep for the next few decades. What I got was a few hours before someone knocked on my door.

I pulled on a pair of shorts and searched for my glasses before stumbling down the hall.

"Hey," Laney said when I opened the door to her. "I'm sorry I'm here so early, but I was worried. I came over last night, and you weren't here. You didn't answer any of my texts. My calls went right to voice mail."

"Oh yeah." I yawned, running a hand through my hair. "My phone was out of battery."

She followed me inside the apartment. "I thought maybe you were pissed at me."

"I was." I shuffled into the kitchen and glanced over my shoulder as I flicked the coffeepot on. "I am."

Her smile dropped. "Oh."

"But I wouldn't have ignored you on purpose. I would never do that."

She dropped into a seat at the kitchen table, pushing her car keys and phone off to the side. "Is that a jab about how I ignored Bobby on purpose?"

I shrugged. I honestly didn't know. My brain too tired to understand sarcasm right now. I focused on filling up the filter with grounds. "What time is it?"

"Six thirty." Once the coffee was set to brew, I sank down into a seat across from her, meeting her eyes for the first time, and I frowned. "What happened? Are you okay? All your last text said was call me, and I freaked out since you didn't answer."

"It was a long night last night."

She winced. "I know. I'm sorry. I didn't—"

I held out my hand to stop her. "Before we get to that part, I was at the hospital last night."

"What?" she nearly shrieked, jumping out of her seat. "What happened?" she cupped my face, as if checking for bruises.

"Justin fell."

"Oh my god. How is he? How is everybody?"

I pulled her into my lap, burying my face in her neck. Even as irritated as I was with her about Bobby, I needed to feel her, smell her, kiss her. I needed her reassurance that everything would be all right.

And because she knew me as well as I knew her, she wrapped her arms around my neck, kissing my temple over and over. My eyes welled up at the concern in her voice when she asked, "Is he okay?"

I squeezed her tighter, brushing my lips over the pulse in her neck. "Broken ankle. It was really scary to get that phone call. Leah was so upset, Trace was screaming. I thought..."

She stayed silent, letting me tuck my face into her shoulder, breathing her in, calming my nerves.

"This is what it's going to be like," I said after a while, voice cracking. "Waiting for a bad phone call."

She wrapped her hands around my jaw, lifting my attention from her shoulder to her eyes. "I'm so sorry I wasn't there with you last night, and even though I can't promise everything will be okay, I can promise you will never have to do any of it alone. I swear it."

I met her halfway for a kiss that did more for my weary soul than any prayer or miracle could have ever done. With her fingers in my hair and her tongue parting my lips, I felt like I could face down anything, as long as she was next to me. Whatever came our way, we would battle it together.

"I'm so sorry," she said against my lips. "You were right. I should have dealt with Bobby months ago."

I closed my eyes, leaning my forehead against hers. "There is no right or wrong way, Laney. You needed to deal with your closure at your own pace. Last night, with...everything..."

She snorted a laugh, sitting back. Her eyes sparkled with mirth. "By everything, you mean that punch you threw?"

"Yeah." I gave in to a chuckle. "That was my own insecurity."

A sly smile crossed her features. "I don't know. I thought it was kinda hot."

My fingers bit into the skin at her waist. "Really?"

She sucked her bottom lip between her teeth and nodded.

"Well, in any case, I shouldn't have done it. Especially not there. I just couldn't stand the idea that you were really considering him again."

"Never." She narrowed her eyes. "I was never considering him." She tipped her head side to side. "Well, that's not the whole truth. For .0003 seconds, I did consider his job offer."

I raised my brow. "He offered you a job?"

"After I told him there was absolutely no chance of me getting back with him, he asked if I'd work for him again. Basically told me I could name my price and title."

"And you told him no?" I asked, because I had to be absolutely sure.

"Of course I told him no. Besides, that was the news I had to tell you. I already have a job offer."

"Really?" I jerked my head back. "Where? Here?"

"Yes, here." She smacked at my shoulder. "I told you I was working with a headhunter. It's the communications director position for Avit."

"Yeah? So you told Bobby to go fuck himself because you already had a job?"

She repositioned herself in my lap, setting her legs on either side of my hips, and I dropped my hands down to her ass. "I didn't quite use those words, and I didn't tell him I already had a job."

I squeezed a handful of her cheeks. "What did you tell him?"

"I told him that he loved the idea of me more than he actually loved me, and that I was with you. There was never a chance of me going back to him because I love you." She lowered her mouth to my ear, whispering, "It's always been you, Ethan. I love you." Then she pressed a hot, wet kiss to my neck. "Is there still room for my stuff in your bathroom?"

My fingers found their way underneath the band of her leggings. "Wherever I am, there will always be room for you. I love you, Lane." When she lifted her head, her smile brighter than the sun, I didn't hold back my grin either. "That's my girl."

CHAPTER THIRTY-TWO

Laney

"Hey, you almost ready?" Ethan asked.

I added the finishing touches to my face. "One minute."

He nodded but didn't move from his spot in the doorway of the hotel bathroom, his fingers tapping on the walls.

I smiled over at him. "You all right?"

He nodded again. He'd gotten his hair trimmed and actually put on a pressed shirt, as opposed to one of his T-shirts. With his chino shorts and white sneakers, he could've passed for a model. Especially when he refolded the sleeves of his shirt up to his elbows.

"You look really handsome," I said, hoping to calm him. When he didn't respond, I set down the bronzer, fluffed my curly hair, and then twirled in front of him. "What do you think?"

"I think if you're trying to sidetrack me with sex, it's not going to work."

I reached for his waist, towing him in for a quick kiss. "Are you sure?"

Tracing his index finger across the swells of my breasts in a new sundress, one that he had helped pick out, he shook his head. "No. But we need to go."

I agreed and grabbed my purse before taking his hand, doing a quick double-check that we had the room key before closing the door to our room.

It probably wasn't the brightest idea to go to Washington, DC, during the July Fourth weekend, but I wasn't going to open my mouth about traffic when Ethan was so excited he couldn't sit still. I had never been to DC, so when the opportunity came up, we agreed to make it a little mini-vacation.

Arlington, Virginia, was only a few miles away, although with the way our car crawled along, it wouldn't surprise me if it would take hours. Ethan touched the GPS on his phone for the fifth time in the last two minutes, as if that would speed us up.

"Do you want to play a game?" I asked.

"A game?"

"Yeah." I adjusted the air vents. "I spy or something?"

He huffed an agitated sound as the car attempting to merge in front of us. "I don't think so."

"Well, okay. Did I tell you that Sam got a job?"

He glanced me way, a hint of a smile on his face. "Yeah?"

Over the last few weeks, Ethan had been inducted into the group chat, now renamed **Four Chicks and Four Dicks** and had taken to the group of boys like he was their long-lost friend. Needless to say, the girls adored him.

"In Chicago," I said.

"Oh, nice. So they'll be close to Gem and Jason?"

I shook my head. "I think they're still, like, three hours away from each other, but at least they're in the same state."

"But that means we could all theoretically be together with a three-hour plane ride, right?"

"Always thinking positive," I said, running my hand along the back of his head.

"Making lemons out of lemonade."

I leaned over to kiss his cheek, knowing exactly how much lemonade we were making and would continue to. For now, Justin was doing well with no signs of the disease progressing quickly, so we'd all drink up that lemonade like it was the best damn drink in the world.

I dropped my hand from his neck, and he laced our fingers together in his lap as I went off on a tangent about Bronte and Chris's dog, Taco, getting lost the other day. They'd been out all day looking for him, and it turned out he'd been hiding under their bed the whole time. Then I gabbed on about sending Gem and Jason a gift certificate in case they needed anything for the new baby, who was due in two months. "So, what else can we talk about?"

He smiled over at me. "Why do we have to talk?"

"Because I'm trying to calm you down."

"Did you ever think that the more you talk, the more nervous I get? You're the one who's babbling."

"Babbling?" I feigned hurt. "I am not babbling."

"You are," he said, checking his mirrors before changing lanes to turn right. We were almost there. He absently kissed the back of my hand then let go of my fingers. "I need you to grab something from the glove compartment." The GPS instructed Ethan to make another turn, our destination was on our left, and he leaned forward, his eyes on the street signs.

"What do you need?" I asked, opening it, not paying much attention as I pulled out random folded pieces of paper and crumpled-up receipts.

"There should be a box." He parked the car and unbuckled his seat belt, turning toward me. He pointed to the corner of the compartment. "Right there."

I ducked my head to get a better look, and I sucked in a ragged inhale, my fingers curling around the small square box. Though I didn't move. I couldn't.

Next to me, Ethan shifted so close, his breath brushed against my cheek when he chuckled. "You scared?"

I dared to look at him. "Should I be?"

He put his hand over mine, and together, we removed the ring box from the glove compartment, and he shut it with a quiet click. Then he unbuckled my seat belt and gently curved his palm around my cheek, his amber eyes shining big and round behind his glasses. "I know we haven't really talked about this, but..." He tipped his head, an embarrassed lilt slanting the corner of his lips. "At this point, I didn't think we needed to discuss it, right?"

I swallowed, bobbing my head up and down, my brain completely empty of anything other than the way his mouth formed my name.

"Delaney Hargrove, I have loved you since I was eighteen years old, and there is nothing I want more than to be with you for the rest of my life." With a flick of his wrist, he opened the box for me, a simple yet stunning solitaire diamond on a gold band nestled in the blue cushion. "I was hoping that when we meet my birth mom in person for the first time, I could introduce her to my fiancée." He took the ring out and held it up to me in offering. "So, Lane, my love, will you marry me?"

I all but threw myself at him, pushing him back against his door, a rush of air leaving him with an "oof." But he only laughed. "Is that a yes?"

"Yes." I held on to his forearms, steadying myself. "Yes, it's yes. Yes, now. Yes, forever. Yes." I kissed him, hysterical giggles bubbling up from my chest. "Yes, yes, yes, yes."

Wrapping his fingers around my left wrist, he slid the ring on to my fourth finger then kissed my palm, and I admired the new topography of my hand. I thought my smile might crack my face right in half. "I'm gonna marry you," I told him. "I'm gonna marry you so hard."

He grabbed my face, kissing a laugh into my mouth then tilted his head toward his door. "Come on. Let's go."

Outside of the car, we linked hands, the metal of my ring cool against my finger. "This is quite the day."

"Goonies never say die," he said, grinning, as he pointed to the townhouse with a colorful wreath on the door. Before we even stepped up to the stoop, the door opened to a woman, smiling sweetly. She held the storm door open, her dark eyes, the same shape as Ethan's, toggling between us.

"It's so wonderful to see you both," she said, her voice breaking, and I immediately grabbed a tissue from my purse, tucking it into Ethan's hand when we let go of each other.

With me following behind, Ethan stepped into the house as Marcela lifted her arms in a welcoming gesture. Her long dark hair was pulled back into a low ponytail, and I could see where Ethan got his thin frame from, but with his skin a few shades lighter and a full head taller than Marcela, the genes from his other half were also apparent.

Almost as if they didn't know what to do, Ethan and Marcela stood and stared at each other.

"Finally," she said, blinking as tears formed in her eyes, and opened her arms.

"Finally," Ethan repeated and curled himself around her. They didn't speak. The only sounds were muffled sniffles and short bursts of air. For my part, I ducked my head from the intimate scene and cleared my own eyes of tears. But it wasn't long before they pulled away from each other.

Ethan lifted his glasses to swipe at his eyes with the tissue, stuck it in his pocket, then held his hand out to me. "Marcela, I'd like to introduce you to my fiancée, Delaney."

I stepped up to the woman, who took my hands between her own, and Ethan pressed his hand against my lower back. "Laney, I'd like you to meet my birth mom."

Marcela enveloped me in a hug. "I've been waiting so long for this day," she said eventually, once she pulled away from me. "Come on, come sit down."

We followed Marcela to a comfy beige couch. She'd set out soda, water, a fruit platter, a plate of cheese and crackers, as well as some cookies on the coffee table. "I didn't know what you liked," she explained, waving her hand over it all. "So I got a little of everything. Please eat."

I grabbed a couple of grapes and nestled into Ethan's side, seeing as how he and his birth mom both appeared a little too nervous to eat anything quite yet.

"So," Marcela said, leaning forward in her chair across from us, running her hand through her hair a few times, exactly like Ethan did. "Tell me everything."

"Everything?" he laughed. "That might take a while."

"Good," she said with a smile, and he glanced at me, taking my hand in his.

"Okay, well…" He met Marcela's gaze. "Where should we start?"

"The beginning."

Epilogue

ETHAN

"It's an actual log cabin," I said, parking our rental car on the gravel driveway as I peered out of the windshield up at the *huge* house.

"Pretty nice, right? Bronte's obsessive with planning. I'm sure she has everyone in assigned rooms with monogrammed towels."

I pocketed the car keys and snagged our coats from the back seat before meeting Laney at the hood of the car. Although it was only a few minutes past six, the sky was completely dark with the stars hidden behind clouds, and our breath fogged in front of us, but Laney shrugged away when I tried to put her coat around her shoulders. "Won't be cold long. Come on."

She ran up the driveway, and I rolled my eyes in exasperation at this woman. "Careful. It's really uneven."

"It's fine. Hurry up, slowpoke!" She opened the big bag she'd carried on the plane and lifted the giant bottle of champagne she'd demanded we stop and get on our way to the house, before kicking open the door to the cabin, shouting out, "Honey, I'm home!"

A chorus of cheers rang out, and I laughed into the night

sky before following her inside our New Year's party place for the next few days.

Laney was in the middle of a group of women hugging in the center of the open kitchen as three men stood in a semicircle. Chris, the famous actor, although semi-retired now, was the first to speak. "We thought maybe she left you at home."

"Nah. She can't get rid of me that easy." I shook each of their hands. Although we'd spoken a few times over video chat, and I'd become friends with these guys, this was still the first time I was meeting them in person.

"How's it going?" Chris asked, slapping my back before tucking his chin-length hair behind his ears.

"Good. When did you get in?"

"We came in yesterday. Bunny had to make sure everything was right," he explained with a smile, tipping his head toward his wife, who was currently holding a baby.

I pointed to them. "And I suppose that's..."

"Hazel." Jason inclined his head toward his few-weeks-old daughter.

"How was the flight with the kids?" I asked, taking off my coat to hang on the back of one of the chairs at the marble island. For as much as the outside looked like a rustic cabin in the middle of nowhere, the inside was completely up-to-date, with no expense spared. Especially when Bronte pressed a button on a panel and a window shade lowered before the chandelier lights brightened.

"It was all right. Hazel pretty much slept the whole time, and we gave Willow fruit snacks and an iPad. Gem was the one struggling," Jason said, wincing as he watched his wife fix her top. "She couldn't get comfortable."

Before I could ask what was wrong, Gem let out a shriek then stomped out the French doors to a deck. A spotlight turned on out there, and with her back to the group, I couldn't tell what she was doing, but the loud sigh she let out sounded like relief as she bent slightly at her waist, her elbows stuck out to the sides.

Sam craned her head to see better. "What's she doing?"

Laney quirked an eye at Jason, and he held his hands out in front of him. "She's overproducing milk."

"Shooting it out like a squirt gun," Laney suggested, finger guns in front of her own chest, and I slapped my palm over my mouth.

"Oh Christ," Mike, Sam's boyfriend, said, dragging a big hand down the side of his face as he sat down. "I don't think I want to know."

Jason chuckled, rubbing Mike's shoulders. "Too much for you, buddy?"

"No. I don't want to know about your wife's…"

"Udders," Gem said, stalking back into the kitchen, her hand shoved down her top, readjusting herself. "You don't want to hear about how I have so much milk stored up in my udders, it hurts to do anything? Well, too bad, Mikey, because that's all I'll be talking about for the next five days. So, get used to it."

We all laughed, chalking the outburst up to Gem being Gem, before Laney handed the champagne to me. "Open, please?"

Sam set Willow, Gem and Jason's three-year-old, down on the floor to grab some glasses. She lined them up on the counter as Bronte handed Hazel off to Gem and took out platters of food from the refrigerator. The four women moved around one another like they'd been doing this dance for years, which, I supposed, they had been.

Once I had the cork popped out of the bottle, Laney took it back and poured it into the eight glasses before handing them out. Jason tugged Willow on his lap as he sat at the kitchen table next to Mike, and Gem held Hazel against her shoulder, her glass aloft. "To Bronte for putting this all together."

Bronte looped her arm around Chris's waist. "To spending New Year's together."

Sam perched herself in Mike's lap, smiling at him then at the group. "To all of us growing one year older and one year wiser."

"Speak for yourself," Mike mumbled against Sam's shoulder, which earned a few laughs.

Then Laney cleared her throat, her arm up high. "To life, liberty, and the pursuit of happiness. Now, enough with the cheers and drink up before the bubbles run dry."

She tossed back her champagne like it was a cheap shot of tequila instead of the expensive bottle of Bollinger she'd insisted we get, but I did as she commanded and drank it all up, then thrust my glass out for more. With a smile, she filled it back up and leaned into my side so I could kiss her temple.

"Now," Bronte said, moving toward the counter, where she picked a printed sheet. She flicked her wrist, straightening it from how it had been folded in half. "I made a small list of—"

"Small?" Sam laughed, snatching it from her.

"No." Gem shook her head. "No lists."

"Or agendas," Laney added, and when Mike, Jason, and Chris all gave in to the laughs they'd been holding back, I shrugged.

"Can I see?"

"Ah, get out of here!" Mike tossed a balled-up napkin at me.

Jason agreed with a nod. "The only plans I have are to take some of Chris's money in poker and to try and seduce my wife."

"Think again." Gem rolled her eyes, barely holding back a

smile, while Bronte sidled up next to me, happy to share her list of activities.

"I knew I liked you."

Chris shook his head in amusement as he pointed between Bronte and me. "Oh sh—" He glanced at Willow, fiddling with a coloring book. "Shoot. There are two of them."

I skipped my focus around my new friends, as they all stared at me, before landing on my fiancée. "What?"

She grinned. "Nothing. You're cute."

I took the printout. "I, for one, really like Apples to Apples."

All seven of them laughed as Hazel let out a tiny whine and Willow sneezed. I supposed this was life now. Marriages and kids and playing Apples to Apples in a log cabin with friends.

A pretty great life.

Acknowledgments

Indie publishing is a wild ride. Thank you, reader, for coming along with me.

I wouldn't be able to put out these books if not for the encouragement of my friends, especially Ellis Leigh and Brighton Walsh, and the help of my editors, Libby and Lisa. I'd especially like to thank my street team for helping me spread the work about my books. I'm forever grateful.

If you'd like more information about me, you can find it at: https://sophieandrewsauthor.com.

About the Author

Sophie Andrews is a contemporary romance author who writes steamy books that will leave you smiling. As a millennial, she's obsessed with boybands, late 90s rom-coms, and will always be team Pacey. When she's not writing, she's most likely trying to wrangle her children or drinking red wine. Or both at the same time.

Also by Sophie Andrews

Tangled Series

Tangled Up

Tangled Want

Tanged Hearts

Tangled Beginning

Tangled Expectations

Tangled Chances

Tangled Ambition